MW01114049

The Children of Doctor Lancing

by Michelle McBeth

To Ronald + Cary,
Keep reading!
-Michelle McBeth

To my friends, who inspire me with their brilliance and strangeness.

Chapter 1

Amelia was everything I wanted in a woman. I knew that from the moment we met as children, on the street in front of my parents' home.

It was the third time that week that I had stormed out of the house intent on running away. My parents had just made me read a passage in our religion's most sacred text, "The Vena Manifesto", that didn't make sense to me. I was smart for a five-year-old child and had trouble accepting doctrine that didn't follow some form of logic. Previously, I never made it past the end of the block before fear would paralyze me and I would shuffle my way back home, defeated. That day, I only made it a few houses down when I stopped just short of running into Amelia.

She was walking past and nibbling on a chocolate chip cookie that her mother had made earlier that day. She stopped abruptly when she saw me, and I watched the skirt of her yellow sundress swing forward then back again, mimicking her short, straight hair. She stared at me, half a cookie gone. Crumbs and a smear of chocolate clung to the edge of her mouth. Her hand squeezed the top of the paper bag with the remaining cookies. I was distracted by the sound of the paper crinkling in her hand.

I looked up into her eyes, and neither of us spoke for what felt like an hour. It was long enough that the tears dried from my cheeks, and at least three cloud shadows passed across her face.

"Where are you going?" she asked me, pulling me from my mesmerized state.

I couldn't answer her. My mouth opened and some noise came out, but I didn't know the answer. Her gaze made me ashamed of my own fear, and I felt the tears welling up again. I stood there trying to compose myself, fighting back the tears with all my might. I looked back at my house to avoid her eyes and wiped my nose with the back of my hand.

"Why were you crying?" she asked me.

That pushed me over the edge. The shame hit as hard as it did just before I left the house. I was a failure. I failed my parents' expectations of me. I failed to run away. I failed to have a conversation with a perfectly lovely little girl. Was there nothing that I could do right?

I lowered my head in the hopes that I would disappear. I felt the tears roll off my cheeks and watched them fall to the ground. Through my silent sobs, I heard the bag crinkle again and saw her feet as she approached me, her Chuck Taylors perfectly matching the bright hue of her dress. I stared down at my bland necktie and khaki pants, wishing for the first time that my parents allowed me to wear more colorful clothes. A cookie appeared in my line of vision, blurred by the tears. With one hand I rubbed them away. The other hand reached out for the cookie. I stopped crying and looked up at her curiously. She nodded in encouragement. I took a deep breath to further calm myself, and then I took a bite.

It was the most delicious thing I had ever tasted. What sort of angel could have produced something so wonderful, I wondered, exactly when I needed it? I figured she must have had some sort of sixth sense, to know I was in trouble and come to my rescue. In that moment I fell hopelessly in love with her.

My parents did not allow me to have sweets, and the hint of rebellion in what I was doing was empowering and seemed just a little evil to me. I had never felt so good. My life changed forever with that cookie. It occurred to me then that running away would not make me happy. I was convinced my parents didn't love me. If I disappeared, they would be relieved. Above all I wanted my parents to suffer for the way they treated me. I wanted it to sneak up on them gradually and consume them, and have them not even realize it was happening. I would stop running away from my problems. I would instead rebel in my own, silent way.

I smiled at her and blinked away my remaining tears, a surge of confidence pushing away the shame and pain. "Thank you."

"Why don't I know you from school?" she asked me.

"I don't go to school."

"Everyone has to go to school."

"My parents teach me."

"Oh."

For a moment I thought that was a mistake, that she would think I was some sort of freak. Even at that young age, and as isolated as I was, I knew the stigma that followed a homeschooled child. The government had outlawed homeschooling years ago. The only exceptions were for a few strict religious sects that claimed infringement on their beliefs. I had just pegged myself as a zealot.

The Order of Vena relied heavily on isolation and guilt as a means to get its members to follow. My parents taught me enough to read and write but left it at that. Technology was strictly forbidden. For a five-year-old child, I was drastically behind my peers, including this girl. I didn't want her to know that I came from a household of people who believed the world was filled with misguided fools, and that I was better off staying away from them.

For a moment, she didn't say anything. I panicked that I had ruined the conversation and she would be on her way, but she stood and stayed. She stared at me with her head tilted to the side, like she was trying to figure me out. Her gaze made me nervous in a way I didn't understand at the time.

I tried to recover. "But I've always wanted to go to a real school."

"Why don't you?"

I remembered my new mission to undermine my parents. "I'm not allowed. But I wish there was some way I could learn the same things other children learn."

She handed me another cookie. "I could teach you the things I learn at school, in secret." Her smile seemed genuine, but there was a flash of mischief in her eyes.

I took the cookie and stood, stunned and excited and paranoid as ever. "What's in it for you?" I asked, trying to ferret out the secret behind her eyes.

The smile fell abruptly. "Have I asked for payment for my cookies? You're in pain. I want to help. I don't like my parents either. Maybe if I help you, somewhere in the future, you can help me."

I considered it. I was frequently left alone for long periods of time to contemplate my innate sinfulness. Sneaking out would not be an option, since my parents would randomly check on me. I thought I could probably sneak her in, and hide her whenever I heard them coming. I ate my cookie and gazed back into her freckled face. A light breeze blew a few loose strands of hair across her cheek: I realized she could ask me to do anything she wanted, and I would do it. "What's your name?"

"Amelia."

"Amelia," I whispered. The name sounded like music in the wind. I brushed the crumbs from my hand and held it out to her, by way of a formal acceptance. She grasped it with unexpected strength for such a slight frame. "Amelia, I accept. I want you to teach me everything you can."

Thus began my real education. It wasn't long before I surpassed Amelia's knowledge. She started finding copies of her books and leaving them with me to study ahead. Even after she was no longer teaching me herself, she still came to see me every day. When I got through those books, she found copies of books from advanced grades to bring me.

Sometimes she would bring cookies, sometimes candy. My parents noticed that I no longer tried to run away when they berated me for some perceived misbehavior. They took it as a sign that I was finally becoming a true believer. I let them think that, and even adapted my behavior around them to make it seem like I was a truly devout believer. They left me to myself more, and I used that time to study and build up my confidence and fall even deeper in love with Amelia.

Things hadn't always been this way, I suspected. I had hazy memories of large modern and sterile buildings filled with people milling about. My parents were two of those people, I was sure of it. They took me with them from time to time, and I got to meet other children whose parents also spent time in that building. I was dreaming it, they told me. When I persisted, they would punish me. In the end, I learned not to argue.

Amelia's life, I learned, was no picnic either. Her mother died shortly after we met, and her father became an alcoholic because of it. Though he never physically hurt her, he was cruel and unloving to her. I didn't mind, since it drove her to me for comfort and company even more. When she was home, she hid in her room and lost herself in fairy tales, dreaming of the day when she would find her own escape.

Biology became my favorite subject. I was desperate to understand the workings of the human body, and how it reacted to the world around it. Even more specifically, I wanted to understand the human mind. I wanted to know how my parents and everyone at my church could be so easily fooled into such a restricted lifestyle. I was convinced there must be some abnormality in their brains that caused them to want this life.

It was at this point that Amelia decided I needed more real world experience. She claimed that books could only tell you so much, and that to truly understand biology, I needed to do experiments. She started setting traps in the woods, and would bring me animals to experiment on. My parents were leaving me on my own more often, and I would take advantage of their time out of the house to hurry to my stash of cages in the woods not far from our house to conduct my experiments. Amelia found nearly empty bottles of drugs—I didn't think to ask where—and I would mix them and observe the effects on my subjects. She was working part-time in a lab and would take blood samples to be tested for me late at night when she was there alone.

I started experimenting with mind altering drugs, finding ways to boost the effects with smaller amounts, and adding other drugs that altered the chemical composition enough to remove all traces of the drug from the body in short order. In a moment of morbid curiosity, I tried the same thing with a small amount of hemlock. I gave it to a squirrel and watched as its muscles gradually gave out, until it gave one last gasp for air then remained still, though there was life in the eyes. I gave the dead squirrel to Amelia to test as thoroughly as possible, explaining why. She glanced nervously between me and the bottle of untraceable poison that remained in my collection before taking the squirrel away.

The next day the bottle was gone. I didn't question Amelia. I figured she didn't want me killing any more animals that way. It didn't matter. Though I had toyed with the idea of using it on my parents, I didn't want to kill them. I wanted them to live through my revelation of abandoning my religion.

I viewed that day on the street when I met Amelia to be a life changing moment. Perhaps that was why she suddenly became the focal point of my existence. My drive to undermine my parents centered on her. Everything I did served a dual purpose; I was surreptitiously abandoning the life my parents wanted for me, while simultaneously dedicating myself to her happiness without her realizing it. I wanted to spend the rest of my life with her, and I knew that still wouldn't be enough. I wanted an eternity with her. I had never known such joy as when I was with Amelia.

It pained me that I couldn't be there for her when her father suddenly died, leaving her an orphan. She had done so much for me in the past decade, and I couldn't even leave my house long enough to stand by her side at a funeral. Though she seemed to take it in stride, it made me more determined to ensure her happiness in the future. She assured me it was fine, but I always felt like she was lying. How could such a lovely creature want to be with someone like me?

We applied to all the same colleges together. I had to take a standardized test to prove my homeschooling had been sufficient, and passed easily. Between that and my perfect scores on the SATs, schools were clamoring to offer me full scholarships. When Amelia was accepted to college on the east coast, I knew I was finally going to leave home to stay with her. It was time to reveal my secret life to my parents. She sold her father's house, having no desire to stay there. Between the profit from the sale and the little money he had left, there was enough that the two of us were able to buy a small place together and still have plenty left over to live on for a few years.

On the day we planned to leave town, I had her bring me a pair of blue jeans and the most garishly colored t-shirt she could find. I hadn't tried alcohol yet, but I asked her to also bring me a bottle of vodka. I dumped it out and filled one remaining swig with water. My parents would never know the difference.

When they came home from some church related event and saw me, my mother nearly fainted. I was sitting at the table, the bottle of fake vodka nearly empty, candy bar wrappers strewn about. My standard uniform of khaki pants, white shirt and necktie lay in a heap on the floor. My acceptance letters to Yale, Harvard, Oxford, Cambridge, and Princeton sat on the table. My father stood silent, an arm on my mother to steady her. I downed the last bit of fake vodka. I gestured to Amelia and introduced her as my girlfriend, an atheist that I was going to live with on the East Coast. That seemed to snap my mother out of her trauma-induced haze.

She grabbed the closest acceptance letter, her hands shaking. "How could you possibly have been accepted to Oxford?"

"I've been studying for years."

"Yes. The teachings of The Order," she said, trying to confirm what she thought she knew.

"No. Math, Chemistry, Physics, Electronics—" I trailed off. "The books are hidden in my closet, you can see for yourself."

Her eyes widened in fear and her breathing accelerated. "No."

I was expecting anger, but I could work with fear. "Biology is my favorite. I'm quite adept at manipulating drugs for alternate effects on the body."

Then the tirade began. "How could you betray us this way?" she screamed at me. She went on and on about what a disappointment I was. I merely sat, not saying a word. Amelia stayed calmer than I would have imagined possible.

My mother then started yelling about how much they had sacrificed for me, snatching a candy bar wrapper off the table and throwing it in my face. I didn't understand that. If they felt being in the church was a sacrifice, why not just leave it behind?

I was thrown, and about to interrupt to ask, when she made disparaging remarks about Amelia and her obviously bad influence on me. My confusion once again turned to quiet rage. How dare she insult my Amelia? I rose from the table, saying nothing. Amelia followed my lead. I left with nothing, the endless stream of high-pitched venom following me out the door.

I always wondered what story they had come up with to explain my disappearance. I imagined they wouldn't have lied to their church. They probably got a ton of sympathy from their co-worshipers. At last they were free of their good-for nothing son.

We walked to Amelia's car and drove off to our new lives together.

Chapter 2

I wanted to get married right away. It was an antiquated notion to get married at such a young age, or even at all, but I was seduced by the romance of the idea. Amelia was not quite as susceptible to being swept up in her emotions. The few years she had with her family taught her to keep an emotional detachment from certain situations and people. It was a quality I admired in her, but at the same time it made me doubt her devotion to me.

I talked myself out of my disappointment by reasoning that she would not have come this far with me if she weren't in it for the long run. Plus, she complimented me all the time. She was always telling me how smart I was, and how she didn't want to detract me from completing my education and getting my doctorate. I had to finish what she had helped me start. I owed it to her. I owed it society. A brain like mine could not be wasted, she argued.

We were living together while both attending Yale. I was working towards dual degrees in Biomedical Engineering and Chemistry. I was learning an incredible amount and Amelia was by my side. For the first time in my life I knew what it was to have freedom of choice for every aspect of my life. I purchased t-shirts with pop culture references I didn't understand just because they weren't plain white. Every morning I had a chocolate croissant for breakfast, and finished my evening with a chocolate chip cookie. Every time I bit into the cookie I relived that moment on the street with Amelia. I would smile at her, and she would smile back. I was in heaven.

My fascination with the workings of the human body kept me scrambling for more information. I took a part-time job with a local laboratory in addition to my research. I could not fill my brain with enough facts. There were not enough experiments to keep me satisfied. As I watched my fellow students, I realized that although I could tell you the processes of the human body down to the molecule, human interactions were foreign to me. I tried to go to a study group once. I took a box of chocolate croissants with me and donned a t-shirt displaying a popular music group of the day. They welcomed me easily enough, and I managed to fake pleasantries with them about the music group they all seemed acquainted with. Things went downhill quickly from there.

They did very little studying. Most of their time was spent in banter and flirting with each other. It was a group from a junior level class and I was technically a freshman. When they finally got around to talking about the work, I had to spend most of the time correcting them on their understanding. I was surprised that a group of people so far ahead of me in rank could be so ignorant of their own major.

The next day one of the group, a woman named Maiia Kischukov, approached me. She was actually a graduate student, so I wasn't sure why she was taking an undergraduate course. She told me I was not welcome back to the study group.

"They don't like you," she explained to me.

"Why not?" I thought I had done everything correctly. I had brought treats, participated in their banter and helped them understand the material better.

"You're younger than them, and it bothers them that you understand the material better. They're jealous."

"But I helped them. They're going to struggle without my help. They were misunderstanding the basic concepts of biomedical signaling."

She nodded. "But they'd rather fail than think they need the help of someone below them."

"Then they're fools," I said. I was angry at the incompetence they displayed. If this was what friendship was like, then I didn't need it.

"I'm not. I can tell you're intelligent. Even more intelligent than me, and I'm well ahead of you. I think we can help each other. As a graduate student, I've been exposed to concepts you haven't even heard of, but I also struggle sometimes to understand them. That's why I need you. I can help you expand your knowledge base, and you can help me solidify mine."

She became my first and only friend, outside of Amelia. I decided this was fine. If having friends meant having to ignore their ignorance, then I didn't want that. We were lab partners any time we could be, and she came to me often for advice on her research. I helped her mold her thesis work into a groundbreaking research project.

Amelia didn't like it. She thought Maiia was using me. I explained that I was benefiting from it as well, not only in being exposed to new material but also by developing a lucrative industry contact. Maiia was offered a leadership position at a highly regarded laboratory just outside of Philadelphia by one of the members of her dissertation committee. She promised me a position there as soon as I wanted.

Though Maiia wasn't as smart as me, she knew how the system worked. I thought she would make an excellent laboratory leader. I promised I would join her lab as soon as I could, so long as Amelia could come with me. Maiia agreed easily, and I was grateful. Amelia was not as smart as me, but she was a good student and was excelling in the field, too.

I tore through my courses, overloading my schedule and using my part-time work for research credits. I was able to finish my degrees in two and a half years. To allow Amelia time to finish her degree, I stayed at Yale to get my doctorate. After finishing my undergraduate work I proposed to Amelia at least once a month. After nearly two years of this, she surprised me.

Amelia had been talking about one of her classes. She was complaining about a professor, who was an idiot in her opinion. She told me that I could do a better job teaching the class than him. She continued to rant about some of the other students in the class who were also incompetent.

I loved it when Amelia said things that made us feel like the same person. It was as though she was the only person in the world who understood my frustration with the mediocre people around me. As it happened often, the need to spend the rest of my life with her surged inside of me. "Marry me," I said.

"Okay."

My fork hovered over my plate of chicken Kiev, halfway to my mouth, which gaped open. "What?"

"As soon as you finish your PhD, I'll marry you." She smiled. She hadn't touched her food. Her fork lay untouched next to her plate, her hands rested on her lap. It was as if she knew what was coming and had been waiting for it.

I blinked a few times and lowered my fork. My mouth still hung open in shock. "Really?" I had asked her to marry me so many times I had become accustomed to her normal response of 'no'. This time she threw me.

She laughed. "Of course I will! You knew this was coming some day." She reached across the table and took my hand. "Finish your PhD, and we can get married that same day."

My heart sped as the realization of what was going on finally caught up to me. "Amelia," I said and got up from the table, pulling her up into a hug. I laughed into her hair. "Oh Amelia, you won't regret this. You are everything to me, and I will prove it every day of our lives together."

"I know," she said simply. "Let's eat." She pulled away and sat again, a slight smile on her face.

I feverishly shoved food into my mouth, desperate to get back to my research.

Eight months later, I defended my dissertation.

The happiness that swelled in me when Amelia called me "Doctor" for the first time was overwhelming. She beamed with pride for days after. I had made her so pleased, and that was everything to me.

Since we still had plenty of money left from Amelia's inheritance, I was surprised when she said she wanted a small wedding ceremony. Given her love of Disney princesses, I had assumed she would want a big poufy dress and fancy party. Instead, we were accompanied to a park by a justice of the peace and two of our colleagues to be our witnesses. Amelia refused to let Maiia come, so two of her classmates attended.

For the first time since leaving home, I relented to wearing a plain white button down shirt with a suit. The tie at least had color this time. I chose yellow, in honor of the color she was wearing when we first met. Amelia wore a plain white floor length sundress. Her sandals matched my tie.

I didn't hear a word that was being said. I stared into Amelia's eyes, holding her hands. I couldn't believe this beautiful, intelligent woman was marrying me. I heard my name and glanced at the justice of the peace. He had just asked me for my vows. I cleared my throat and smiled as I began. I had spent months adjusting and memorizing what I wanted to say. I finalized my vows even before she had agreed to marry me.

"My dearest Amelia, from the moment we met I knew I wanted to spend my life with you. You saved me from a life of certain destruction, and it is only because of you that I am the man I am today. I owe you everything. I owe you my life. I will forever be devoted to you. I will do everything in my power to make you the happiest woman alive. I will never fail to be there for you again. Never."

Saying it out loud, I realized it didn't feel strong enough. It was as if mere words had no way to convey the depth of my feelings or the strength of my conviction. Amelia smiled at me, and I forgot all my feelings of inadequacy. I swayed, dizzy with delirious happiness. I couldn't believe this was happening.

"I know I cannot hope to live up to your impression of me," she began, "and words cannot express what you have meant to me so far. You have saved me in ways you don't even realize. I promise to strive to be that person you see me as, as a way of honoring your love and dedication to me."

I found it amusing that we both felt we deserved each other so little, and couldn't express how much we felt for each other. I took it as a sign that we were destined to be together, that we would forever strive to be better for the other person. That seemed a worthy cause to enter into a marriage for.

The rest of the ceremony passed in a blur. I vaguely remembered saying "I do," at some point and putting a ring on Amelia's finger. When she finally put her arms around me to kiss me, the rest of the world disappeared. I flashed back again to the day we met, never thinking at that time that she would make my dream of forever come true.

I often flashed back to the first meeting on the street. It was the day I felt like my life really started. Every day since that day my life got better and better with Amelia by my side. I eventually forgot about my parents. They were a distant memory that I rarely dredged up. A part of my life I no longer associated with.

I pulled away long enough to smile and say, "I love you, wife."

She grinned back. "Same here, Doctor."

I lost myself in her kiss again.

A few days later we moved to Westchester, Pennsylvania and started working at Maiia's laboratory. She had moved up through the executive branch and was now in charge. She had convinced the board to change the name of the laboratory to her own: Kischukov Laboratory. I thought it was a smart move, since she was now well known in the field of biomedical engineering. In my mind, it gave the laboratory more creditability. Amelia thought Maiia didn't deserve such recognition. It turned out, Amelia was right.

Chapter 3

I was in my office at the Kischukov Laboratory when I had my breakthrough. Maiia and I were having yet another argument about my research. I wasn't bringing in enough money with my "off-kilter" experiments, as she called them. She kept harping about how research labs need to do more popular work with promise of returns if they expect to get funding. She absolutely believed that my ideas had no basis in reality and that I was doomed to failure. I had been taking care of little side projects, I tried to pick ones that would take little of my time but yield a high return. She didn't like it. I think she was just jealous that I was able to breeze through these projects and still have time to work on my own dreams.

I was arguing that my work did have promise. Science had already managed to slow the aging process for human beings, and agelessness was merely a step further. I knew there had to be a way to do it. Maiia disagreed. She kept me around though, because she knew how intelligent I was, and that I was doing good work. Even if that work wasn't what she wanted me to be doing, it was important. More important though, the lab got excellent publicity for everything I accomplished.

My own dream was one of immortality. 3D printed organ transplants were quite popular several years ago, but costly and impractical. It also didn't work for the brain. Cloning could never gain enough approval to overcome the ethical issues of growing an empty shell of a body.

Ketelzene, the drug that had been developed to slow the aging process had one flaw that prevented it from halting ageing entirely. The whole body works together to maintain itself, and Ketelzene helps with that process. At some point the body cannot catch up with healing itself and the Ketelzene, while delaying and slowing the timeline, cannot completely halt it. The interdependencies of the cellular systems means that one part will inevitably neglect itself while tending to another, and the next time around, will not be able to assist in repairs as quickly or thoroughly.

My theory was that cells needed to be able to replace themselves with new, younger cells instead of just repairing themselves.

It was at the end of this frustrating discussion about the use of my time, that she stalked out and slammed the door behind her. The force of it fluttered the papers on my desk, and the sound of it hitting the frame was almost like thunder. I grimaced, knowing it would not be the last time we had this talk. For what felt like the hundredth time since I started working there, I felt the urge to give up on trying to work with Maiia and leave to start my own lab. The biggest detractor there was funding.

I swore under my breath and stood up to pace in my office. I glanced at the papers that had been ruffled by the door closing. They were white papers from some of the projects I had recently completed for her. I swept them off my desk, enraged. It was completely unfair. In a few weeks my work was able to bring in more money than anyone in the laboratory could get in a year. I was keeping this place afloat, and all it did was put me further behind in my own research. I needed to stop cooperating with Maiia's demands and fend for myself.

That was when it hit me. Cooperation is what kills us. The body needed to stop cooperating with itself.

I would reprogram the brain. I would teach the body to use Ketelzene to fend for itself rather than working together as one giant machine. If each part was able to focus entirely on it's own maintenance and preemptively help out with other systems when it had time, then it would never fall behind.

My heart fluttered as I thought the idea through again, but in my core I knew I could make it work. "Lancing to Amelia Pope." I waited for her to respond, but it was taking too long. She must have been unable to talk at the moment. I sat back down at my desk. "New message to Amelia Pope." A picture of Amelia opened on my monitor next to a small text box and waited for me to speak further, but I was wary. I looked at her picture and thought back to our first meeting as children.

I was suspicious that Maiia checked up on my correspondence. She knew things about the status of my work that she couldn't have known otherwise. I didn't want her to know about this. I wanted all the glory of this for Amelia and myself, but I didn't have the resources to fund the research on my own. I thought about the early years of my life, how I defied my parents without their knowing. That defiance brought me to this place and made me the man I was today. I never once regretted it.

I'd keep this between Amelia and myself. I'd continue to work on my other method of stopping the ageing process and Maiia's pet projects in public, but I'd find a way to keep her from seeing this. I'd find someone I could trust to create a way for me to develop and test my theory without Maiia being able to see it on my computer. I'd protest from time to time, to make things seem like normal, but I'd undermine her and leave when I had the first opportunity. Take her by surprise and leave her with no recourse and no credit.

I walked back around to the front of my desk and cleaned the papers back up. I stepped into the hallway, intent on heading to the security department to ask someone there about it, but I stopped short when I realized I couldn't use someone from the lab. I had no doubt that I couldn't trust any of them to keep this from Maiia.

Instead I headed for the exit. I waved to Kathy, sitting at the administration desk on my way out. "Going out for lunch a little early today, Kathy."

"Skip out on breakfast?"

I faked an appreciative smile at her and left the building, wondering what Amelia was doing.

It was a clear, brisk day. I had not taken my lab coat off before leaving the building, and buttoned it up to shield myself against the wind. There was a small French cafe a few blocks away that Amelia and I frequented. I knew it would be quiet this time of the morning, so I headed in that direction. The traffic was sparse, most people well into their workday by now.

The woman behind the counter waved a familiar hello to me. I nodded in greeting and by way of ordering my usual pastry and coffee, and sat down at a table. "Computer security consultants." A screen appeared on the tabletop and showed me a map of businesses close by that specialized in computer security, several spots that had stories related to computer security and a list of related news links below.

"A coffee and a galette," said a waitress as she laid them on top of the map. "Oh, you looking to bring that kid in to check out his brain or something?"

I glanced up at her, certain she was mistaking me for someone else. "I'm sorry, what did you say?"

"That whiz kid they've been talking about who lives over in Mt. Airy."

"What whiz kid?"

"Don't you ever read the news?" She stabbed a finger at the top link

The truth was I had very little time or concern for what was going on in the world around me. I had ruled out politics as a field of study almost immediately upon learning about it. Outside of the lab I only talked to Amelia. It was always just Amelia.

The waitress walked away as I shifted my food around to read the article that she pointed out. The headline immediately brightened my mood; "NSA Hires Child Prodigy After He Confounds Their Surveillance Programs."

An eight-year-old child had developed a device he could carry with him to ensure that any access he made to the Internet or communication network could not be monitored or traced. Like most articles, the headline was misleading. The boy had been offered a position with the NSA but turned it down. He was quoted as saying he didn't trust anyone, least of all the government.

I didn't need his trust. I only needed his advice. I flagged down the waitress again. "Can I get this to go?"

She took the dishes away and came back with a paper bag and a disposable cup. I packed my food up and then I was out the door intent on finding the nearest shuttle stop. Before I could reach one my eyes were drawn to Amelia, just a few yards away from the cafe. It happened all the time, as though I could sense when she was near even before seeing her.

When she was within arms reach of me she grabbed my coffee as she gave me a quick kiss. She took a sip for herself then grimaced as she saw the pastry bag and handed the cup back to me. "You and sweets, Doctor."

I adopted a sheepish grin. "It's all your fault, wife. Care to give me a lift to Mt. Airy?"

"What's in Mt. Airy?" she asked as her eyebrows rose in curiosity.

"The means to rebellion."

"My car's back at the lab," she said.

I noticed a quick grin flicker across her face as she turned and I followed her back down the street. Another thing that I loved about Amelia, she never felt the need to ask too many questions. We drove in silence and she occasionally stole the coffee cup back.

The article did not list his address, but I learned years ago how to track people down. Perhaps not a young child who didn't want to be watched, but I could at least find his parents. The one thing I definitely had going for me was my lab association.

The house was a large Victorian, and I spotted at least one news van still hanging about, hoping for something to add to the story. I sent Amelia over to distract him as I went and knocked on the door. The last thing I needed was for Maiia to see me on the news that evening, visiting a child genius.

A well-dressed, middle-aged woman answered and took in my lab coat with a sense of distrust. "Good morning Mrs. Bledsoe. My name is Doctor Lancing. I work with Kischukov Laboratory on the other side of town."

"I told that other doctor, I'm not interested in having Tommy's head examined."

I filed that bit of information away for further investigation. "I'm not here to dissect him, I promise. I was a bit of a child prodigy myself you see, and I'm certain I have some projects at the lab that Thomas would find intriguing."

She glanced out at the news van and glared back at me again. "Did Doctor Kischukov send you?"

So it was Maiia. She was constantly trying to get children who showed increased mental capacity to come to the lab for studies. The problem was, she refused to offer them anything in return. She felt that furthering the cause of science should be enough incentive for anyone. "I assure you, though I work with her, our projects are vastly different. I didn't even know she had been here."

She hesitated another moment before letting me in and closing the front door behind me. She gestured into the living room. "Take a seat." I did as she asked. "He's bored. We weren't thrilled about the NSA thing, but we don't want to stifle his learning. He's surpassed his classmates by years now. We're trying to get him advanced learning classes, but at his age, it's difficult for him to socialize with the other students when he's so much younger than they are."

I tried to smile in a friendly, reassuring way. "I had the same problem as a child. I know boredom, if not guided, can lead to dangerous pastimes for a child of great intelligence." Like fatal experiments on small mammals, I thought to myself. "And the beauty of this is, for now at least, he would be able to work from home. He's too young to do any real lab work, but he could do research and simulations remotely."

She glanced into the next room before looking back at me. "It would be nice to be able to keep him at home."

She seemed like she was nervous, almost afraid of something. I couldn't be sure why. "Can I speak with him? Explain the sort of work I do and see if it's of interest to him?"

She hesitated before nodding, and walked out in the direction she had glanced in earlier. She returned, her hands on the shoulders of a young boy, guiding him into the living room where I sat. I stood and offered my hand. "My name is Doctor Lancing, Tommy. It's a pleasure to meet you."

He shook my hand but said nothing. I retook my seat and he sat in a chair on the opposite side of the room. He stared out into space, obviously bored.

"I work at the Kischukov Laboratory," I said. "My research is mostly in cellular biology, but it branches out into various technologies. I understand you weren't interested in a job with the NSA, but I think you'd be very interested in some of the projects going on at the lab. We're doing very exciting stuff."

He still said nothing and didn't make eye contact with me at all. His mother spoke up on his behalf. "Perhaps if you explained some of the projects?"

"I'd like to, Mrs. Bledsoe, but I'm afraid I'd have to ask you to leave the room for that. The work isn't classified, but it's highly sensitive and I can't broadcast it to more people than necessary."

She frowned and looked a bit put out, but squeezed Thomas's shoulder and said, "I'll be in the kitchen when you're done, Tommy." She glanced nervously over her shoulder as she left the room.

I picked up on a slight eye roll as she said his name. I realized he didn't like being treated like such a child. I decided to play to that. "Do you know what extreme intelligence is, Thomas? It is power."

His gaze turned to me and for the first time since he entered the room he looked engaged in what I was saying.

"I was like you before, Thomas. I felt like I didn't belong. My parents forced my isolation upon me. I didn't get to go to school, I found someone to bring me books and I taught myself. But even after I entered society, I felt the distance that comes with being far superior to your peers. I know how it is. Your intelligence isolates you. But you can turn that isolation to your favor."

"I'm smarter than the rest of them," he said and paused. He seemed like he was trying to penetrate me with his gaze. "I'm smarter than you."

I couldn't help but grin at his arrogance. "We'll see, won't we?"

He responded to my grin with one of his own. I could tell he wanted to take on that challenge.

"What sorts of projects do you work on?" he asked me.

"How would you like to live forever?"

Thomas paused for a moment and stared at me, measuring me. "What do I need to do?" he asked.

"I have the answer, but I need privacy to develop it. I need to hide my work from the rest of my lab. Doctor Kischukov is always watching what we do. So we'll start with this: I need some way to mask my work."

"It'll be done by the time you get back to your lab." He stood and I followed him into the kitchen.

"Thank you, Mrs. Bledsoe. Tommy sounds interested in the work." I caught his smile, and wondered if he had picked up on the fact that I had intentionally used his full name just for him. "I'm sure he'll enjoy the chance to expand his mind. We'll set up an account in the lab for him and supply him with a cutting edge computer in a few days."

"Well that sounds just lovely, doesn't it, Tommy?" She squeezed his shoulder again when she looked down at him, and I watched him give her a fake smile.

"I'm glad you think so, Mrs. Bledsoe. Now would you mind if I went out the back? I'm not crazy about news vans either."

She smiled and led me to the back door. Amelia had pulled the car around the corner, and I walked through the yard behind the house to meet her.

Chapter 4

"Now will you tell me what's going on?" Amelia asked as we pulled away from Thomas's house.

"I've done it, Amelia. I've found the secret to immortality." I relaxed in the car, confident that Thomas would be more than able to complete his task.

"You found a way to regenerate cells? That's amazing." Even in an impressed state, Amelia had a graceful calm that I always appreciated. Anyone else would've mistaken her flat tone as sarcasm.

"No, I didn't." We had had many discussions on the impracticalities of that solution, but I had insisted it was the way to go. After all, I had been working that angle for over a year and I wasn't about to give up on it. Immortality was the ultimate reward. Amelia and I together, forever. She wasn't as obsessed about the "forever" idea as I was, but she granted that being able to live at least several lifetimes was an intriguing idea.

She glanced at me and raised an eyebrow, but waited, knowing I would explain myself in due time.

"I was going about it the wrong way. The body spends way too much time making certain systems help out other systems, when they should just be fending for themselves."

She turned and gave me a wary look. "The human body has been a vast network of cooperative parts since we apes climbed out of the muck. What makes you think it can survive turning on itself? Won't you just further the problem of individual decay?"

"Think of it as turning the brain into a multi-threaded operating system," I said.

"It already is!"

"But it's not taking advantage of that to its maximum extent, especially not with regards to how it utilizes the Ketelzene drug."

We were back at the lab. She turned into the parking lot and turned off the car but made no move to leave the vehicle. "So what you're saying is that you're going to reprogram the brain to use Ketelzene at opportune moments of low processing?"

"It's a bit more than that, Amelia. I'm going to rewrite the priorities of each system in relation to one another and remove, or at least reduce, the unnecessary tasks." Talking it out with Amelia made me even more certain that this would work. She had a knack for throwing wrenches into my plans that would force me to further develop my ideas into fully realized proposals.

"Reprogramming the brain…" She seemed doubtful.

"Think of it more as retraining the brain. This sort of thing has been done, Amelia. It's just rerouting neurons."

She turned to me and smiled, an act that always filled me with warmth and made my heart flutter a little, even after all these years. The idea of still feeling this way, two or three hundred years later, was inspiring.

"I look forward to poking further holes in your hypothesis, Doctor," she said with a half grin.

"I look forward to filling them, wife." I smiled back, and we both exited the car. "I'm not telling Maiia about this, just to make you aware."

"So that's why you wanted to talk to that hacker kid?"

"You know who he is?"

"Of course. I read the news."

Her voice was flat, but I knew the jab was there. She often chastised me for being so disconnected from the world. The truth was, outside of Amelia, I had no interest in the rest of the world. I wasn't at the laboratory to save other people; I was there to help myself, and to help Amelia. The rest of the world could die in a fire for all I cared.

She walked me to my office and gave me a peck on the cheek before turning to leave. "Good luck with that."

I watched her walk away until she had turned the corner and was out of sight, and then entered my office. A message was waiting for me from Thomas. He had already infiltrated our inter-office communication system. I could only assume, since he was sending me email, he had also managed to set up an invisible work environment for me as well. "Open message."

> *Lancing,*
> *Weren't you listening? I get bored easily. Try something harder.*
> *Thomas*

It hadn't taken half an hour for Amelia and me to return to the lab. This kid was definitely good. I knew for a fact that younger people were more susceptible to the type of brain reprogramming I was looking to do, since their brains were not completely developed yet. Thomas was certainly young. Theories and proposals are all well and good, but nothing beats a test subject. "New message to Thomas Bledsoe."

> *Thomas,*
> *It's not like the security here is super tight, anyone could have hacked into it in short order. But you've passed the first test. If you want a real challenge I've got one for you. First, I've realized we'll need some lab space after all, and some equipment. Find me an empty warehouse space that won't ask too many questions. I'm sure you can hack into my bank account and deal with the initial investment, but you may need to find some additional sources for funding. Be aware, I will turn you in if I find you're being unreasonable about costs. I'll put together a list of equipment and send that along as well. Try to spread the orders out to various companies. I don't want questions. Once we're set up, the real challenge will begin for you. You may find programming computers to be a simple task, but the brain is a whole different story.*
> *Lancing*

I knew that last sentence would intrigue him, albeit for the wrong reasons initially. He'd think we were reprogramming someone else's brain, and given his excitement at my talk of power, he'd probably think that was the power I was talking about. He'd think I was suggesting power over other people, not himself. Within a minute I had my response.

> *Lancing,*
> *What do you think I am, an amateur? A different person will order each piece of equipment and the lease for the space*

won't have your name on it. Send me this list, I'm anxious to
get started. Whose brain are we going to reprogram?
Thomas

I knew Thomas was driven and wanted a challenge. I was also sure he would see through any ploy of mine to suggest we need a young vibrant mind. I put together the list of equipment and sent it to him along with a simple message:

Yours.

It was a bit of a gamble, but if he was as anxious as I thought he was, I knew he'd be flattered. Once he realized we'd be improving the capability of his own brain function and not exerting external control over it, he would be eager to be the test subject. I stepped away from my desk to invite Amelia to lunch. Though we had been gone all morning, I knew no one would make note of our absence other than Kathy. Kathy would not care.

We went back to the French cafe. I realized on the way that my pastry had remained in Amelia's car, untouched. I often forgot to eat on days when I was consumed with work. Usually, the only thing that got me out to lunch was knowing I would be there with Amelia.

She didn't produce quite as much work for the lab as I did, but she got away with skipping out often because she was with me. Maiia didn't understand her attachment to me, but accepted that there were certain things she could not deny me if she wanted me to stick around and produce funding for her. She knew that we were a package deal.

"There's a bounce in you," she observed after we had ordered.

"Thomas has already been more productive than I expected."

The corners of her mouth twitched upward slightly. "I'm glad you're doing this for yourself. You've been a slave to that woman for far too long."

"This could be it, Amelia. This could be the big payoff. We could leave that stinking lab behind and go into business for ourselves. I can find tons of people to fund my research once they know what I'm capable of. And not just those busy work projects Maiia has me doing. I mean real, life altering work."

"I'm proud of you."

Amelia often told me how proud she was of me. Today though, there was sadness in her tone. In most people I would interpret that as jealousy, but I knew Amelia was never jealous of my mind. "What's wrong?"

She shook her head. "I've just been tired. Working too much." She smiled faintly, but it didn't reach her eyes.

It seemed like she was tired all the time these days. "Soon you won't have to work at all if you don't want to." I smiled and lifted my water glass in a toast. Her returning smile was genuine this time, and she clinked her glass against mine. "To breaking out of this hell hole."

When she laughed I forgot about the rest of the world. We sat in silence, and I stared at her until our food arrived. I watched her eat and wondered what I could do to her physiology to cure her tiredness. By the end of lunch I had five ideas.

*   *   *   *

A stab of panic ran through me as I arrived at my office and saw Maiia sitting at my desk, looking at my screen. "Maiia," I said and nodded hello.

"Ah, Lancing. I noticed you finished the paper on amino-peptide reordering, very nice." She gestured to the paper sitting on the corner of my desk but remained seated in my chair.

"Go ahead and take it. Were you looking for something else?"

"Nope, just noodling around while I waited for you to return." She leaned back in my desk chair as though she was sitting at her own desk instead of mine. "How's the cellular membrane restructuring going?"

I cringed at the obvious privacy infringement but tried not to show it. "Done by the end of the week."

"Excellent, excellent. I'm glad to see you've taken this morning's conversation more seriously." She finally stood up. She walked over to me and put a hand on my shoulder. It was not heavy, but I sagged under the weight of it and wanted to shove it away from me. "You're an excellent asset to this laboratory, Lancing. I'm glad to see you're finally taking that to heart and being a team player." She let go of me and left.

I couldn't move for a moment. My shoulder felt soiled from where she had touched me. After the glorious morning I had just had, it felt like a crushing defeat to find her in here. I would play my part though. Just like with my parents, I would do everything I could to rip the foundation of her success out from under her, and she would never see it coming.

I was pleased when I sat down at my desk and found a message waiting for me from Thomas that Kischukov hadn't been able to see.

> *Lancing,*
> *3 weeks. The scanner was the longest lead item at 6 weeks, but I talked them down to 3. The warehouse paperwork will be done by the end of the week and the first shipment should arrive there the following day. My mother will be there to take delivery until we can find someone to staff the place in the interim. The only people I know are children or my parents. Any ideas?*
> *Thomas*

I had to admit, Thomas was good. I was intrigued to know how an eight-year-old child could talk a company down three weeks in a delivery time. Thomas was proving to be an invaluable asset, and he had been working for me for less than three hours. A sense of pride swelled in me. Even though he wasn't my own son, I knew him better than his own parents did. Without knowing it, in that brief conversation in his house, I had taken him under my wing as one of my own. It was fulfilling to be guiding him to expand his potential.

I also felt vindicated, and couldn't help but smirk. This child and I would show Maiia.

Chapter 5

"Ow!"

"Stop complaining, Thomas," I said. "No one ever said progress doesn't hurt."

I had fully developed my plan for reprogramming the brain at the lab. Now I was working with Thomas, mostly on the weekends. The procedure seemed to be painful to him, so I was insisting he take a full week to recover between training sessions.

Thomas was lying on a hospital bed. A neural helmet surrounded his head and electrodes were attached to various parts of his body. The damage I was inflicting was muscular so far. Deep enough it wouldn't leave a mark, nothing critical to his survival. At this stage, the worst he would suffer for his undeveloped control was a few sore muscles. Though at the end of every day he claimed to feel fine.

"Come on!" he half yelled, half whimpered.

"You're better than this, Thomas. You can control the pain with your mind. Practice. Focus."

He took a deep breath and was quiet for a while. His face was set in concentration and his eyes were closed, but I saw a tear glimmer in the corner of one of them.

I hadn't told him that part of what I had him hooked up to was intentionally damaging some of his cells to see how the repair process would go while his neurons were behaving properly. So far, it seemed to be working. However I needed a lot more data to confirm that it would actually work on a long-term basis.

At some point I would have to show Amelia how to do this and try it on myself, to make sure he wasn't just putting on a brave face. I never trusted test subjects to be completely honest with me, especially when it came to their own development.

"Just imagine yourself 80 years from now, young as ever and all your classmates old and withering."

"I'll be eight forever?"

"No. You will continue to age to a point. The body grows and with it, systems will mature. But you will never reach the point where things start to break down. Your muscles will always be strong, your bones dense, your mind sharp."

He smiled on that last one. I knew he valued his intellect above all else. I felt the same. Even if this didn't work and my body slowly decayed, I dreaded the idea of my mind going. My mind was everything to me, apart from Amelia. I stopped the helmet from transmitting and let him sit for a moment. "How do you feel?"

"Fine."

"How does your mind feel?"

"Tired."

"You're showing signs of improvement, but that's all for today. I've nearly got the neural pathway limits figured out. I'd say within a month, you'll be well on your way to immortality."

He smiled again but was breathing heavily. He was hiding the pain. It had me slightly concerned. Emotional detachment from test subjects was normally quite easy, but I liked Thomas. I saw much of myself in him, and I wanted him to succeed. I felt a little bad about using him like this, but I knew I would get further faster with him than a normal person. I walked over to the bed, took the helmet off him and laid a hand on his shoulder.

"Really, Thomas, how are you?"

"It's fine. I can keep going."

"Just because you can, doesn't mean we should."

"You just said yourself, we're nearly there right? Well I can't give up now. I want this."

I looked down at my hand, resting on his shoulder and wondered what he really thought of me. I was definitely too attached to a test subject. We both knew though, that pushing him like this was the best course ahead. "Why don't we give you a two week rest this time. The closer we get to mapping your limits, the worse it seems to be on you."

"No. I'm fine."

I couldn't argue with him. He'd see through any excuse. "Ok. Sit here and rest for a bit. We'll pick up again next Saturday, as usual. Water?"

He nodded and kept his eyes closed as I brought him a bottle of water with a straw. As he started to sip at it I removed the rest of the electrodes. I had told him they were measuring the cellular repair rates, but in reality, it was how I was damaging him. Everything I wanted to know about his cellular processes, his brain was already telling me.

His eyes snapped back open as we heard the door open. They relaxed again when he saw Amelia. "Hello, Ammy!"

If I thought I was getting too close to the kid, Amelia definitely was.

"Hello, Thomas," she said. "Good session?"

"Lancing says we're nearly there!"

I watched him perk up and force his breathing to slow. He put on an even braver front for Amelia that he let slip for me. I patted him on the head as I removed the last electrode and wheeled the cart away. "He's making excellent progress. I don't think we'd have made it this far without such a dedicated candidate."

Amelia walked up to the side of Thomas's bed and took his hand. I was momentarily hit with a pang of jealousy. I pushed it aside. Thomas was more like a nephew to Amelia than anything else. The idea of her and an eight-year-old child was utterly absurd, and I knew that. She was my wife.

She swept a lock of hair off Thomas' forehead that had been displaced by the helmet. "Well, I'm very proud of you," she said. "You've been very brave to submit to this experiment. And I'm sure the reward will be well worth it."

His mouth broke into a wide grin. "I'm certain of it. Just think of all the time we'll be able to spend together, once we're all immortal. The things we can accomplish!"

Amelia's smile wavered just a touch. "Absolutely. Especially when we quit Kischukov's for good and start our own lab, right?"

Thomas almost laughed in his excitement. "I already have a few ideas for projects!"

This was news to me. "What sorts of project, Thomas?"

He turned his attention back to me but clung to Amelia's hand. "You know how they never really got cryogenics working? Well, I have the solution!"

"Care to share?" I was intrigued. It was a problem I flirted with briefly, but it never held my interest well enough for me to fully pursue it. What possible use could I have for cryogenics when I could simply live forever instead?

"Let's just say there are other ways to stop bodily functions that don't involve freezing. And if you don't have to freeze the body, you don't have to worry about everything rupturing as it expands." His grin turned into a boastful smirk. He was convinced he could solve this problem, I was certain of that. And that meant that he could. I had never known anyone quite as gifted as Thomas, except for myself.

"We'll make it our top priority once we've escaped from Kischukov's lab," I lied.

Thomas hopped down from the bed. "My mom will be here any minute to pick me up. I better go wait for her. Thanks."

Amelia patted him on the head and he took it as an invitation to hug her.

"Until next Saturday, Thomas," I said as I watched them embrace.

"Bye," he said to me, as he released Amelia and headed to the door. He looked out the window to confirm that his mother had arrived and he was almost skipping as he left.

Amelia turned to me, her smile returned. "So, it's going well?"

"A few more weeks, though I think he's hurting more than he lets show," I said with a mischievous grin and held my arms out to welcome her into a hug. She approached and placed her head against my chest as my arms wrapped around her. "He's really quite brilliant. I think this could work out very well for us. I'll be free of Maiia and we can work on really fringe research projects."

She sighed into my chest. "That will be nice. I feel like I haven't accomplished anything in weeks."

I pulled away from her to gaze at her face. "What's wrong? You seemed down when Thomas mentioned how close we were to solving this problem. You can't possibly be jealous."

"No. Just tired."

I left it at that and pulled her into an embrace to hide the nervousness in my face. The concern for Amelia that I had been burying for weeks returned to the surface again. She wasn't telling me something. I knew Amelia though, and believe that she would take care of whatever was ailing her. "What projects are you interested in that Maiia has shot down?"

She pulled away on her own and smiled up at me. "You'll laugh."

"Never."

"I want to make human gills."

I started at her and fought very hard against the laughter. I tried to twist it in my brain to think about the scientific hurdles it would involve but my mind kept failing me. After about twenty seconds of trying I gave up and laughed.

"Told you."

"I'm sorry," I said in between giggles. "It's very...fantasy. Not so much science."

"I always thought it would be fun to be a mermaid." She shrugged and giggled a little herself. "To be able to swim in the ocean, unassisted, nearly weightless, for as long as I like. But it is a very impractical project."

"I'll fund it. Hell, it would be an amazing feat. Did you actually pitch that to Maiia?"

She rolled her eyes at me. "I'm not crazy. I didn't want to get laughed out of her office, then potentially fired."

"They'd never fire you. I mean too much to them," I said.

She looked up at me with a gaze that was both grateful and hurt. I took her face in my hands and planted a kiss upon her lips before pulling away to take in her face again.

"Seriously, to hell with Maiia," I said. "When this is over, we'll have enough money to fund anything. I say, the crazier the idea the better. But why would you want to be a mermaid? Do you have some unnatural sort of attraction to fish?"

She swatted my shoulder and pursed her lips at me for a moment. "Let's just say I watched "The Little Mermaid" way too many times as a child." The smile on her face faded to a frown. I knew she didn't like to talk about her childhood.

"No idea what you're talking about," I said.

She gave an aggravated sigh. "Figures. Come on, let's go home and I'll introduce you to a Disney classic."

I groaned. Her previous attempts to introduce me to Disney classics had not gone well. The only movie she had shown me so far that had any merit was an animated commentary on the decline of society called "Wall-E". The robot in control of the ship carrying the remains of humanity had reminded me of Maiia. The movie also gave me my first idea for how to erase memories. I regretted telling Maiia about that idea. She pounced on it, and the next thing I knew one of my duties was dealing with government agency employees sent to us to erase their knowledge of secret programs when they had unfriendly partings with their jobs. I mollified myself by believing that these people were real dangers to national security. I reasoned leaving them alone would be the more harmful action to the general public than erasing a few years of their lives.

Amelia helped me shut down the rest of the machinery and we drove back to our place. Five minutes into "The Little Mermaid" I was ready to just accept her dream and move on. When she became engrossed enough in the movie, I stopped watching and gazed at her. There were dark circles under her eyes as though she hadn't been sleeping well. Her skin looked sallow as well. I grabbed her hand under the pretense of holding it, but examined it shortly after. She had lost some weight. The veins in her hand were readily apparent. It looked like the hand of an old woman, not my vibrant, young adult wife. I gave her a quick kiss on the cheek and said, "Bathroom break."

"Shall I pause it?"

"Why not."

I heard her say, "Pause movie," as I went to the bathroom. I opened up the medicine cabinet, but none of the prescriptions in there seemed out of the ordinary. Vitamins, mild pain killers and birth control.

We had discussed children several times. She wanted to try, but I had never been ready. There was always too much work. Both of us were always staying too late at our jobs. We could never sustain that sort of schedule and feel good about raising children as attentive parents. The issue was often shelved with a promise of "some day." We had plenty of good childbearing years ahead of us, so it never seemed to be a pertinent problem. I closed the medicine cabinet and headed back to Amelia.

"You know, once we open our own lab, things will be less hectic."

"What do you mean?" She left the movie on pause.

"Well, we won't have to work these ridiculous hours to satisfy our own intellectual pursuits while at the same time producing for Doctor Kischukov's benefit. We can set our own hours, based only on our drive to solve the world's problems."

"Like you ever won't be driven to solve the world's problems, Doctor."

"The world can do without me for a while, wife."

She studied me. "You wouldn't know what to do with yourself if you weren't working."

"Sure I do. We've been putting off a family for a while now. Maybe starting our own lab would be the perfect time for us to ease back on our research and let our employees save the world for a while. We can let Thomas create human gills after he's solved the cryogenics problem."

She stared at me, speechless, for a moment. "What brought this on?" There was sadness in her question. She turned her face away as I saw her eyes begin to glisten with tears.

"Probably the fact that I'm watching a children's movie." I smirked at her and she once again swatted my shoulder.

"Resume movie."

I was glad for the distraction. In her current state, she didn't look like she could survive carrying a child to term, and that frightened me more than I wanted to admit.

Chapter 6

"There's something I need to talk to you about," Amelia said.

It was early in the morning. Thomas had not shown up yet, and we were powering on equipment and getting the space ready for him. I was one or two treatments away from finalizing the methodology for the brain reprogramming, I was sure of it. The immediacy of a solution had been fueling me for days. I hadn't slept, but I had been wide-awake with eagerness at the approaching end of this project.

I suddenly found that energy drained, as though someone had hit me with a stun gun meant for an elephant. I set down my computer pad and turned to face her directly. I tried to brace myself for the worst, not entirely sure what that could be. "Yes?"

She worried her lower lip slightly, something she did when she was hesitating on saying something. I walked over to her and grasped her frail hands in mine. I looked into her eyes and nodded my silent encouragement. I tried to keep my face serene, though my mind was screaming in fear.

"I've been diagnosed with Sunithe's disease."

The room swam for a moment and I staggered back from her. It made me feel ashamed, it was the exact opposite thing I should be doing. I leaned against the bed for a moment in an attempt to steady my breath and gather myself, then approached her and took her hands again. "You're sure?"

She nodded again.

"Have you gotten a second opinion?"

She nodded again.

I knew Amelia wouldn't leave a diagnosis like this to chance. She would've been thorough in her research into her state. "How long?"

"About a month."

"A month!" I was blinded by anger. She must have known for a long time now that she had the disease. Why wait until she only had a month left to tell me? I was filled immediately with regret, and a new pain. My plan for immortality would do nothing for her. I could have spent the last few months working a cure for her instead. "Why didn't you tell me sooner?"

"I know how important this work is to you. And I thought maybe— Jenson has been working on a cure you know."

"Jenson is a moron. *I* could have been working on a cure." I seethed with rage.

"And if you failed?" She glared at me, though in her weakened state it had little effect. "You'd never forgive yourself."

"It would still be better than not giving me a chance to try at all!" I fed on her anger, sweeping the pad off the bed onto the floor. It wasn't enough. I was angry with Jenson, angry with Maiia. I was angry with myself for not realizing what was going on. I wanted to smash my equipment in my anger. Everything I had accomplished here seemed so pointless all of sudden. Nothing else mattered, not immortality, not screwing over Maiia. Nothing mattered but being with Amelia, and she was being taken away from me. "I can't believe your lack of faith in me!"

Hurt crept into the anger on her face. "It wasn't a lack of faith in your abilities, but a desire to not have you obsessing over this merely for my benefit."

"*Merely* for your benefit?" I said, mocking her voice. "You're more important to me than immortality. How could you possibly think otherwise? What good is an unending life without you by my side, sharing it with me?"

"Think of the bigger picture. I'm only one person. With this work, you'll be able to help the entire world."

"To hell with the world!" I shouted.

The door opened and Thomas entered. Amelia gave him an impossibly cheery greeting. I tried to control my fuming breath. It was unfair of her to wait until now to tell me. I wanted to yell at Thomas to get the hell out, but she was already preparing the bed for him. "Good morning, Thomas." The hollow words came out of my mouth in a snarl.

He stopped short and glanced between the two of us and at the pad, still on the floor. "Good morning?"

I swooped down and snatched the pad back up off the floor. Amelia had won this round. We wouldn't be able to talk about it again until Thomas was gone.

The session went even better than I expected. My drive to control my anger meant I had even more focus on the scans than prior sessions. Thomas's body was healing itself entirely as a background process. No resources that were needed elsewhere were being redirected. It was a bittersweet victory.

"Congratulations, Thomas. With Ketelzene, you will now live forever." *Assuming you don't get Sunithe's disease,* I added silently. I should have been thrilled. This was what we had spent the past few months working on. I only felt hollow.

Amelia hugged Thomas and me, and excused herself. Thomas looked satisfied, but not as excited as I would have expected. Again, I cursed myself for not being able to deal with Amelia's situation earlier.

"What's going on?" he asked.

"Didn't you hear what I said? You're immortal." I nearly spat the words at him. I was angry that he wasn't elated. He was supposed to distract me from my anger, not remind me of my problems.

"Yes, great. What's going on?" His concern over the two of us was more immediate than anything else we might have accomplished today.

I was disarmed by his reaction; my anger finally began to turn to pain. I looked to where Amelia had gone. He might as well know. I felt defeated, I didn't have the strength in me to try and steer the conversation elsewhere. "You've heard of Sunithe's disease?"

He looked over after Amelia as well, then looked back at me and nodded. "How long does she have?"

"About a month."

He caught me by surprise by clapping his hands and rubbing them together.

"Well then, now that I'm immortal and your project is finished, we better get moving on my cryogenic machine."

I almost laughed at him. The idea was ludicrous. For a moment I thought perhaps I had damaged his brain in the process. I wanted to laugh, but knowing how intelligent Thomas was, I couldn't. An acceptance of the idea tugged at the back of my brain.

I allowed myself a moment to believe it. To believe in the glimmer of hope that we could find a way to safely freeze Amelia, then find the cure and wake her up. After all, we were about to become immortal. It wouldn't matter how long it would take to find a cure. I shook my head at him. "No."

"Why not? Give me a month. What's the harm in that?"

I thought about it. "No. There's no point. We don't have the funding."

"You must not pay much attention to your bank account. You've had a bunch of small anonymous donations from various sources building your savings back up. You can afford to fund this. And you can't afford not to try this. I can tell."

"What do you mean?" I asked him.

"I can see how much you love her. I know you won't survive losing her."

"That's ridiculous. I will live on."

"But it will be a shallow life without her."

I glared at him. He was right. How could he know me so well? I'd lose my drive to continue on. Without Amelia, I wouldn't even want to be immortal. "What does an eight-year-old child know about love?"

"I'm no normal eight-year-old and you know it."

Neither of us spoke for a few moments, just glared, measuring each other. I was fighting the urge to let him try to fix things for me. I knew I would give up the rest of my work to spend every last second with Amelia. What difference did it make what he did?

"Give me a month," he pleaded. "Just one month to at least try."

"Back up power? Containment?"

"Don't you worry. I'll sort it all out."

I fought against my pessimistic side, let myself be defeated and cling to the small glimmer of hope he could provide. He was right. I could afford it. It was his project, so I would only be minimally involved. We wouldn't have much time for testing, though. Amelia would have to be the test subject, and that worried me. I didn't even know if she would submit to the idea. At the very least, it was worth a try. "Okay, Thomas. One month. I'll convince Amelia."

"Yes!" He thrust his hands up in a motion of victory.

Sometimes I forgot how young he was, but every now and again he would do something to remind me. I had to smile at his enthusiasm. He deserved to live forever. "What do you need?"

He hopped down off the bed and walked up to me. "I'll have the list for you in an hour." He left me alone in the laboratory area, waiting for Amelia to return.

I tried to refocus. My work on immortality was mostly done. I had to write up the results and conduct the final procedure on someone other than Thomas to prove the final mapping was accurate across all brains. Given the need for secrecy, that left Amelia and myself. I doubted Amelia would subject herself to the procedure, even to help me. I would have to program the computer with the final mapping and have her perform the experiment on me.

She returned, smiling at me, which only made me feel worse. I tried to apologize for my behavior. "Amelia, I'm-"

"Shh." She pulled me into a hug. "It will be alright, Doctor."

I wanted to believe it. I buried my head in the crook of her neck, rocking back and forth in her arms. "It's so unfair." My previous anger had dissipated. The glimmer of hope that Thomas's project would pull through still lingered in the back of my mind. "What do you want to do?"

She pulled her head away to look into my face, but kept the embrace. "What do you mean?"

"I mean where do you want to go? We've got a month to spend together. This work is basically done. I've got plenty of time off coming to me. Where should we go? Paris? Buenos Aires?"

"Somewhere quiet, and secluded."

"Quiet and secluded. I can manage that. Standard amenities?"

"Whatever," she said, and took her turn to bury her head into my shoulder. "So long as we're together."

My mind scanned about for places we could visit and have some relaxing, quality time together. Having something to think about helped to distract myself from the pain that I knew would have to surface at some point. A colleague had once told me about a remote island he knew of with a run down hotel, not far from the Atlantic coast. It was no longer maintained, but the infrastructure was decent enough. I decided to call him and inquire about it again. With any luck, I could send a team of people ahead to clean the place up and stock some food for us. It would take a few days for me to finish up my work and get Amelia to run the brain reprogramming on me. Then Amelia and I could live out the rest of our days in solitude.

"I'll work it out," I said, and kissed the top of her head.

We stood there, in each other's arms for a while. I fought off the tears by plotting my next moves.

"So it's done?" she asked finally.

"Yes." I reluctantly pulled away from her again. "Thomas responded very well to the final mapping. I'll need to try it on another patient before publishing my results."

"I guess I'd skew your results too much."

I kissed her forehead. "You're not exactly a standard patient, even ignoring your current state." I hadn't told her about Thomas's plan, and I wasn't sure I would for a while. I didn't want to risk giving her false hope. The very hope that even now, kept my heartbeat a little surer than it would have been otherwise. "I'll run the mapping on myself at some point."

"I can help."

"I'm counting on it, wife." I grinned at her again.

"Okay, Doctor." She smiled back.

Her smile made the hope in the back of my mind swell. She was strong, and Thomas was brilliant. This would work, I told myself. "But it can wait a while. First, I think we're overdue for some vacation."

With Sunithe's disease, she would be weak, but functional up to the last day or so. The mind would start to have spurts of incomprehensible activity that gradually increased into a constant state. We had to get her into a frozen state at the first sign of degradation. I'd use my programming as an excuse to get her back here for Thomas's experiment. If it was ready in time, that was.

My belief in him was strengthening. I wasn't sure if it was actual belief in his ability to solve the cryogenic problem or if I was just that desperate to save Amelia. It would be a lonely period of time without her around me while we tried to cure the disease. Though I knew it would go quickly with a purpose. And what better purpose could I find for living than saving Amelia's life?

Chapter 7

I told Thomas to go ahead and put together whatever he needed. I explained that it needed to be portable, and have a temporary power source that could last a few hours, for transporting it to another location. A few days ago I had a geothermal generator installed in the center of the island, which we could use to get the initial setup and freezing done. My plan was to get Thomas to a point where he could freeze and revive a mammal, and then he would bring the device to the island to try it on Amelia.

Amelia had a slight phobia of open water, so instead of chartering a sailboat to the island we booked passage on a seaplane. It wasn't a long flight, and Amelia would be able to distract herself well enough to not notice when we could no longer see land.

We met our pilot at a private dock in Rehoboth Beach, Delaware. Amelia was frail enough that she needed my assistance getting up into the aircraft. I could tell she was nervous about the vacation, but I couldn't be sure if it was because of the flight or because she thought she would die on this trip. I helped the pilot put our bags in the small cargo hold and climbed into the copilot seat next to him. I glanced back at Amelia and smiled. She gave me a thumbs-up, but could not wipe the look of apprehension off her face to smile back.

I shook my head and laughed. "Why would someone who hates open water want gills?"

"With gills I won't drown," she said.

I nodded and smiled. "Makes perfect sense to me."

She gripped the back of the seat in front of her as the propellers began to spin, and I turned back to the front to watch as we took off.

The island was not more than a few miles in circumference. I didn't even see it until we were descending and the pilot pointed it out. I looked back to ask Amelia if she could also see it, but she had her eyes closed and was breathing deeply to keep herself calm. I turned quickly away from her. In that state, she already looked dead.

I watched, as the island became a larger land mass packed with palm trees. The pilot glided to a stop in front of a disused dock. He left the engines running while I got out and helped Amelia. I grabbed our bags out of the small cargo hold and left them by the side of the plane. The pilot glanced at the island as I stuck my head back into the fuselage to bid him farewell. "You sure you'll be okay here?" he asked.

"Perfect." I smiled at him as I closed the door to the plane, then stepped back to watch while he took off. Amelia stood by my side and slid her hand around mine. We watched for a minute as the plane grew smaller, then I turned to her. "Let's see what we've gotten ourselves into."

Amelia smiled. Even in her diminished state, the unknown and the idea of us fending for ourselves excited her. I smiled back and tugged her along the wooden planks. The dock was not in great shape, but at the edge of the beach, a small hut looked promising. There was a group of half a dozen more huts surrounded by an overgrown landscaped garden. Most of them were in disarray, but one had obviously been repaired, as I requested.

The door was open. The inside was dated, but clean. To my satisfaction, the lights and the refrigerator, which was well stocked, worked. I turned the tap to run the hot water and waited for a minute before steaming water worked its way out. "Not bad."

Amelia was taking it all in: the art on the walls, the design on the bedspread. Someone had left a chilled bucket with champagne by the side of the bed. She fingered it idly and continued her survey. She disappeared into the bathroom for a while so I decided to unpack. We had brought enough clothes to last a couple weeks, assured that a washing machine would be available. I knew her patterns well enough to know in which drawers she would want which clothes, and the proper order to hang garments in the closet. She was still in the bathroom when I finished, so I opened the champagne and poured two glasses. A quick survey of the fridge revealed a lot of prepackaged meals. We would have to explore the island and see if we could find fresh fruit. At least, I would.

I handed Amelia a glass of champagne when she emerged from the bathroom shortly after my survey of the food. I held up my glass and said, "To vacation."

She clinked her glass against mine and gave me a coy glance before setting it back down and sitting on the edge of the bed. She patted it briefly and gave me a look that would normally have me flying to meet her. The state of her body had me wary. "I don't know."

She could tell why I was nervous. "I'm not dead yet, you know, Doctor."

I laughed once, with only a slight bit of humor, but met her on the bed. "Okay, wife."

*   *   *   *

Two weeks passed before Thomas got in touch with me. Amelia and I had grown into a pattern of sleeping in, eating, reading by the beach and making love. Despite her frail frame she still had plenty of vigor, and I learned after our first encounter to not take it easy on her. She had stormed out of bed with such rage and ferociousness that it made me want her even more. At that point, I stopped treating her like a sick person.

She tried to read inspirational writings like Randy Pausch's "The Last Lecture" and Joanna Avery's "The Moment I Lived," but she quickly became tired of them. "I've accepted that I'm dying, and I'm ready for it," she had told me. She switched back to reading technical journals and trying to come up with a few last hypotheses.

I promised her I would do my best to prove whatever she came up with, though secretly I thought to myself: you'll be able to work on that yourself some day. I was reading everything I could about Sunithe's disease. When it was first discovered, the work that has been done so far, what types of people get it and what results they've had with early medications.

If caught early, a person's life could be extended for a few years with a new drug. The problem was, there were no warning signs until you started to feel sick, and government regulations did not allow for regular testing to be covered unless there was a family history of it. Since Amelia's parents both died young, there was no way she would have known if they had it.

It took years for Sunithe's disease to fully manifest itself silently inside your body. Even if it had been caught early enough in Amelia, it wouldn't matter. A few extra years would not have been enough of a match for my eternity.

I also thought about my own work. A concern had arisen in me that there could be ethical issues with supplying people with eternity. Not to mention the cost. The equipment was expensive and at the moment we only had the one machine. It would not be hard to replicate the equipment and share the mapping with people, but then what? How much do we charge? Is this the sort of thing the government would demand be released to public domain so that rich and poor would have access to it the way they had with Ketelzene?

More than that, I wasn't sure most people could handle it. Thomas was a brilliant child and he understood what was going on and did his best to not fight against it. I knew it was painful, not just from the damage I was intentionally inflicting on him, but the actual remapping of the brain pathways. He told me it felt like his brain was on fire at some points. I wasn't convinced the average person would be able to cope with that, and anesthesia wasn't an option since the brain had to be receptive to the signals I was trying to send to it.

I decided that the next candidate for immortality, before I published my work, would definitely be myself. By going through the process I would have a better understanding of what it would involve for an average person. It was this decision that I was solidifying when I got an incoming call notification. I excused myself from my chair next to Amelia and went back into the hut to answer it.

Thomas looked like he had aged. I knew he would be just as driven to accomplish this task even without the motivation of saving Amelia, so I didn't let it bother me that he looked so tired. "Thomas, you're looking well."

"Stuff it, Lancing, I know I look like I haven't slept in weeks."

"Have you?"

"Barely." An enormous grin spread over his face. "But it was worth it. Yesterday I managed to stop a mouse's vital functions, then bring them back."

Two weeks. I was stunned. My heart fluttered. Thomas was bright, but I had no idea he was that bright. His theory of a biological EM pulse had merit, but I thought it would take months to get it right. A mouse was a very different creature than a human being though. "Congratulations."

"Ha! I need to adjust the settings, but I think I've worked out the pulse parameters relative to the organism. I was a bit overzealous at first, I think. I tried a monkey this morning." He paused for a moment. Though he didn't need to finish the thought, he did. "It didn't go well." He looked a bit ashamed.

"If the next one does, I believe you will have sorted it out. It's a big step from a mouse to a monkey, but if you think you know how the parameter changes relate to the organism then—"

"I do. At least, I'm pretty sure I do. The next monkey will confirm that I've worked out the equations, I'm sure of it. And then—" It was his turn to trail off.

"And then. I'll have to talk to her soon. How long will it take to get it packed up with the portable power source and shipped here?"

"A day, once we're done. I talked to that pilot who took you to the island. He pointed us in the direction of another seaplane with a larger cargo hold."

"I'm monitoring Amelia. When I think she's down to her last few days I'll contact you to set up the flight. I assume you're coming as well."

"Of course. This is my baby; I'm not letting anyone else touch it. For now."

I had to laugh at his protectiveness. "I understand completely. How's that immortality thing going, by the way?"

"Ask me again in 50 years."

"When we get back it's my turn. I'll have to show you what to do."

"I think I figured it out already, but at the very least, I'll run it by you."

"How did you—never mind. I should get back to Amelia. Contact me again with news on monkey number 2."

"Will do. See ya, Lancing. Tell Ammy I said hi."

I nodded and switched off the display. I sat for a moment and debated what to tell Amelia. It was almost certain that Thomas's theory would hold for a human. I called Thomas back.

"Lancing, I won't get the second monkey till tomorrow."

"That's fine, Thomas. Just one more thing." I hesitated, and he waited. I wasn't sure how deep his devotion to this cause ran, or his feelings for Amelia. "If the monkey works—find someone off the street who won't be missed. Get it?"

He stared blankly at me, and then apprehension crossed his face. "Got it." He paused for another moment and the apprehension turned sour. He frowned and furrowed his brow. "Yeah."

48 – The Children of Doctor Lancing

"Would you rather your first try be on Amelia? When you won't know the final results for who knows how many decades? I need something better than you thinking you've worked out the equations."

He gave me a curt nod. "Got it. I'll call when I have news." He cut off the call. I didn't want to take any unnecessary risks with Amelia. I would see how far Thomas's devotion to my cause went. I went back out to Amelia's side.

"Who was that?" she asked, setting aside the journal paper she had been reading.

"Maiia. Wanted to tell me about this great new project she has lined up for me. It's something to do with herpes. She says hi."

She laughed and the sound warmed me more than the blazing sun. She had been laughing a lot since we had come here. It was definitely the right move after the insanity of working for both Maiia and on my immortality project. She looked healthier, stronger. I knew it couldn't last. I stretched my arm out to her chair to rest my hand on hers.

Chapter 8

"What's wrong?" Amelia asked me.

"Nothing." I knew it was a pointless lie. Amelia could see through me.

"You're nervous about something."

I was. Thomas had called. Another week had gone by, and he had worked out his stasis apparatus. He explained it a little better in our conversation the prior day. It didn't involve freezing so much as a complete shutdown and preservation. The chamber the person stayed in after the biological EM pulse was cold, but didn't freeze the body completely. Instead, he pumped a preservative gas into the chamber as well. He couldn't test the longevity of the system given his time constraints, but he was convinced it would work.

He had gotten a random, homeless stranger off the street to be a test subject and three days later, dropped the man off where he was found. He was extremely disoriented but healthy. Thomas had wanted to observe the man for a few days to be sure. I argued that we couldn't risk the stranger remembering anything about his time at the lab. I wasn't about to cut time out of my vacation with Amelia to sneak him into Maiia's lab to erase his memory.

Thomas was coming with the chamber and power supply. They would arrive this afternoon. I was running out of time. That meant I had to tell Amelia about my plan. I didn't want to talk about it. We had been so happy here the last few weeks, and I knew she would not like that I had been secretive about his plans. "I will miss this place," I said to her.

"You have to go home?"

"Not just yet. But soon. And I'm hoping to take you with me, so we can come back at some point and enjoy more glorious days like this together." I gestured at our surroundings, trying to sound nonchalant.

She looked at me, confusion coloring the features of her face. I could tell she was trying to sort it out in her head. "What have you done?"

"Me? Nothing. Thomas, something extraordinary."

She lowered her eyebrows in concern and gave me a distrusting look. "What?"

"He thinks he's solved the problem that's been plaguing cryogenics."

Her face went blank for a few moments before turning furious. "How could you be so selfish?"

"What? Me?"

"Yes, you!" She launched herself out of her beach chair with a surprising amount of force, and kicked at the sand as she began pacing. "You've been planning this since you found out, haven't you? And you pushed that poor little boy, just like you pushed yourself. Pushed him into solving your problems for you without any regard to how I would feel about it!"

"I did no such thing! I told him you were dying, he's the one who decided he needed to save your life." I left off the part about me encouraging him.

"And he just happened to have this equipment lying around."

"I didn't want to agree to it," I tried to explain. "I didn't want to believe it was possible only to have to go through the disappointment all over again. Finding out I was going to lose you in a month was the worst thing I have ever gone through in my life!" I was fuming, but she continued to stare me down. "I gave him access to my resources and left, denying myself the hope that he would actually get it done. I'm as surprised by this as you!"

Her stare broke me down.

"Okay, I'm not surprised by it. Thomas is a special kind of child genius. But what could I do? Tell him no? He was so excited by the idea, Amelia. It was like when you figured out the cure for Lesch-Nyhan syndrome. Remember how driven you were as the solution finally emerged from out of depths of your research? Remember how you reveled in the idea that you would be saving the lives of so many? Well what Thomas has done is make it possible to save the lives of everyone! Think about it. Anyone who has an incurable disease can be put into his stasis chamber and reawakened when the cure is found."

She continued to glare at me. "So I'm your latest lab rat."

That stung. I tried to keep my rage submerged. "Amelia—"

"You should have turned him down!"

"How was I supposed to turn it down, Amelia? Do you have any idea how hard it will be for me—"

"For you?" she asked, cutting me off. "This isn't about you! Did you ever stop to think that maybe I'm ready for my life to be over? It hasn't exactly been a picnic, you know. Growing up with my father the way he was, then finally getting out of there only to spend the rest of my life in your shadow!"

"My shadow? How could you think that? We're not even in the same field of research! And you've had plenty of accomplishments at that lab."

"Not nearly as many as you. And it's always been quite clear they would have left me behind a long time ago if you weren't so dead set on having me there!"

I found the idea that Amelia considered herself less than me ridiculous. I might have been smarter, but she was ten times the person I was. "You made me what I am. You and your compassion and dedication to me. If you hadn't given me that damn cookie on the street all those years ago I'd be sitting in a church in khaki pants and a stupid necktie, reciting meaningless dribble that I didn't even believe but was too afraid to stick up for myself and leave over.

"It was you, Amelia. You gave me the courage to do this. Everything I did and everything I continue to do. It has always been because of you. I'm nothing without you. Because without you—" I couldn't continue. Tears welled to the surface.

Amelia's scowl broke and her own tears formed in her eyes.

"Amelia," I said in a broken voice. She moved to embrace me and we stood together, crying. "I'm sorry I didn't tell you," I said. "I didn't know if he could do it and I didn't want to give you false hope either."

"Shh. Shut up," was all she said.

We continued to cry together until my eyes felt dry and my feet started to hurt from standing in the sand. I pulled away and wiped the tears from her cheek with my fingers. "I'm sorry. But he's done it, Amelia. He's been successful! Please, you're so young. Think of how much we could still do together. A majority of that involving being here on this island." I raised an eyebrow at her, trying to lighten the mood.

She closed her eyes, shook her head, and waited a few moments before she spoke again. "I'll give you five years."

"What?"

She opened her eyes and looked at me again. "You can freeze me for five years. If you can't find the cure in that time, I want to be let go."

I could swear the beginnings of a smile crept up at the sides of her mouth before disappearing again. "Deal." It was the first time I had ever outright lied to Amelia. I was convinced it wouldn't take that long anyway, at which point the lie wouldn't matter.

"When do we go back?"

"Thomas is coming here, with the equipment."

"When?"

"This afternoon. But you haven't started showing the signs of disorientation yet, so we could probably wait—"

"Yes I have."

She caught me off guard, and my heart sank. I was thinking I still had days left. Now I was left with just a few hours. "When?"

She gave me a wry smile. "Don't worry about it. It was short lived, and you clearly didn't notice." She looked downtrodden. "So I guess that means, I only have a few hours left?"

"You have years left. I'm the one who has to find some way to survive without you for the next three."

"I told you, you have five years to find a cure."

"I'm being optimistic." I couldn't help but give her a conceited grin. She punched my arm with a surprising amount of force. "Think of it as a long break. And an interesting experiment."

She avoided my gaze, but I knew she was excited by the idea of being involved in something groundbreaking like this. I didn't bother to tell her about the person Thomas found on the street. If she started having doubts again, I would. For now though, I would let her think she was the first.

I glanced out from the island as a flash of light caught my eye. I could see the seaplane. Thomas would be here within the hour. "We don't have to do it this afternoon. We could spend one last night together."

"The sooner you freeze me the sooner I'll wake up." She kissed me passionately and pulled away again. "We've got at least half an hour, you think?" She raised an eyebrow at me.

I scooped her up into my arms and sprinted to the hut with her.

*   *   *   *

We had dinner with the pilot, who agreed to help lug the equipment around, and Thomas. He didn't want many people to know what was going on, so he had limited his help for the past three weeks.

Amelia took an extra long time arranging her hair and picking out what she called her "Snow White" garment. I had no idea what that meant, but she figured if this worked, she might be on display. She wanted to look her best for everyone who would come to see her sleeping.

Thomas had set up the stasis pod on a lev-cart in the garden area. I wanted her surrounded by flowers and sheltered by trees when she went to sleep in the cold, sterile pod. The portable power source was on a cart nearby, behind a bush. Since the portable supply was not strong enough to power the biological EM pulse amplifier, that part was connected to the thermal generator on the island.

Amelia was to be given a sedative so she would fall asleep. The pod would be sealed and the gaseous preservative and a sort of antifreeze would be pumped inside at that point. Thomas had calculated the precise amount of time for the gas to be absorbed into the bloodstream through the lungs and spread through the body as the temperature dropped to 35 degrees Fahrenheit. After the appropriate amount of time, the pulse would be generated and stop all bodily function. It sounded rather trivial to me for such a momentous procedure.

There were two gas tanks with hoses connected to the pod. One tank held the sedative and the second held the preservative mixture. A computer controlled the valve to time how long each one was pumped into the chamber. Thomas had gotten accurate mass and lung capacity measurements from Amelia before dinner.

He was convinced he was ready as he pulled the lid open on the pod. The scene seemed ridiculous. An eight-year-old boy was fiddling with knobs and running through parameters on the computer screen while gnawing on his fingernails and shifting his weight in a never-ending march.

"This is going to work," he tried to reassure me.

I could only give a shallow nod in response. It was like having a child tell you he knew exactly how to perform the open-heart procedure you were about to undergo. The immediacy of the situation was hitting me. I wanted to delay, to have more time to mentally prepare myself. If Amelia was already showing signs of deterioration though, we had to stop that as quickly as possible.

She appeared in the doorway, and my heart stuttered in my chest. Her hair was done up on top of her head in some loose, twisty style. Stray strands softly framed her face. She rarely wore makeup in normal life, but I could tell she had applied some. Not so much to look done-up, but enough to flatter her facial features. She wore a dress of soft yellow, and for a moment I was transported back to the day we met. I tried to cling to that memory, to remember her that way forever.

For a moment, she didn't look sick. She looked radiant.

"This is just like a fairy tale," Amelia said as she approached the pod and saw all the flowers. She ran her hand over a fern and then bent to smell some of the flowers. She plucked one from its stem and tucked it behind an ear.

"Nice dress, wife," I said.

"I know how you like yellow, Doctor. You better be there to kiss me the moment I wake up."

Thomas interrupted our moment. "Technically it'll be an hour or so before you're coherent enough to know what's going on."

The two of us gave him an exasperated look. I shook my head as I took her hand and helped her climb into the pod. I lingered by the side. "I'll be there," I said. I held Amelia's hand as she lay down in the pod. Thomas waited silently. I struggled to let go of her hand. I leaned into the pod and kissed her for the last time for who knew how long. "Good night, my princess."

I found her fascination with fairy tales immature, but I would indulge her for this.

"I'll miss you," she said, and tears filled her eyes again as her breath sped. "You sure this will work?"

"Don't you have faith in Thomas?"

"Thomas, if this doesn't work I will find you in hell and kill you all over again!" she called out from inside the pod. The joke was marred by the crack in her voice. "Well then, here we go," she said and pulled her hand from mine to touch the side of my face. "The things I'll let you talk me into for science."

Her hand trembled as she pulled it to her chest and clasped the other one. She looked so frightened; but I couldn't do anything. I knew this was her best chance. All I could do was smile reassuringly at her as Thomas closed the lid to the pod. *This will work*, I repeated to myself over and over again, to keep from pulling her out in panic.

As the pod sealed, her hand shot up to the window. I could see the tears she had been holding back overflow and spill down her cheeks. She focused on me. I pressed my hand on the opposite side of the glass and tried very hard not to let myself cry, but continue to smile. I knew she wouldn't believe it. I knew it wouldn't reach my eyes, but I tried all the same. It would be almost instantaneous for her but years for me. Years without Amelia. I focused on her face, avoiding her eyes, and I saw her mouth the words, "I'm scared," as the sedative began to fill the pod. Her other hand shook as she raised it to her face wipe away some of the tears.

This will work, I told myself again, trying to remain calm. I breathed deeply, but it didn't work. Panic overtook me. This was a mistake, I was suddenly sure of it. My breathing accelerated as I watched her frightened expression. I had to remove myself from the moment. I plotted, even as I smiled at her. In less than five years I would cure Sunithe's disease. I would clean up this entire island

and get it running again. I would hire people to come here and manage it and rent it out while we weren't around so it would be profitable. She would wake up here in this paradise as though nothing had changed. I would be the same age. It would work. It had to work. My breathing slowed, and for once my smile was honest. I imagined the moment when she woke from the pod, unaware that anything had even happened.

Her eyelids fluttered a few times and then closed. Her hand drifted back to her side. Her breathing slowed. Thomas gave me a look, his eyebrows raised in question. This was my last chance to change my mind. As much as he liked Amelia and wanted to see her live, he was leaving the decision to me. My hand was still pressed against the glass, but I felt more resolved. I had a plan, and the drive to see it through was starting to surface. I nodded with conviction.

Thomas turned the knob off on the sedative and opened the valve on the preservative. The computer attached to the pod beeped. I heard the hiss of air moving through a valve. A fog started to form on the glass as the temperature dropped. Though I knew it was invisible, I expected to see something when the EM pulse fired. A quiet beep sounded and the pod was still when Thomas said with finality, "It's done."

I removed my hand from the glass and put it on Thomas's shoulder. My hand had blocked the fog from forming on that area of glass. Through the clearing I could see Amelia, asleep and beautiful as ever. We both stood there silent as the spot clouded over and I made a vow to myself that if this didn't work—but I stopped. There was no "if". This would work. This had to work. There was no other option.

The detachment of work was kicking in. Amelia became an emotion that I would suppress and deal with at a later date. Finding the cure to Sunithe's disease became the foremost thought in my mind. That would trump any lingering feelings or doubt about what had just happened. "Thomas," I said as I squeezed his shoulder and gave a final glance at the tropical paradise scenery around me. "We have work to do."

Chapter 9

I slammed my fist down on my desk. Thomas didn't even cringe, he had long ago gotten used to the temper I had developed during this project. The latest results from the drug trials were staring at me, and they weren't good. At least, they weren't what I needed. They had slowed the development of the symptoms of Sunithe's disease but had not cured it.

"At least we're moving in the right direction," Thomas said.

I glared up at the boy. "Maybe we need a different direction altogether."

"You really want to change tactics now? We have less than a year left."

"I don't intend to keep my promise."

It was Thomas's turn to glare. "She said five years. You agreed to five years. You know she didn't want you to devote your time to this."

"It was an arbitrary amount of time, it didn't matter. I would've agree to a year if that's what it took to get her in that pod."

"You want to start over? We're nearly there."

"We're not nearly there." I scowled at him and got up to pace. "This is the same problem I had with immortality. This method will only get us closer and closer to delaying the inevitable. It's an asymptote; it will never be a cure. I need..." I stopped pacing. I thought back to that moment in my old office at Maiia's lab when I was struck by inspiration. "I need a moment of clarity." My head sank in despair. "And it's not something I can force."

"We've delayed death by at least a few years. Wake her up and let her decide what to do next."

"We haven't tried the drug on someone with symptoms as advanced as hers were. We don't know if it would help."

"Is it not at least worth a try?" Thomas asked.

The pleading in his voice caught my attention. I stopped pacing to look at him. He had approached my desk. His hands gripped the back of a chair. His face was desperate.

"If it didn't work we'd have to freeze her again almost immediately—"

"Don't call it that!"

When he yelled like that he sounded like a petulant child. I had to remind myself sometimes that he still was a child. He had grown touchy about people referring to his method of stasis as "freezing" someone. The word had negative connotations from all the prior failed attempts where cells exploded as they froze and swelled. It was still considered a hoax, or "fashionable" science. Although we had three more clients whose families were paying a lot of money to keep them in stasis, the end result had not been revealed.

Our forth client was a very rich eccentric who made a deal with us. He didn't have a terminal disease; he just wanted to see the future. Since my immortality procedure had proved to be deadly to people who couldn't handle the brain remapping, this was his next best option. He gave us an obscene amount of money up front, to handle the initial fees and maintenance costs, accounting for inflation, for the next 50 years.

It was enough money to buy a large amount of land and build a new state-of-the-art laboratory. I even had some apartments built next door, so anyone who wanted to could live there and never be far from work. We had about three-dozen scientists free to research whatever they wanted without having the pressure of producing research grants hanging over their heads, and a small support staff. It was the sort of environment I had always wanted. We were producing world-recognized research.

Even Maiia, whose lab fell apart after I left and took a handful of people with me, had asked for a job. After initially rejecting her request out of spite, I decided keeping a close watch on her would be a better decision. She took a significant pay cut as a researcher. She had no executive role, which was how Thomas and I wanted it.

A few people balked at the idea of a nine-year-old being the co-chair of the lab, but when they realized how gifted Thomas was they forgot about it quickly. He had moved into one of the apartments with his older sister, Emma, as part of an agreement with his mother. She still didn't trust me, and thought Thomas needed a family connection there with him. Although Emma was not as brilliant as Thomas, she was gifted with an advanced intellect as well. Since she had no interest in science, she took it on herself to become head of security instead of a researcher.

There was very little security needed, aside from keeping an eye on Maiia, so it was mostly an empty title. She took the position to heart though, and installed invisible security systems. She had taught Thomas everything he knew about network security, never thinking he would go so far as to defy the NSA. She was also the third person to undergo the immortality programming, after me.

The fourth person did not survive. In the back of my mind I had feared that this was a possibility. The remapping technique required a great strength of mind and trust in the process. Instead of presenting my findings to Maiia, I went over her head to present to the Science Advisor of the President. Unfortunately, the man had used his influential contacts to get the position, and was not terribly smart. He also was mistrustful of major scientific breakthroughs and had developed a rather tedious process for getting anything accepted into the scientific community. Had I known about this prior to our meeting, I would have presented my findings at a medical conference instead and dealt with the public response later.

He sat through the presentation with a bemused and greedy look on his face. In the end he decided he needed proof for himself. We kept our meeting private, understanding that this could have a tremendous impact on society, and we made plans to bring him to the warehouse space a few days later so he could experience it for himself. He wanted proof, but it was hard to prove immortality without letting it play out. I explained the process and the way the body healed itself in the background, but he remained unconvinced. He said he needed to feel the effects.

It didn't go well. In the end, I was grateful for his secrecy about our meeting. Thomas cried as we disposed of the body, and no one came asking questions after. The news reported him missing, but there were no leads to go on, since he hadn't told anyone what he was doing that day. He was replaced as Science Advisor and quickly forgotten. The project was shelved, but not destroyed. Thomas vowed that after we saved Amelia's life, he would figure out why the remapping didn't work, and whom it would be safe for.

I disagreed, and took it as a sign that general society wasn't ready for such power. That it was a sort of Darwinian filter for humanity.

Thomas, I felt, was letting too much of what had happened get to him. While I admit the death of the science advisor was gruesome and entirely our fault, I was able to approach the situation with the detachment of a scientist. It was an experiment gone wrong, just like his first attempts at freezing mammals had been. Not freezing, I thought to myself as my mind drifted back to our argument.

"I'm sorry, Thomas. I meant that we'd have to put her back in stasis almost immediately. And she wouldn't agree to that. Are you going to sit there with me and watch her die?"

He didn't say anything. His glare faded into a desperate but silent plea. "I can't."

"It's not always easy to keep the emotional detachment necessary for this type of work."

He looked hurt only for a moment before his face became a mask again. "You're right. Waking her early will help no one." His voice was emotionless. He had let go of the chair and was standing with his hands in the pockets of his lab coat. "We'll try a new route, even if it means starting over." He was all business now. It was the same personae he adapted for meetings with sponsors, and whenever someone questioned his ability as a scientist.

I nodded. "Sometimes abandoning your work is necessary. Don't think of it as having wasted that time, but learning from it." It sounded trite even to me. I was the worst role model possible for Thomas.

I watched him leave my office. His frame sagged with the weight of too much pressure for a child. I tried to keep my emotional detachment aimed at him. Thomas was no ordinary twelve-year-old boy, but he didn't deserve to have this sort of stress thrust upon him at such a young age. He never got to have a childhood, though that was his decision. I couldn't blame him for abandoning it, given how his childhood had gone already.

He was strong, I told myself. He could handle it.

My door chimed almost immediately after Thomas had left. "Yes," I called. I expected it to be Thomas again, having thought up another point to argue. Instead, when the door slid open, Emma entered.

"I see you've been upsetting my brother again. He's got that fake, composed, I'm a responsible adult, look on his face again."

I rubbed the bridge of my nose, frustrated at her bravado. "Surely that wasn't the reason you were heading to my office."

"No. I've got this wicked cool idea."

"Wicked cool?"

Emma was able to better integrate into society as a child. Though she still abandoned school when she was 14, she kept in touch with friends she had made. Instead of fearing her, they admired her and were jealous that she already had what they considered to be a real life.

She ignored my gibe. "How annoying is it to have to sit there and say 'yes' every time someone comes to your door? Or to have to speak to the computer to get it to open files for you, or call someone to your office?"

She stopped, but rather than play into her sales pitch I waited for her to continue.

"So I had this idea. I don't know if it would work for most of the people here, or if you'd even want it to, but I thought, you'd be way more productive if you could kill off the time you spend doing a lot of this manual searching around and performing tasks."

She stopped again. I raised an eyebrow to show interest, but kept silent.

"Thomas tells me you've got this amazing brain. That you can process more information than anyone he's ever seen. It's like your brain computer is way more organized and well structured than most people."

"Enough flattery, Emma. Get to the point."

"I think we can integrate your brain directly into the laboratory environment."

My first instinct was to laugh, but I learned a long time ago that sometimes the craziest ideas were the best. Rather than letting that instinct show and possibly deflating a researcher's drive, I would foster the idea long enough to see if it had actual merit. Emma was not a researcher though. She was in security. "An intriguing thought, but I don't think you have the resources or background to make it happen."

"Maybe not the brain side, but certainly the technology side. It's a simple matter of some injectable wireless electrodes and some upgrades to the security system. Give me a researcher to worry about the other half."

"Give you a researcher? They're not my property to give."

"Ask one if they're interested in helping."

"Did you have someone in mind?" I had plans for Thomas that I wasn't about to push aside.

"Someone working on artificial limb control would be about the right area. I don't know if there's anyone here, or if you know of someone in the outside world who would be cool."

There was no one in the lab doing that sort of work, but I had outside contacts in the military world that could help find someone. "I'll ask around. Would this interfere with your normal work?"

She looked slightly taken aback. This was certainly not a question she wanted to answer. "Maybe a little. But it's all maintenance. I can hire someone part time who can keep up with it while I do this. At least give me a month to see if it's even feasible. Just one month."

I remembered Thomas making the same request of me over four years ago. I saw the similarities in their faces as she looked at me with anticipation. There was no doubt in my mind that she could make it work. She was almost as talented as her brother. She seemed bored with the work she was doing now. Who was I to deny her the opportunity to work on something that excited her? "Find your replacement, I'll find you a researcher. Then you'll have a month to develop your plan and we'll see where it stands from there."

"Really?" She looked at me with astonishment.

I nodded. "Really."

"Yes!" She leapt around the room making various victory gestures until I coughed for her attention. "Sorry. Thanks! I can't wait to let Thomas know, this is super awesome!" She laughed and headed for the door.

"Not wicked cool?" I asked.

She paused and turned back, "That too!" Then she was out the door.

Chapter 10

I was reading Thomas's latest progress report on the cure for Sunithe's disease when the lights in my office went off and an alarm sounded. Emma's program had only been working for a few months and I still wasn't used to it, so when her panicked voice filled my head it startled me. I could tell she was on her way to the power grid, and she was very concerned. I grabbed a lightdisk from a drawer in my desk, clipped it to my lab coat and ran out of my office and down the hall to meet her there.

Her mind was a jumbled state; it was hard to pick out thoughts from the mess. My pace picked up when I heard something about a fire and the pods. I met Emma outside the power grid room. She was nervously looking through a window into the room.

"What's going on Emma, I can't make out your thoughts through your panic."

"Something must have short circuited, there's a fire in the power grid room. The automatic suppression system has kicked in, so it'll be another minute or so before I can get in. Why are you here?"

"You called me here."

"No, I sent you to the pod lab! You're supposed to meet Thomas there."

"It was a bit hard to understand you. You need to work on your crisis management skills."

"It's a bit hard to focus when people's lives are in danger, Lancing! Go help Thomas at the pod lab, the back-up power is out!"

I wanted to ask her how that could have happened, but my feet were already carrying me back into the lab facility. Unfortunately the pod lab was all the way at the other end of the building. It felt like an eternity, and I was out breath by the time I arrived at the door. My heart pounded from the exertion and the fear of what might happen.

Thomas was inside with a few people, yelling orders at them. To his credit, he had proven himself over and over again well enough that they didn't hesitate to listen to a teenager.

"What happened, Thomas? Why is the back-up power out?"

"Not now, Lancing. Briggs, find me an adaptor for the generator, now!"

Another laboratory technician was sitting on the floor next to Amelia's pod. He had several uranium batteries clipped together and jury rigged to the power cord. "This won't last much longer, Thomas."

"I'm working on it!" He was bent over a lab bench, fiddling with some electronics and a soldering iron.

I wanted to yell at him and find out what was going on, but I was too distracted by the fact that four of the pods seemed to be leaking gas. Amelia's was the only one still sealed. I knew I had to leave Thomas be if he was going to fix the power issue. It was infuriating to not be able to do anything. *"Emma,"* I said in my mind, *"what's the power grid situation?"*

"I'm inside the room now; it's not looking good. The main transformer is burnt out. It will have to be replaced before we can get the main power back online."

"And what's going on with the back-up generator?"

"It was taken off-line two days ago for repair. I'm sorry, but we have no back-up for the pods at the moment."

"Why was the back-up system taken off-line with no replacement?" I was furious that I hadn't been notified about this. I stared at Amelia's pod, frantic action going on in the fringes of my vision.

"The repair was only supposed to take a few hours. We ran into some snags. I never dreamed something like this would happen while it was out. I mean—"

"What, Emma."

"This shouldn't have happened. I think—I think someone did this. Someone who knew the back up was out. This is just too coincidental, and nothing that would happen naturally."

"Sabotage." I didn't realize I had said the word aloud. A technician glanced in my direction and quickly away again. I glared at him for a few moments, trying to remember his name. *"We'll look into it later, Emma. Get whatever you need, fix the power now."*

"Give me an hour, I should be able to fix it."

I looked at the pile of batteries sitting on the floor next to Amelia's pod. I tapped the man sitting next to them on the shoulder. When he looked up at me there was fear in his eyes. "How long?" I asked him.

"Maybe fifteen minutes. This pod pulls more current than these batteries are meant for."

I looked back over at Thomas, but he was still focused on whatever he was doing. "How long was she without power?"

"We're not sure, sir. Maybe three minutes?"

I looked back over at the other pods. They had stopped leaking whatever gas was inside them. I went over to one and opened the lid. The patient was unconscious. It was the eccentric millionaire who had wanted to be awoken in fifty years. Unfortunately, he was about to be awoken almost forty-four years too early.

"I've got it, Thomas!" Briggs, the technician, had returned, dragging a power cable from somewhere.

"Finally. Bring it here!" Thomas attached leads to the battery cables, snipped them from the batteries and plugged the other end into the power cable Briggs had dragged in. The console on Amelia's pod flickered slightly. Thomas went over to it and pushed a few buttons, seemingly satisfied. "She's okay for now." He finally looked up at me. "But we have to deal with our other patients."

I nodded at him. "What do we do?"

"My first human experiment was sedated immediately upon awaking, so I'm not sure how the body handles this part. But I'd suggest we sedate these four, before they wake up completely. As soon as Emma gets the power back up we can put them back in stasis."

"Agreed. Get on it."

I turned to leave. Now that Amelia's pod was back on a stable power source, I had a saboteur to track down before things got worse.

"Emma, what's your status?"

"Another half hour."

"Meet me in my office when you're done. I'll be reviewing security logs and surveillance video."

The lights were still out. I sat down in my chair and closed my eyes. I wondered how Emma managed to keep this mental link functioning without a power source. My mind searched out for the video link of the power grid room. A quick scan showed only one person entering it, but I couldn't see his face since it was downcast the whole time. Either he knew where the cameras were, or he was a very depressed employee. The entry was three days before, so unlikely he was the cause if it was indeed some sort of sabotage.

I saw Emma coming down the hall and allowed the door to open as she approached. "Someone definitely broke that transformer. That damage couldn't have happened naturally."

"There was only one person who has been in there in the past few days. I can't tell who it is though."

She closed her eyes and I pointed her to the time index in the surveillance file. "Matthew Porter."

"How do you know?"

"I recognize the bad comb over. He must have planted something."

"Something that wouldn't damage the transformer for three days?"

She paced, thinking. "Must be something that either gradually degraded the transformer's shielding or was on a timer. But I didn't find anything in there that looked like it was on a timer."

"What about the back-up power source. Why was it taken off-line?"

She hesitated for a moment. "Porter said he found a vulnerability in the system. He said he could fix it within a few hours, but after he started he said he found more problems and needed to get some parts to strengthen up the supply. He's been a good employee, really helping out with some installation stuff for the security systems. I had no reason to suspect him."

"It could be coincidence."

She gave me an impatient look in between paces. "No way you believe that."

"No. But we must give him his chance." I folded my hands on my desk. "But I've no reason to think he'll tell the truth if it is him."

"So how do we prove it, either way?"

"I need a way to read his mind."

She stopped pacing. "You want me to hook him into our system?"

I shook my head. "It's not good enough. He'll only share what he wants to share. I need a way to pry into his subconscious."

"That's beyond me. You'd need to get help from Jenny Flack. She helped me with this system," she said and pointed at her own head. We both froze as we heard Thomas call to me.

"It'll have to wait," I said.

Emma nodded, then we both ran back to the pod lab. Thomas was having an argument with one of the techs. I gave Emma a glance and a silent order to get Matthew Porter into a secure space, and then I ordered everyone to leave the room. She followed him and the other technician out.

"What's going on, Thomas?"

He was sweating and agitated. "Something's wrong. That millionaire guy, he woke up before I had a chance to administer a sedative." Thomas refused to look me in the eyes. He fiddled with one of the buttons on his lab coat.

I glanced at his pod and saw the man sleeping. "He seems fine now."

"He's gone crazy," Thomas said and stood next to the open pod. He stared down at the face of the sleeping man and took a deep breath before continuing "He screamed that he was awake. Well really, what he said was 'We've been awake.' I'm not sure whom he meant by that. But he also screamed for you an said, 'We're going to kill him. We're going to kill Lancing.' And then he asked where you were. He didn't seem to recognize me. Just kept asking where you were. I finally got him sedated again a few minutes ago."

"We? We're going to kill Lancing?"

"I think he might have a multiple personality disorder. I think..." He trailed of and looked upset.

"What."

"I think he's been awake this whole time. Awake, and trapped in an unresponsive body."

I glanced at Amelia. "Thomas, if that's true, is everyone awake? Amelia? Rig now? Is she thinking and feeling that she's trapped in that body?"

His voice was quiet as he answered. "I think she might be."

"How could this happen, Thomas?" In a second I was across the room and shaking him by his lab coat. "You think? She's been in there for 6 years now! Do you have any idea what that would do to a person?"

"I don't understand what happened. The biological pulse should have stopped the brain's synaptic pathways. It must not, must not have been powerful enough." He still couldn't look me in the eyes, but I saw the threat of tears glistening in them.

I let go of his coat; I knew if I kept at it I would hurt him. I glared at him and the bodies still in their pods. I tried to breath deeply to calm myself. "What do you suggest we do, Thomas?" I said through my clenched teeth.

He looked uncomfortable, and straightened his lab coat. "We put the three whose families paid for them back under. And pray that no one finds the cure to their diseases."

"And if the families decide they can no longer afford to wait?"

He began to pace as he sorted his way through the options. "We convince them to donate their loved ones to medical science. We'll find some way to spin it to convince them that they're better off not being awoken only to face their death soon after. We can come up with some bogus case studies of other patients who have gone through it."

Underneath the anger I felt a small amount of pride. Thomas had become a true scientist. He was not letting his mistake get the better of him. He had the cold exterior of a true professional. "And the millionaire?"

He finally turned to look at me. All evidence of the potential tears was gone. "We get rid of him."

"That seems unnecessarily cold, Thomas. He may prove useful in some other way. We'll find him a room and keep him locked up for now. No one need know where he came from. We'll make sure that he was really awake. We'll find out what caused it, and then we'll know about the others." I stopped and watched his face. He knew the question I was about to ask, and didn't want to answer it. "Amelia."

"If we pull her out, we can give her the partial cure. Extend her life by a few years. Maybe it'll be long enough to find the real cure." The optimism in his voice did not reach his face.

"And if it isn't, she lives out the rest of her days insane." I sighed and ran a hand through my hair, turning back to her pod. "Maybe we should leave her be."

"How can you say that? You know what she's going through in there. If we can help her recover from this, we have to."

"Don't let your guilt cloud your mind, Thomas. Walk yourself through it," I demanded.

He took a few deep breaths to calm himself again. His face took on the flat detachment of a scientist again. "The damage has already been done, but who knows how much worse it could get. If we keep her in there— even if we find a cure, it might not make a difference. If we take her out now, we could work on helping her regain her mind." He looked devastated. "Just in time for her to die." He looked up at me and pleaded, his emotional wall barely staying in one piece. "We can't leave her in there."

"What's the point of taking her out just to kill her?"

"I can't imagine-just can't imagine what she's going through."

Guilt hit me. She hadn't wanted to live. She said she had been through enough for one life, and now I was putting her through much worse. I ran my hand along the glass of her pod. "Amelia is a brave soul and has an exquisite mind. She'll survive this."

I willed myself to believe it as I left Thomas to his pods.

Chapter 11

Amelia had now been in stasis for ten years. The guilt of leaving her in there weighed against my heart. Every day, I pushed it down and focused on the tasks at hand. I was becoming an expert on "handling" situations. Between the four people who had been accidentally woken up, to Matthew Porter, I was adept at making people disappear.

To my surprise, Matthew Porter admitted to the sabotage. He had a whole speech prepared about the evils of mental and biological experimentation. I only heard about ten seconds before I left the room and locked him in.

Matthew Porter, it became known to his next of kin, had accidentally contracted a deadly virus and had been quarantined and put in stasis for his own good. It was a potential hazard he had been warned about when he signed the contract for his position here. We sedated him and let his family come say their goodbyes through a window. I felt no pity as I watched his parents cry. I had saved them from finding out what a malicious monster their son was.

A year later Matthew was to be taken out of stasis and left to the care of Jenny, the researcher who had helped Emma with her security system. Jenny believed she could tap directly into the brain to repair the damage done by the years of isolation. I would not allow her to try the experiment on Amelia, after her work on the millionaire turned out so poorly. Matthew Porter became a willing and able volunteer.

The millionaire was being kept under surveillance and had been given the codename Rich. He was suffering from multiple personality disorder and was severely bipolar, but he was also showing signs of heightened intelligence. We gave him pads of paper and pens and were hoping at some point he would produce something of value. He continually scribbled down numbers and made line drawings that were inscrutable. Thomas often argued that the man was just crazy, and should be put out of his misery.

The lab had grown in the past four years since the initial incident. Emma hired more people to help her keep the security systems up to date and invent new ways to keep tabs on what was happening in the lab. I knew every project that was being researched. I knew where everyone was at any moment. The information was overwhelming at first, but with Jenny's help I was able to sort through it all and find a way to suppress superfluous things.

Even still, it was taking my time away from helping Thomas with a cure. It was the only thing he ever worked on. I tried to get him to step back from it from time to time to gain some perspective, but his guilt would not allow him to rest.

In addition to my increased duties in keeping tabs on things, I had started to branch out for research scientists. Thomas and Jenny needed help, and the researchers who were already at the lab could not keep up with them. I started scouring the news for hints of children like Thomas: children who had exceptional minds. I took on fake personae and would go to schools to talk to counselors about smart kids who just didn't seem to fit in. I would visit their homes and talk to their parents about wonderful opportunities for them to expand their minds.

When each one arrived, Jenny subjected them to a cognitive evaluation. She would scan their brain while asking a few simple questions. By watching how various sections of their brain reacted, she was able to tell me what areas of research they might be most suited for. We would then give them a small project in that area to prove their worth.

Today, it was shortly after one of these scans that she came bursting into my office with a piece of paper. She practically shoved it in my face before asking me, "Does this look familiar?"

I snatched it out of her hands to hold it at a proper distance and glanced at it quizzically. It contained a few mathematical formulas and pictures of tubes swirling about. "No." I handed it back to her.

"A few months ago I started giving our recruits paper and pen to doodle or write whatever came to mind while I was doing their brain scan. It helps them focus and I get better readings. Our latest recruit came up with this." She waved the paper in my face again.

"And?"

"Computer, display files 'Rich-tubes', one through seventeen."

17 drawings filled the air between Jenny and me. I didn't have to look very hard to recognize the tube pattern. I stood up from my desk to look at the formula on one of the pages and compared it to the paper Jenny was holding. They were

exactly the same. I snatched the paper back out of Jenny's hand and stared at it. "Bring him here."

Jenny left to retrieve the boy. As she walked him through the hallways back towards my office I could hear the murmurs follow him when he walked past people. News spread quickly in this place. I closed the files and waited as calmly as I could, smoothing his paper out on the desk in front of me.

The boy was younger than Thomas was when I first found him. Jenny introduced him as Larry Genway and left us. I remembered meeting him. I remembered the conversation with his mother as he sat playing with blocks on the floor of their living room, creating some grand freestyle structure. I thought he showed promise. I hoped I was about to be proven right.

I gestured to a chair on the opposite side of my desk. He sat quietly on the edge of the chair and waited, his feet swinging a foot above the floor. He didn't seem frightened, just curious. "Hello, Larry. I'm Doctor Lancing."

"Hello, Doctor Lancing."

I smiled at his good manners. "Do you remember meeting me a few weeks ago?"

"No, sir." He looked down at his lap and frowned.

"I met with you and your mother in your house. I told her we could find ways to help you develop your already astounding intellect. That's why you're here."

"Yes, sir."

I held up his paper. "I understand you drew this while Doctor Jenny Flack was doing your introductory exam. It's intriguing."

He squirmed in his chair and looked around as though identifying the exits. "She told me to draw anything. She said it wouldn't matter what it was."

"You're not in trouble," I said as I put the paper back down. "The exercise is meant to help bring subconscious understanding to the front of your brain. Do you know what this picture means?"

"No."

"Do you remember what you were thinking about when you drew it?"

"Transporters."

"Transporters?" I asked. I picked up the paper again, staring at the symbols in the equations. My heartbeat sped as I moved to the edge of my seat.

"Yeah, they take something from one place and put it in another place. I read about it in a book."

I tried to keep a straight face and opened the Rich files again. I stood up from my desk and paced to mask my excitement. "Do these look familiar, Larry?"

He looked at the pictures, stunned, and then his eyes widened. "Who did these?"

I stopped pacing but kept the files between us. "A scientist here. Would you like to meet him?"

"Yes!" Larry had jumped out of his chair and was scanning the drawings.

I sat back down at my desk and closed the files again. Without their distortion in the air I saw disappointment fill Larry's face as they went away. "You can meet him." His face perked up again. "But I need to warn you, he's been through some rough times." I paused, uncertain how to explain multiple personality disorder to a child. "Do you have any imaginary friends?"

He nodded. "Oh yes, a few."

"But you know they're imaginary."

"Of course."

"Why did you create them?"

"I get bored with the other kids at school. They don't talk to me like they should. And sometimes they're mean." He frowned and stared at his lap again.

"So your imaginary friends are interesting and never mean. They keep you entertained and happy?"

He thought for a moment. "Mostly."

76 – The Children of Doctor Lancing

His answer caught me off guard. Why would he invent friends who didn't have a positive influence on him? "Well, this scientist went through a rough time. And to help him cope with it, he made up his own imaginary friends."

Larry nodded again.

"The problem is, he doesn't know they're imaginary. He thinks they really exist."

"But they do exist. He created them."

"Yes." I began to rethink letting the two of them into the same room. I worried how Rich's mind could end up effecting Larry's. I silently called to Emma. "But we both know they don't exist outside of his head, right?"

Larry nodded. "Right."

"That's where you and I are different from him. We know they don't exist in the real world. He doesn't know that. He thinks they are actual real-live people."

"Oh." He fidgeted in his chair.

"And it's better if you don't mention that sort of thing. He gets upset if you imply that his friends aren't real. And one of them is not really a friend. He's a bully."

"Oh." Larry pushed himself back in the chair and looked worried, his brow furrowed. It seemed an unnatural expression for such a young child.

"Do you still want to meet him?"

Larry looked at the paper with his drawings and gripped the edge of his chair, thinking for a moment. "Mm-hm." He nodded, but the enthusiasm from before was gone.

"Okay." I smiled and gave him a nod. I tried to look reassuring. *"Okay. Emma,"* I said.

The door to my office slid open again and Emma came in.

"This is Emma," I told Larry, gesturing to her. "She's going to show you around for a few minutes while I make sure the scientist is free for visitors."

Emma smiled and held her hand out for Larry. He took it and the two of them headed back out to the hallway, past where Jenny was waiting. She came back into my office after they had passed. "Jenny, I don't want to mess this boy up."

She shook her head. "I think it will be okay. He's very grounded."

"Is there anything we should do to prepare Rich?"

"I'll go show him the picture now, and see how he reacts. Give me a few minutes." She picked the drawing back up off my desk and headed for Rich's room.

I watched in my head, as she managed to get his attention then showed the picture to him. Rich started to cry and nod his head. Jenny patted him on the shoulder and spoke to him for a few more minutes before she came back to my office.

"He feels relieved. He thinks we finally found someone who understands him. I think it will be okay, but I'm going to stay in there with them, in case he takes a bad turn."

I had called Emma back. She came back through the door with Larry's hand still in hers and guided him over to Jenny. "Okay, Larry, let's go meet Rich," Jenny said. The two of them headed back out to Rich's room.

I sat back at my desk and closed my eyes to focus. Larry was hesitant at first, especially when he saw Rich crying. Rich held his arms out to invite Larry into a hug, which he cautiously let happen. Then Rich held the piece of paper out and started pointing to various parts of it. They talked about pathways and quantum physics and other things that went over my head. Within a few minutes they were feverishly organizing equations on a new sheet of paper.

I let my mind drift from the scene and smiled while sitting at my desk. A transporter would be an amazing and profitable discovery for the laboratory. I briefly wondered if the scientific community would claim it couldn't possibly have come from such a young child. If there were too many questions, Rich's history might come to light. I definitely could not allow that to happen. I'd have to come up with a fake backstory for him.

I pushed the worry aside. This was a moment to revel. A transporter would change the dynamic of society on a global scale. For the first time in years, I felt light-hearted and excited about a project. I would devote my full attention and resources to developing their work.

As always, the guilt crept back up into my chest. I had completely forgotten about Amelia today. I walked to the pod lab and sat next to her. I told her about Larry and Rich and my hopes for developing an actual transporter. I stopped after a few minutes and was overcome by the guilt. Talking to her had been an empty gesture to make myself feel better.

I hadn't done any work on a cure lately, and I still didn't intend to.

Chapter 12

Thirteen years of Amelia in stasis. Sitting on my desk was the latest report from Thomas about his progress toward a cure. He thinks he has it. The problem is the well of patients to try it out on has dried up. The patients we've given the partial cure to don't want to risk taking a new cure until they're closer to dying in case it changes the way their current drug works.

I worried about what was happening to Amelia's brain during her extended time in stasis. The immortality brain remapping destroyed weak minds. Even if we cured Amelia of Sunithe's disease, there was no telling what would happen if we tried the remapping in her current state.

Jenny was still working with Matthew Porter. She had hired a new assistant, Eliza Phillips. Jenny found her last year and she proved to be an exceptional candidate for the immortality process. She even managed to alter the remapping to stunt her growth as well. I tried to warn her she wouldn't want to be a twelve-year-old girl for her entire life, but she assured me when she got bored with it, she'd be able to fix that.

She seemed jealous that when she arrived there were children younger than her working for us already. She also didn't seem to care that while she technically would be older, she just wouldn't look it. I told her she needed to keep the change to the remapping a secret; that I would allow her to do it, but no one else. She was to tell people that she had an aging disorder that slowed her aging process even more than people already on Ketelzene. I found it disturbing that she would remain a child while her mind grew into an adult.

Ketelzene itself had become a way of life. Like fluoride in the old times, our water supplies were being laced with it. The government decided that it was beneficial enough to the public's health that everyone should be on it. It was also starting to spread to other countries.

With Kischukov Laboratory closed, we were the government's go to for scientific research and consulting. I kept most of our research secret from them, including the immortality remapping. I knew they would want to start pushing regulations on work that touched on ethically questionable areas. I considered immortality and mind alteration in general to fall into those categories.

Teleportation was a different story. If Larry and Rich managed to get that working, I couldn't deny it would need government regulation. Some day soon, I would have to let them in on that project.

There were plenty of other researchers doing vast amounts of important work. Enough to sustain our funding needs. As much as I disliked doing projects for the government, they were a steady source of income. Much of the research going on was involved in enhancing soldiers. In addition to enhancing their bodies and minds, we were implanting devices inside them to heighten their situational awareness. Our networked intraocular displays kept entire platoons aware of everyone's position and status. We were constantly improving on the interface and the amount of information we could organize in a soldier's field of vision. A less advanced version had been released to the general public, and our patents had given us a large boost of funding.

The number of researchers had grown too big to fit inside the lab, so I added another structure to my sweeping complex. I kept the younger researchers in the same building as me, where they could be more closely monitored and supported and kept from prying eyes. Thomas had moved with the rest of the researchers-a decision on my part that he was furious about. He had told me in a recent conversation that he would not being staying in the publicly visible lab once the cure to Sunithe's disease had been found.

He had grown into an adult, but retained some of his childish impetuousness. Whenever we argued I could still see the eight-year-old boy I met all those year ago. I rubbed my head and tried to think of where I could come up with another patient for him.

My thoughts were interrupted my Jenny approaching my office again. She had Eliza with her. Neither of them seemed pleased. I let them enter and put Thomas's request aside.

"Yes?" I looked from one to the other.

Jenny started. "She's made it worse," she said, gesturing to Eliza. "We've been developing that helmet that we can use to tap into peoples' minds, as you know. Well it's working. The problem is that it's freaking Matthew out even more. He knows there's someone in his head that doesn't belong there. And somehow, he's managed to shut us out."

"It's only a matter of time," Eliza said. "I'll find a way back into his brain."

"And probably make him worse!"

I glared at each of them in turn for silence and thought for a moment before I spoke. "I would think him being able to tell the difference between the voices in his head and the ones that don't belong there, and finding a way to shut that voice out, is actually quite an interesting result. He may still be crazy, but he has a vast amount of mental control."

Neither spoke. Eliza seemed unnerved by my statement and Jenny seemed horrified.

"Can he still talk to you normally?"

"Yes," Jenny said. "But it jumps from one personality to the next so quickly it's hard to keep track of where he is, and what sort of tactic we should be using with him. His paranoia has not let up at all."

"Do you think, if he started to show signs of fatigue, that he would be able to express that to you?"

Jenny glanced at Eliza, as though she thought Eliza should be heading the conversation. "Well, probably. Maybe not voluntarily, but if we asked him directly, yes."

I placed my elbows on my desk and pressed my hands against my face. Sunithe's disease was the priority here. Mind control would not get me very far with Amelia if she died shortly after she came out of stasis. "Stop your work with Matthew."

"What!" Jenny looked affronted. She glanced at Eliza, who remained unaffected and curious.

"Matthew has just volunteered to help Thomas out with his test of a cure for Sunithe's disease. Turn him over to Thomas for as long as he needs, and try doing some more research before you jump back into testing."

I hoped she picked up on the admonishment. I didn't exactly approve of Eliza's approach of jumping in without fully developing theories on what she was doing. This would give Thomas time to check on his potential cure and Eliza a feel for a more disciplined approach. It wasn't like I was going to be able to supply her with a steady stream of mentally imbalanced patients. Given that this was more secretive research, it was harder to find test subjects.

"I also want a full report of what you've tried so far and what results you have seen from it. Matthew is a precious commodity, Eliza. It's not like I can just pick anyone else up off the street for you to play with."

Her eyes narrowed at what I assumed was the "play" comment, and then took an air of condescension. "If Matthew's so precious, why give him to Thomas to be killed anyway?"

I wanted to leap across my desk and slap her. I kept my face as neutral as ever and hid what I was really feeling. The pain that would come with yet another failed cure, the frustration at not having Amelia by my side for over a decade, and the protective instinct that welled up at having Thomas criticized. Eliza could do powerful things; I could not afford to get her on my bad side.

"Write the report. And when you're done, I have another research project I think you'll enjoy." I let the corner of my mouth creep up enough to attract her attention.

I could see the eagerness in her eyes. She knew I would have something exciting for her to do. She knew I wouldn't waste her talents on something trivial.

"You'll have the report tomorrow," Eliza said. She glanced at Jenny, and left my office.

Jenny watched her go, then turned to give me a wary look. She didn't speak.

"What is it, Jenny? I'm a busy man." I said.

She looked back at the door again and shook her head. "Nothing. Never mind." She dropped her head and left.

I assumed Jenny was disappointed at losing her test subject, but didn't feel brave enough to question my judgment; a wise choice. I wasn't in the mood for more arguments, and another was on the way.

I called to Thomas. While I waited for him I pondered a project for Eliza. She had a knack for tapping into the brain like no machine ever could. If she could extend that into the world around her, perhaps she could tap into matter as well. I firmly believed that telekinesis was a possibility with the right training of the right mind. Eliza presented me with a chance to test that theory.

It was a long shot, but if anyone could do it, Eliza could.

Thomas entered my office. He had aged into young adulthood well, but there was no mistaking the fatigue in his face. "I got your request."

He slumped into a chair and sighed. "And?"

"You're not going to like it."

"You have no one."

"Oh no, I've got a subject for you." I gave him a smile.

He didn't seem to know if he should smile back or worry. "Where did you find them?"

"It's Matthew Porter."

"Matthew has Sunithe's disease?"

"Not yet," I said and raised an eyebrow.

I watched comprehension dawn on Thomas's face. The comprehension turned to a cross between regret and disgust. It wouldn't be the first time he compromised his ethics for his work.

"Would you prefer a bum off the street?"

He laughed once without humor, and then grimaced as the memory of his first human stasis experiment hit him. "I might. Then I can just let them go if the cure doesn't work, and not have to know their day to day progress towards death." He sighed and once again his fatigue aged him. "Does Matthew even have the mental capacity to know what's going on with him?"

"Matthew betrayed us a long time ago. As far as I am concerned, this is his penance for that betrayal."

"You didn't answer my question."

"You can tell him exactly what you're doing and no, I don't think he'll comprehend it."

"You don't think."

"I've allowed you to get by with less than that, Thomas."

He nodded.

"I'll take care of the gene modification necessary to infect him, if it will make you feel better."

Thomas glanced thankfully at me. "Only slightly."

"Think of it this way. We can't release him into society. He has no life outside of this place. We can either put him to good use or get rid of him. Either way, I think it's a win situation."

"Okay." Thomas got up from his chair and turned to leave. "I'll leave you to it."

He left, and I worked on detaching myself from emotion once again. Even though it was the opposite of detaching from emotion, I decided to go visit Amelia.

The pod lab was further into the depths of the complex from my office. The way it was set up, a person had to go through my office to gain access through a locked door that only I could open, to get to the remaining stasis pods. The door opened with me barely having to think about it as I walked towards it.

We had put the terminal patients back into stasis in the hopes that some day cures would be found to their diseases, and Jenny would be able to get their brain function to a normal state.

I walked over to Amelia's pod and wiped the condensation away so I could see her face. "Hello, wife."

Of course, she didn't respond. I watched her face intently, for any sign of cognitive activity, as I did many times before. There was no visual indication that she was mentally alive in there. Every now and then I tried to imagine that it had worked for Amelia. That she wasn't trapped, cognizant, in a frozen body. That she was just sleeping.

Every time I walked away, I knew it was just wishful thinking.

"Thomas thinks he's finally done it," I told her. "That we'll be able to wake you soon, and we'll be together forever." Even if your brain is mush, I added to myself silently.

I was tired of this routine. I wanted her out of that pod and back in my life, even if she was insane.

Chapter 13

Larry was giggling with glee. It was the sort of emotion that only worked with a teenager. At thirteen he was old enough to be flirting with adulthood, but still young enough to have that child-like wonder. I hadn't even been paying attention to his work with Rich, but for some reason this outburst caught my attention.

I had been reading through Thomas's latest heart-breaking report about the lack of a cure for Sunithe's disease. I had begun to give up on the idea altogether and thought that five years, the lifespan our incomplete cure provided the infected with, would be enough. I could take a five-year sabbatical with Amelia, go back to the island, and we could spend her remaining years in the blissful peacefulness of the tropical paradise.

I had hired a couple to renovate and run the island. They cleaned the place up, added some modern amenities to the huts and added some self-sustaining gardening areas. They only relied on deliveries from the mainland once a month, as I understood it. It became one of the perks of working for our lab; vacationing on the island. I wouldn't even care if other people were there with us. Most of the researchers here didn't know who I was, and those that did seemed to be afraid of me. Anyone who happened to be on the island at the same time would leave us alone.

But I knew I was kidding myself. Five years with Amelia would not be long enough, though I ached for the time with her. There were so many things I still wanted to do in my life. Going back to the island seemed like an extended version of defeat. Sure, it would be nice while it lasted, but it wouldn't last.

I pushed Amelia and the feelings of defeat out of my mind as I stood from my desk. I walked over to the door of lab C, where Rich and Larry spent most of their days. Rich looked terrified of something. He cowered back from Larry and made a whimpering noise. Larry was holding a metal sphere while pacing and talking very excitedly at Rich. Neither of them noticed my entrance. They seemed to be arguing about the sphere. I only caught a few words, but "time" and "pathway" captured my attention.

Normally at a time like this, Rich's internal bully would take over his mind for him and fight back at Larry. I wondered why he wasn't making an appearance.

I coughed to make my entrance known. Rich scurried away to a corner, continuing to whimper. Larry turned towards me with a strange look in his eyes. I'd call it mischief but it was grander than that. When he spoke, his voice had an air of condescension. "Hello, Doctor Lancing." He mangled the word "doctor" as though I wasn't worthy of the title.

"What's going on, Larry?"

Larry glanced at Rich, who continued to cower in a corner and had started to cry. "It's not a teleporter after all."

I glared at Larry. If it wasn't a teleporter, it wasn't much use to me. "Then what have you created?"

Larry fiddled with the sphere in his hands. He turned it over and over again before pausing to flip open the lid. There was a simple red button on the inside, glowing red. He left the lid open and held it out to Rich, who retreated further, though I thought it not possible, into his corner. Larry stomped his foot and frowned at Rich. "Come on, we've got to show him."

Petulant child, I thought to myself.

"No!" Rich shouted. "It's wrong." His last words were a whisper. He closed his eyes and curled into a tighter ball, crying. His body shook with silent sobs.

"Larry, I don't have time for these games. What the hell is going on with you and Rich?" I asked.

Larry held the sphere out to me. I hesitated before taking it, and looked it over as he spoke. "Push the red button. Wait about ten seconds, then push it again."

I glanced at Rich, cowering in the corner, and thought this might be a mistake. However, I rationalized to myself, I didn't get to my current position by not being able to take risks. "Okay," I said to Larry.

Larry closed his eyes and scrunched his face up to focus on something. I pushed the red button. Larry and Rich suddenly disappeared. I was in the same room, but it was dark and deserted. I stepped backwards towards the door I had come through and turned as it opened. It was my office, as it should be, but it was also dark and deserted. I walked over to my desk. It glowed to life as I approached and the lights turned on as they normally would. Since I didn't want to push Larry's directions I walked back into the lab area and pushed the button again.

In an instant, the room filled with light. Larry and Rich were in the places they had been when I left.

Larry clapped his hands and jumped around. Rich cowered some more and cried, "It's not right. You can't. You'll mess things up."

"Larry." I waited for him to stop jumping. "What just happened?"

"You traveled back in time!" Larry said, throwing his hands up in an exultant gesture.

It was as though my brain had stopped working. I couldn't quite comprehend what he was saying. I placed my hand on the desk next to me to steady myself. "Explain."

"I sent you back in time. Twelve hours, to be exact, though I could have sent you further," he said, bragging. "Twelve hours back in time and then back here again! What do you think?"

I paused and tried to parse the information. "I think I don't believe you."

Larry groaned, exasperated. "Try it again. Push the button, and give yourself thirty seconds. Check your computer, check the time and date, then push the button again when you're sure."

I wasn't sure. I didn't want to push the button again. "Where did you get this?" I asked, while holding out the sphere.

"I had the quantum physics labs throw it together. Push the button!"

I stared at the sphere, half thrilled at the idea and half terrified. I pushed the button again and suddenly the world around me changed. As before, I walked back into my office. As the computer and office buzzed to life before me I said, "Computer, time."

The default computer voice, which always sounded like Sean Connery to me, said "22:55."

"What date?"

Again the computer answered, "October 15th, 2059."

It was eleven hours prior. I walked through the door and pushed the button on the sphere again.

Larry was smirking but no longer laughing. "So?"

"That was eleven hours, not twelve."

"Well naturally. I couldn't send you back to a time when you had already been there. Imagine what sort of fright you would've gotten the first time I sent you back to see another version of yourself!"

I closed the lid to the sphere and tried to sort through what was going on. "You can send people back in time with this?" I asked and shook it at him.

"Yes," said Larry.

"I thought you were working on a teleporter device."

"So did we," Larry explained. "But after we got it up and running we realized, it wasn't just equations for transporting matter through space, it was also time."

My mind whirled at the idea. "You didn't move me through space."

"I could have," he countered. "But I thought for an initial demonstration, this would be adequate."

"How—" I couldn't even think of a question to ask.

"I can see your path. I can see where you've been, where Rich has been, where I've been. Anyone who touches that sphere, I can see where they've been. It's like a portal into their past."

"What is the sphere made of?" I was trying desperately to understand how this could be.

Larry frowned for a moment. "I don't know exactly. Like I said, the physicists threw it together for me. I gave them some equations that didn't really make much sense to me, but Rich and I both came up with them, so I figured it would be right. The sphere somehow creates the pathways for me. And I can control where it goes."

"So—you created a teleporter that can also transport in time?"

"Yes!"

"I need to think about this."

"What?" Larry asked, but I was already locking the door behind me as I left.

I felt trapped and panicked. Transporting was a useful tool; but time travel in the wrong hands could be a massive weapon. I heard Larry pounding on the door to be let out. "Computer, flood lab C with sedative."

Shortly after, the pounding stopped. I hid the sphere in my desk and sent a note to the physics labs that they should destroy the plans for the sphere and not communicate with Larry again.

"What have I done?" I asked myself. I called to Emma, who came to my office with another security person. They walked straight to the door to lab C and dragged Rich out to the pod lab. They put him in stasis, and then went back to Emma's security area, no questions asked. I needed time to think.

Time travel. It was a discovery I could not have imagined for years to come. A thirteen-year-old boy and an insane millionaire had figured it out. Teleportation was an amazing discovery on its own, but time travel—time travel would have to have massive regulations. The damage someone could do to his or her own timeline was unthinkable. If Larry couldn't separate the two from each other, then teleportation would die. I couldn't risk leaving the power of time travel to the general public.

I would have to tell the government about it. I groaned internally and sank my head on the desk. The last thing I wanted was the government poking their regulations in where they weren't wanted. This couldn't be ignored though.

I supposed I could tell the government the lab was working on it and get their opinion. Could it be a useful tool? Or was it just too dangerous to be playing with? An opinion could be rendered without the knowledge of the application being fully known. I scheduled a meeting with the chief science advisor.

It might not matter in the end. As long as Larry was the only one who could control this time travel, then it would be much easier to control. If I kept him under guard, had Eliza monitoring him, then he couldn't do too much damage. could make sure the only trips into the past were safe. Perhaps I could take ju a few short trips to check some things out. I'd love to be a stranger on the stre watching, on the day I met Amelia.

I tried to push the thought from my mind. That was exactly the sort of thing t should be avoided. It would be irresponsible of me to use such a tool to reliv old life with Amelia.

Amelia! If I could travel back in time, once the cure to Sunithe's disease was discovered, I could go back and present it to myself before she ever went into stasis.

I wasn't sure how that would affect my present though. Would the world just change around me? Would I get back here and find that Amelia had been working by my side for these past nineteen years? Would I remember those nineteen years with her, or would it seem foreign to me? Would it seem like should still be inside that stasis pod?

I breathed deeply to try and calm myself. Rich may have just volunteered himself to be a candidate for exploring a cure for Sunithe's disease, but Larry definitely had promise. He had the potential for greater things, if I could just control him.

What was to stop Larry from sending me back to the prehistoric age and leaving me there if he got angry with me? This sort of power in the hands of thirteen-year-old boy was not something to trifle with. Rules would have to b made, and he would have to be controlled.

I canceled my meeting with the science advisor. I could handle this, I decided My initial panic had subsided and my scientific curiosity was taking over. La couldn't do anything without the sphere, which was one safeguard. I'd make sure he couldn't mentally do anything outside of what was directed with Eliz mind control. That was the second safeguard.

My panic subsided into excitement. I thought about all the places and times I would love to see: the Roman Empire at the height of its glory, the pyramids being built, dinosaurs. I couldn't help but smile at the idea as I sat at my desk could just keep this discovery between Larry, Eliza, and myself. I didn't hav let anyone else know.

When a cure was discovered, I could go back in time and give it to myself and just see what happens to the future. Perhaps it would all just work itself out. Perhaps my mind would not know that Amelia had spent the last nineteen years in stasis, but would think she had been here the whole time. Whatever happened would just be filled into my memories. Then what happened if this lab didn't progress as it had? Without the drive to find the cure or find the mind control abilities of Eliza, would I even be here? Would time travel have been discovered? Would I be able to get back?

There were many questions to be answered. I would take small steps first.

Chapter 14

Thomas had almost given up. I couldn't blame him really. He'd been working on a cure for Amelia for nearly two decades now. I didn't want to tell him about Larry's ability to send people back in time. For one thing, it was my back-up plan for Amelia if Jenny and Eliza were never able to fix the minds of the stasis pod people. For another thing, it was dangerous. I had only gone on two trips myself, but I could see how harmful it might be in the wrong hands. It had to be controlled, and unfortunately, the only way I could see to do that was to get Eliza in on the process.

I feared Eliza. I hated to admit it, even to myself, but she had mental abilities far beyond anyone else at the lab. She still looked like an adolescent girl, but she could destroy anyone's mind in a heartbeat if she wanted. I had a way to keep tabs on Larry, but Eliza was a different story.

Eliza's control over Larry affected his ability to function. My first trip had been seamless. Afterward, I told Larry we needed to study the process, and that I would be taking a few more short trips, further back in time with Eliza monitoring him. I didn't know exactly what Eliza did to keep tabs on his mind at the time, but when I arrived back in the present I was violently ill.

Larry said he had struggled to keep track of me with Eliza watching over him. I believed it. Eliza could be very intrusive on a person's mind. With her constant monitoring of him, Larry had a harder time getting me back to the present, and that difficulty reflected back on me. Larry protested, but I assured him it was as much for his protection as for the traveler.

There was still a question of what to do about the discovery. This was a great advancement, but to what purpose? I couldn't put the burden on Larry of shuttling people around in time for their own pleasure. My first trip had been back to the day I met Amelia. I watched from a little way down the street as she handed me a cookie, but couldn't bear to stay for the entire interchange. When I think back to that day, I can't remember seeing someone there on the street, though my mind was fully focused on Amelia at the time. Nothing here seemed different either. Then again, I only observed the past. I didn't do anything or interact with anyone. Perhaps trips back for the purposes of observation of important events would be allowable.

The truth was the laboratory was financially unstable. Our publicly acknowledged projects were bringing in money, just not enough to sustain the secret ones. It felt like bringing the government in on the other projects might end up being necessary. Who else would have tons of money to throw at towards their curiosity about the past? Millionaires too, I supposed. I'd start with millionaires. They tended to understand the need for discretion and respect things like non-disclosure agreements. As a bonus, once the technology was shared with some of the outside world, it would be harder for the government to try and control it.

I'd find people to do the travel work for us. My own employees would be easier to control than outsiders. I could expand the apartment section again and make it a requirement of employment that these researchers live there, so I could keep an eye on them.

The apartment complex was already getting large enough to necessitate some autonomy. I could add an agricultural department to grow our own food as well as do research. I could ensure the researchers never left my sight or talked about their work to the outside world.

A construction project of that magnitude, including the necessary infrastructure, would be vast. Given the current financial state of the lab, I would need a huge infusion of grant money to get started. That likely meant I would have to allow someone very rich to go back in time.

I scoured my contact list, trying to think of who might be interested in funding this sort of project, but would also be capable of being trusted to go back in time.

Rachel Tidwell. The name popped into my mind with a groan. Rachel, of course, would be perfect. She was incredibly rich, partly from family money but more so from her own enterprises. She was ruthless against those who stood against her and rigid in her business practices. I had no doubt she would be capable of understanding the importance of secrecy. My only concern was that she wouldn't be interested. She had the imagination of a brick wall. I would have to make her see it as an investment.

I was distracted by Thomas approaching my door. I didn't want to let him in, but he surely knew I was in here from Emma, and I had never turned him away before. The door slid open and he took a seat on the opposite side of my desk. "Thomas."

"How are you?" he asked me.

"Distracted. What do you want?"

My bluntness caught him off guard. He retreated into his seat before continuing. "I'm done with Sunithe's disease, Lancing. And before you try to guilt trip me into continuing with the work, remember that you haven't donated a second of thought to a cure for Amelia in well over a decade."

That wasn't entirely true. My trip back in time to see my first meeting with Amelia had stirred some powerful emotions up in me. I knew that no matter what the consequences turned out to be, I would travel back in time to give her the cure well before any of this mess occurred. I could afford to wait for it. Even if I couldn't spend the rest of my life with her, some version of me would. If it didn't change my own timeline, so that she was here when I returned, then I could live with that.

"Well, Thomas, what do you want to do?"

"I want to know what you have going on in here. I think I have that right."

His arrogance angered me slightly. "What makes you think you have that right?"

"I've been here since the beginning. But more importantly, I am the co-founder! This lab wouldn't even be here if it wasn't for me. Amelia would be dead and you'd probably still be working for Kischukov."

Despite what he said about me not giving him a guilt trip, he never hesitated to attempt to use it on me. He was unsuccessful this time. I had been prepared for it. I did owe him though, that much was certain.

I tented my hands and stared at him from across the desk. I really didn't know what to do with Thomas. His usefulness to me had dwindled in the past few years. I stared at the man he had become. Aside from the bags under his eyes from stress and lack of sleep, he was handsome. He deserved better than being stuck in here with nothing but work to fill his days. Thomas had never actually had a real life.

His dedication to me had never wavered until this current outburst. I knew I could still trust him with anything. He needed a break, though. I had to give him some time to recover and remember what a life was. "You're right. You're the only one who has been here for me since the beginning, the only one I have
96 – The Children of Doctor Lancing

trusted from the start. It's been unfair of me to lock you away in your own area and keep you out of the big picture. We built this place together, and together we will continue to make it grow."

He seemed relieved. Was I really such a hard-nosed person that he thought I wouldn't understand? "There have been some major developments happening here," I continued, "and I'm going to need your help bringing them to fruition. But first, you need a vacation."

"You expect me to take time off?"

"It will be a working vacation. I have a job for you, which will require you to spend some time on the island. We're in some dire straits financially, and I need to convince a potential investor that this place is worth her money and her time. I can't leave, so who better to explain to her the sort of work we're capable of."

"But I don't know what's going on in here."

"You will." I called to Eliza and silently requested she bring her latest project along with her. "I have a way to fill you in rather quickly and thoroughly."

The door to lab C opened on the side of my office, and Eliza entered carrying two helmets that were linked together with wires. She glanced at Thomas. Since they both worked in separate lab areas they had never met, not even in passing. That was partly coincidence, but mostly because I kept Eliza under tight control.

"Thomas, this is Eliza. What she's holding in her hands are two brain helmets we've adapted for instantaneous communication. It's similar to the link Emma had installed in my head, but not permanent and not as wide-reaching."

"You mean you're able to link two brains together to share thoughts and memories in an instant?"

I had to hand it to Thomas; he was quick, and still useful to have around. "Precisely. Eliza and Jenny have been working on it. It's proven useful for some other work that's going on as well."

"What other work?" He eyed the helmets curiously.

I knew anything involving the inner workings of the brain would get his attention again. "It'll be a lot easier if you just share Eliza's mind."

"Why not you?"

"Eliza's been linked with most of the people in this section of the lab. She knows more about what's going on with everyone than I do at this point."

That was only half the reason. I wanted Eliza to scan Thomas's mind. I wanted to know more about how he thought. I trusted Thomas, but even your most trusted companion could be broken. I needed to know his weaknesses, like I knew the weaknesses of almost everyone here.

"She looks rather young," he said, eyeing Eliza.

"She's older than you were when you started."

He laughed, and didn't notice the scandalized look on Eliza's face. It was precisely the right thing to say. If he had a weakness, there was no doubt Eliza would find it now. She handed him a helmet and sat in the chair next to him as she put on her own. Her eyes bored into him as she waited for him to put on the helmet. He gave me another look and shrugged before putting it on. He immediately gripped the arms of the chair and gritted his teeth.

"Don't fight it, Thomas. Open your mind to her and it will be much easier for both of you."

I could tell he was battling with the idea of letting go. Thomas had been through a lot with the experimentation necessary to find the proper brain mapping for immortality. His mind was possibly the only one here that could present Eliza with a challenge. I would have to remember that if I ever needed help in subduing Eliza.

His arms relaxed and it was Eliza's turn to grip the chair. A few seconds later she relaxed and was breathing heavily. Thomas seemed unfazed and rather amused. He smirked as he took the helmet off and held it out to her. She snatched her own helmet off in frustration, grabbed his and stormed out of the office.

"Nice girl. She seems a bit jealous of me."

I smirked. "Eliza is affronted by the idea that anyone younger than her could be more useful to me."

"Time travel," he said with amazement in his voice. He smoothed his hair back from where the helmet had ruffled it.

My lips curved up. I knew he would be interested in it. "Yes."

"And you've already tried it, and it worked! I'm amazed!" He had jumped up from the chair and was pacing. He had the same excitement in his step that he used to get when he was young.

It was nice to see he was still capable of it. The research on finding a cure for Sunithe's disease had been steadily taking its toll on Thomas.

"Where did you go?"

His question threw me. I had been limiting my exposure to Eliza, so she wasn't aware of that trip. I saw no reason to lie to Thomas at this point. "I went to see Amelia. I went back to the day we met." The smile left my face.

He was silent for a moment. "I'm sorry." He sat back down and avoided eye contact.

He didn't say what he was sorry for, but I knew it wasn't just about giving up on finding the cure.

"You've seen what we have going on in here, Thomas. Do this thing for me, and you can work on whatever you want, no matter how crazy the idea may seem."

He perked up a little at the idea and the corner of his mouth twitched upward. "What if I can't convince your investor?"

"I'm certain you'll find a way. You have a certain charm about you." Now that energy had filled his face again, his features were striking. Though he hadn't been successful in finding a cure, I was immensely proud of Thomas's other accomplishments. In some ways, he felt like my prodigy. No, my and Amelia's prodigy. He was the closest thing we had to a child.

"When do I leave?"

"Tomorrow. I'll give you a few days on the island by yourself to mellow out and enjoy yourself. I'll tell her one of my researchers has a business proposal for her and get her to join you there. We need this money, Thomas. Be creative in your offers."

He stood back up. "I'll make it happen."

I watched him leave and felt very confident that we would soon have a rather expansive laboratory complex. I walked to Eliza's room, now feeling a little guilty about having her dig into Thomas's mind, but anxious to hear what she found all the same.

Chapter 15

Things were falling into place. Thomas had convinced Rachel to join the lab and fund our research. I had to make several concessions to her, but that was to be expected. She decided to sell her primary businesses and join the lab as the head of the time travel section of the laboratory. She and Thomas were co-chairs of an executive board, which would hire the researchers to do the time travel, and decide what trips were to be made. Rachel had many equally rich contacts in the outside world that were willing to pay a lot of money to fulfill their curiosity. Within no time Rachel was well on her way to making back her initial investment.

Most people wanted to know reasonable things, like how the pyramids and Stonehenge were actually built. Requests were pouring in and we hadn't even started sending people back yet. It became apparent very quickly that not everyone had honorable intentions in the manner of scientific pursuits.

Suggestions that came up repeatedly in various forms were to find Jesus Christ to see him perform miracles or Moses when he parted the Red Sea. This came both from people who were overly zealous and extremely atheist. Rachel refused to even entertain the idea of sending someone back there, since it could send millions of people into depression or worse, self-righteous evangelism.

Rachel was also shocked at our lack of security other than surveillance. She chastised me for not taking more precautions after the Matthew Porter incident. I assured her that it was handled ably. Her concerns were well founded though. I knew we would have to be more proactive about protecting the sphere, and keeping people from snooping around in sections they weren't cleared to be in.

Since Rachel had joined us two years ago, the lab had turned into a series of buildings. At the core was an enormous bio dome that she had built around the apartments. It became a requirement to live in the apartments in order to work here. A few researchers balked at that idea and had left, but most people found it convenient and rarely thought about the outside world since they were so absorbed in their work. Only the people working with time travel would be necessary to keep under control, but we also didn't want to single them out.

Several labs spread out like buds around the central dome. The largest one was the agricultural research wing. There was enough room for an enormous garden, several small fields and an orchard with various trees. It encompassed an old farmhouse that had been on the grounds when I purchased them, and had since been renovated.

There was now only one publicly known entrance and exit available to the outside world. Emma had worked with Rachel to make sure it was a secure one. All employees now had vast information files on them, including biochemical energy scans, which controlled their access to various areas. I worked with one of the construction workers to get two things added to my satisfaction. The first was a secret tunnel from the basement of the farmhouse to a field in the distance that was still part of our land. An escape route, so to speak, that only myself, Eliza and Emma knew about. When the work was done, Eliza helped me make sure the construction workers wouldn't remember it. Eliza didn't share my qualms about erasing memories from people. She seemed to enjoy the power.

The second part I requested was a small apartment for myself inside the lab, just off my office. I was becoming more withdrawn from the other researchers, and I didn't like having to interact with any of them now that Thomas and Rachel were handling most of the administrative roles of the laboratory.

In a move that Rachel found odd, but Thomas completely understood, I had Amelia's pod moved into one of the rooms with me. The promise of the time travel section coming to fruition renewed my drive to find a way back to Amelia. I kept her closer now. Every morning I wiped the moisture from the glass and said "Good morning" to her as I left for my office. In the evening I bid her goodnight on my way to bed. I would often sit and talk with her about my day. Even a one-sided conversation with Amelia was better than nothing.

My interaction with animated people dwindled to those involved in development of the time travel department, and my remaining researchers, the children I had found over the past two decades.

And Rich. A second round in a stasis chamber had not been good for Rich. He was even more of a recluse now and refused to help Larry or even interact with him. I was beginning to think we should just get rid of him, but I kept him around just in case. Eliza might need more volunteers to work with her on mind control issues, and since Rich's mind was already so far gone, I figured she couldn't make him any worse.

Hiring for the time travel department was difficult. I sat in on the first few interviews, to reassure myself that we would be hiring quality people. The problem was, we had no idea what sort of skill set would be most useful. Spies were the natural choice that we came to. They were adept at remaining inconspicuous and getting out of tricky situations. Spies had the downside that they were usually trained only for one country, and modern warfare scenarios. Historians would be more useful for interacting with cultures that were long outdated.

We stuck to recruiting people who already worked for the government with high level security clearances, since we knew they were trustworthy. Then we tried to find people within that restriction who had an interest in history or hobbies that could prove useful, such as theater or historical literature buffs.

Our first hire was a man named Jim, who had worked for years at the Pentagon as an intelligence analyst. He was exceedingly well read and liked watching historical documentaries in his free time. His first and only mission was a disaster.

Even though the files on Kennedy had been released and nothing controversial was noted in them, Rachel didn't believe it. She thought for sure his assassination was part of a larger plot and cover up. Given her fanatical security measures, I wasn't surprised by her disbelief in the released information.

The plan was simple. Jim would be sent back to Dallas in 1963 and stake out the grassy knoll. When he could confirm or refute the existence of a second shooter, he would return. It would be an hour for him, but only five minutes for Larry. We reasoned that it gave Larry a chance to recover from the initial part of the process, but not take too long. Our own impatience led us to rush the return.

When Jim arrived back at our time it was with a bloody eye and a few bruised ribs. The pain of both of these injuries was exasperated by the fact that he immediately doubled over and vomited, then collapsed on the ground.

Rachel had people clean him up and tend to his wounds before sitting him down to find out what had happened. The mission had been a complete failure. As soon as he arrived in 1963, he was spotted by some secret service agents, appearing out of nowhere with a metal sphere in his hand. He was immediately "subdued" and taken into custody. By sheer luck, custody turned out to be the Texas School Book Depository Building's lobby area. When the shots were fired Jim managed to grab his sphere and escape in the chaos.

It wasn't that he didn't find it fascinating to go back in time. It was more that Jim enjoyed the logistical side of it more. He wasn't exactly an exciting person, and felt he was much happier reading about history than reliving it. We decided to keep him on as an intermediary between Rachel's new board and the researchers. Aside from Thomas, Rachel had hired an ethics philosopher and another historian to help sort through mission requests and discuss any problems that might arise. The four of them ferociously debated the ethics of missions. I didn't understand why Thomas wanted to be involved, since he seemed to detest those sorts of discussions. From what I watched, he mostly observed and supported Rachel.

Given the nature of Jim's mission and how much attention he attracted, Rachel decided to forgo finding out about Kennedy until the researchers were more practiced.

Also, given Jim's experience, it was decided that spies would in fact be necessary. If no interaction with society was required for a mission, then a spy could simply remain under the radar and do the research independently. If the mission were going to be more complicated, as in Jim's case, the spy would go first as a scout. They would assess when and where things were going to happen and what would be the most advantageous use of the researcher's time.

Everyone's return to normal time had the same effect on the body as Jim's. There was disorientation and almost always vomiting. We decided to build a room that was padded, but easily cleaned for people to return in.

Thomas, working with the historian, was able to create a machine that could reproduce money from any time period or culture. He also hired a stylist to help produce period appropriate clothing, hairstyles, and if necessary, minor cosmetic alterations like skin pigmentation.

The next few missions were simple scout based fact-finding missions. They went more smoothly. We hired a few more researchers and started assigning them more complicated tasks. There were a few breakdowns in security. One researcher brought an artifact back from his mission with the intent of selling it to make a little extra money. From there onward, researchers were stripped, and anything they brought back with them was taken away to be checked upon their return. The researcher was removed from employment, after Eliza managed to erase any memories of this place or his mission from his mind.

Another researcher returned, covered in sores and incredibly weak. Why she waited so long to return when she was obviously ill, I will never understand. She didn't survive long enough to explain herself. The support staff that would normally strip her and take her things away was horrified at the sight of her when she returned. They refused to touch her and demanded HAZMAT suits from there on out. Though we were able to cure the plague, she was just too far along to be helped. Thomas and I decided cremation was the safest way to dispose of her body. Her family was sent a picture of her, and a vial of ashes.

We hired Anne Crebbs, a general practitioner, to do pre- and post-mission exams. After the incident with the plague, every researcher was vaccinated against any possible disease of the time before they left. When they returned they were screened for any possible contaminants and their general well-being was checked. The symptoms of nausea and dizziness continued, but at least they did not appear to get any worse.

We were accumulating more and more information about the past. It led us to an unexpected question—what were we to do with all this knowledge?

The ability to travel through time was still unknown outside of the lab and even inside most of its sections. We couldn't publish papers documenting our travels and present them to the public. We had to find ways to release the information without letting the source of it be known.

It was Thomas who came up with the idea of planting evidence in the past as well. The problem was, it had to be done in such a way that it wouldn't be found until our current time, or the future. Putting information like that to be discovered too far into the past could damage our time line to an unrecognizable state.

Given that we were still uncertain about the effects changes we made in the past would take, we didn't want to take any unnecessary risks. If evidence could be manipulated to look like it was from the past and planted somewhere that it wouldn't be found until very close to our timeline, that was what we did. To minimize the risk of scouts or researchers running into their own past selves, we hired yet another group of researchers to take care of planting evidence.

I told Rachel repeatedly that it was all terribly convoluted, but she told me that I was too lax in managing security risks, and told me that she wasn't about to let her investment destroy itself.

Confident that they had sorted out all the complications, I left the time travel folks to themselves and refocused on my children.

Chapter 16

Jenny sat across from me, fidgeting. She kept crossing and uncrossing her legs. She seemed nervous. She always seemed nervous when she was in my office. I would have to remember to be friendlier towards her. I smiled cordially. "How is Eliza doing, Jenny?"

She froze for a moment before speaking. An insignificant moment of time, but I caught it. "Eliza is as brilliant as ever."

"What is she working on these days?"

"She's managed to automate Larry's mind control through the helmet so she doesn't have to be there when he sends people or retrieves them."

She was silent at that point, but I could tell she was holding something back. I fixed my smile and tried to encourage her. "And?"

"I'm a little worried about Larry. She seems to have suppressed him to an unhealthy state."

"What do you mean?" I found Jenny to be far too empathetic with her patients. She lacked the ability to separate the human from the test subject, as I was able to.

She sunk into her chair and gave me a wary look. "He doesn't eat of his own will anymore. He doesn't do anything of his own will anymore. He seems almost—" She trailed off and bit her lip.

"You know you can tell me anything, Jenny."

She looked up at me. Her brow was furrowed and she had a frown on her face, but she nodded slightly before continuing. "He seems like a shell. Like he's not actually there. It's almost as though he only exists when Eliza tells him it's time to do something." She stopped again and looked down at the floor. "It's no way for a person to live."

I could sympathize with her pain, but I knew Larry was too important and too dangerous to be left to his own devices. He wanted this, after all. He wanted the power to send people back in time. "I'll see if I can get Eliza to ease up on him when he's not working."

"Thank you." She went quiet again.

"So what else is Eliza doing if she's no longer busy with Larry?"

"She's working on your telekinesis project. She thinks she's close. She says she can feel the world around her when she closes her eyes. It doesn't extend very far. But she can feel objects and people who are around her, even if she can't control them yet."

"People?"

Her eyes flicked up at me and there was genuine fear in them. "Yes. She says she's getting used to my mind. Since I'm around her all the time. That she's learning how to delve into it, without the helmet interface."

I tried to mask my own fear. If Eliza was starting to pierce people's minds without being connected to them, then she could start reading anyone's mind. She could start reading my mind. There were plenty of things I wouldn't want her to know. I'd need to find some way to shield my mind from her, but I couldn't even think about it when she was around. It would have to be something so subtle and buried that even she wouldn't know she was being controlled. "Does it go both ways? Can you feel her at all when she's doing this?"

"No." Jenny shook her head and looked downtrodden.

"Eliza's a special case, I didn't expect you would be able to."

"It's not that."

"Then what is it?" I tried to ask the question in a caring way instead of a prodding, exasperated one.

"I don't like the lack of privacy. I don't like that she knows everything I think now. That she knows it bothers me, and still does it as though my feelings don't matter at all." She quieted and looked at the door. She gasped, and fear tainted her features. "She'll know I said that." Her head fell into her hands and she started to cry.

I was completely wrong about Jenny. She wasn't nervous about me, she wasn't jealous of her coworkers. She was terrified of Eliza. "Why don't you take the rest of the day off? Go relax, get your mind off work. Do whatever you like to do in your down time. I'll talk with Eliza about boundaries."

She looked up at me suddenly, the fear in her eyes intensified. "She'll know it was me! She'll know I complained!" Tears streamed from her eyes again though her gaze remained fixed on me.

"Go home and don't worry about it. I'll bring it up as relates to Larry, you'll have nothing to do with it."

"But the next time I see her, the next time she goes into my mind—"

"She'll have learned to respect people's privacy. She won't test me by breaking that respect again. She knows better. She knows I can eliminate her. Now go home. I don't want you coming back tomorrow either. We'll tell Eliza you're sick. Go on."

Jenny stood, swaying for a moment, and looked at me one last time before turning to go. I called to Thomas before realizing he was in a meeting with the board. "*When you're done,*" I said to him.

When Thomas and Eliza had linked minds he gave her a run for her money. The truth was I was a little frightened of getting near her now too. I wanted Thomas as an intermediary. I still had to figure out how to get her to behave, especially around me.

I realized though, that I didn't need her to behave, I needed her to act like she was. I still wanted to be able to know what was going on in peoples' minds. I just wanted to keep mine to myself. I could try threatening her, but that was a hollow victory that would eventually fail. I needed her love and respect. Unfortunately, Eliza didn't seem to respect anything.

If I tried to prove I was smarter than her, she'd merely get jealous. If I tried to be a peer she would think herself above me. I needed to find a weakness that I could exploit, and Thomas was the only one who might be able to help me with that.

The boardroom meeting ended and Thomas arrived at my door shortly after. He picked up on the concerned look on my face and sat, focused and ready.

"I need a way to control Eliza. I need a weak point."

Thomas sat back and smiled. He remained silent as he thought. "Perhaps you could use her jealous nature against her. Present her with a task that she should be able to do handily that is actually impossible."

I laughed once without humor. "I already did that and she's excelling at it. What's behind the jealousy?"

"A tiny ball of rage."

"What does she have to be angry about?" I asked.

"A traumatic childhood for starters. Isolation. She knows people fear her, and although she enjoys that, she's incredibly lonely. Her father left when she was very young, and her mother blamed Eliza and beat her because of it."

"Are you telling me the only difference between the two of you is that you had loving parents?"

"And a cool sister."

"So Daddy issues and a lack of trust in anyone." I sighed and ran my hand through my hair. This would not be easy. "Thomas, I need to rescue her somehow. I need her to trust me."

"She respects you. Honestly, I think that's the best you'll get. You already rescued her from her life. What more could you do for her?"

"Be honest," I said.

"What do you mean?" Thomas asked.

"I need to be honest with her. Completely. But I need to not be afraid of her first."

"Good luck with that. She's a terrifying little girl."

"She's nineteen, Thomas. Anyway, she can't harm me." I paused as I thought. "Yet. If she respects me, she has to know that she needs me to be able to continue her work here. Any other lab would've dissected her head by now."

Thomas remained silent. The look he gave me told me exactly his opinion on head dissection.

"Go on, get out of here," I said. "I'll give it a try. What's the worst that can happen, she finds out my deepest darkest secrets?"

"What really happened to Matthew Porter? The rest of the pod people?"

I gave Thomas a look of disappointment. "Maybe she'll respect me more, knowing what I'm capable of."

Thomas didn't move. "Amelia."

I nodded. Amelia would always be my weak point. Amelia was in stasis though, and I had access to all of eternity. So how could Eliza possibly use her against me?

Thomas rose and left. I headed to the door of the lab where Eliza and Jenny spent most of their time. Eliza was lying on some cushions on the floor, staring at a small red ball. I hadn't been in here in a while. I didn't realize the changes they had made to the place. Eliza either hadn't noticed my entrance or didn't care.

I said her name in my mind and her focus shifted immediately to me. Her eyes bored into mine and I could feel the intrusion. It felt as though something was winding its way through my thought processes. I tried to take in the sensation fully, letting her explore as she liked. Because I had just been talking about him with Thomas, Matthew Porter popped into my head. Eliza gasped and broke her eye contact.

"I hear it's going well," I said. I walked over and sat down on the floor next to her. She continued to lounge on a cushion, the ball a few inches from her face.

"I never knew. Jenny never told me how Matthew got that way."

I let my face remain a mask as I looked at her. Let her see the detachment necessary for my job.

"You killed him."

I frowned at her. "That's not true, you know very well he's alive."

"But he's insane. And you gave him that disease and couldn't cure him and put him back in that stasis pod and he'll get even more insane."

"That's part of why you're here, Eliza, to eventually help those people. Though you have more important tasks to be focusing on first." I gestured at the ball but she ignored me.

"How could you destroy his life like that?"

I refrained from pointing out her own hypocrisy. "He wronged us terribly. We couldn't let him go, he knew too much. Back then we didn't have you to erase people's memories. What would you have done?"

She stared at me again, not probing, just thinking. She looked away and I knew she couldn't come up with an answer. She shrugged and shook her head.

"I have to protect my people here. Someone has to do the dirty work. I've managed to compartmentalize my brain very well over the past—many years. I do what needs to be done, and don't think twice about it."

"You did it for love."

"Yes."

"No one has ever loved me that way."

I smiled at her. "You left society when you were twelve. That's hardly enough time to develop a passionate love affair." I wondered if she learned that I met Amelia at age six.

"Not even my parents loved me. They were afraid of me."

I was surprised to see tears glisten in her eyes. "People fear what they don't understand."

"You don't," she said, challenging me.

"I'm something people don't understand."

She gave me a half smile.

"I have faith in you, Eliza."

Her smile broke. For the second time that day I unintentionally made a woman cry. A woman, trapped inside the body of a twelve-year-old girl. "I can't do it," she said between tears. "I can't make it move. It's just a stupid ball. It's nothing. Why can't I do it?"

I thought back to Thomas's anger at me when I had been neglecting him. Perhaps Eliza just needed attention from someone who mattered to her. "It's an incredibly difficult task, Eliza. That's why I gave it to you, because I have faith in you. But I know not to expect results overnight." I put my hand on her shoulder. "Tell me where you are."

She wiped the tears away and sniffed a few times. "I can see it. I can see all of it, every molecule. I just can't control it."

"Let's start more simply. What are you trying to do to it?"

"Push it so it rolls."

"But how are you pushing it?"

"By making the molecules move away from me."

"Relative to what?"

She stared at me blankly. "I don't understand."

"Something has to physically push against the ball to make it move. The only thing there is air."

"You want me to blow on the ball?"

"No, that's cheating. Here, let me show you." I lifted her hand up. "Spread your fingers." She obeyed. "Now wave your hand through the air," I said as I let go. "Feel the motion in relation to the space around you."

She waved her hand back and forth before yanking it back down furiously. "This is stupid. There's nothing there."

"There is something there," I let the anger resound in my voice. Eliza needed more discipline. "You're being impatient and arrogant, that's your problem."

"This is impossible!"

"Nothing is impossible!" I yelled at her. She retreated from me into the cushion. "You're better than this. You can do this, Eliza."

"I can't!"

"Focus." I stared into her eyes, but I wouldn't say anything else. She had to come to things on her own.

She huffed and held up her hand again. She closed her eyes and remained still for a few moments before slowly waving her hand through the air. She put it down on the cushion and pushed against it, then moved it through the air again. The expression on her face turned from despair to curiosity. "The air," she said. She froze for a moment and the look of focus on her face intensified. Her closed eyes scrunched up even more. Out of the corner of my eye, I saw the red ball twitch.

Chapter 17

My joy at Eliza's progress was short lived. Later that day, Emma called me into her office to give me a printed photo I requested of Eliza and me. The surveillance system had caught the moment when Eliza was finally able to levitate the ball. It rose just a couple of inches out of her hand. I placed my hand on her shoulder, as a proud father would. I planned on giving it to Eliza as a way for her to remember that I'm on her side and pleased with her work. I was the father she never had. The proud father who was not afraid, would stay by her side, and believed that she could do anything. I looked at it with a detachment that surprised me, and nodded in satisfaction.

"Thank you, Emma. It's perfect."

"We have another situation that needs to be handled," she said to me, ignoring my gratitude.

"I don't like it when you use the word 'handled'," I said and lowered the photo in irritation.

"Fine, we have a situation that needs to be dealt with by someone in charge."

I didn't attempt to hide my frustration at her. "What?"

"Jenny has killed herself."

The words didn't register at first. My knees felt weak, and I gripped the back of a chair for support. "What?"

"She was found in her apartment bathroom. She overdosed on sleeping pills."

"How could she possibly have gotten enough to overdose? Drugs are kept under tight control."

"Doctor Crebbs mentioned she'd been having trouble sleeping for a few weeks. She must have been hoarding them and not actually using them." Emma's voice broke. I had forgotten that she was the one who hired Jenny in the first place to help her sort out the mental aspects of my surveillance interface. "She left a note." She held her hand out. A crumpled piece of paper was in it.

"Who found her?" I asked as I took the note.

"I did."

I lowered the note to my side and looked at her. I hadn't noticed earlier that her eyes were puffy and red. I felt like a selfish fool. "Emma, I'm so sorry."

"She didn't meet me for our post breakfast jog this morning. I meant to stop by at lunch to make sure she was okay, but I just got so busy."

"This is by no means your fault, Emma. Do you understand me?" I waited, but she kept her head lowered. "Emma!"

After a moment she looked up at me. "I know."

"What did you do when you found her?"

"I called Doctor Crebbs. I knew she could be—discrete."

"Where is Jenny now?"

"Still in her apartment. Doctor Crebbs thought it would be better to wait until tonight to move her."

"That's probably wise." I sat down in the chair and flattened Jenny's note out on the desk to read it.

> *To whomever finds me, please know that no matter what, Eliza cannot be left to her own devices. She is evil itself. Though she may play along she will one day destroy us all. I've seen inside her mind and know that there is no means of redemption there. At some point, she would have figured out what I know, and I don't know what she would do then. Rather than wait for that day I have decided to deny her access to my mind any more. Let her torture some other researcher if she must, but I cannot go on like this. There is no life for me outside of this place. I've never wanted to be anywhere else. I loved this lab. I hope it will go on for years to come. Good luck to you all, and goodbye. I'll miss you, Emma.   Jenny.*

Emma stared at me as I leaned back in the chair, leaving the note on the desk.

"She told me Eliza frightened her," she said. "I didn't know how bad it was."

"She told me too. Just yesterday, in fact. I told her she needed some rest. I thought it would help." It was my fault. I should have taken her more seriously. I should have paid more attention to what was going on even before that. I looked away from Emma. "Eliza has been managed."

"You read the note," Emma said angrily. "Jenny spent more time with Eliza than anyone in this place. Their thoughts intertwined on a regular basis. She knew what she was talking about."

"Eliza has been managed," I said again, and glared at Emma.

"Oh I see." Her eyes narrowed when she looked at me. "Eliza's more important than Jenny."

"Do you really think I'm so callous as to not feel the loss of one of my scientists? One who was here from nearly the beginning? Jenny was equally as important to me as Eliza!"

"You never asked me to get you pictures of you and Jenny."

"It's part of my handling of Eliza." I was partially a lie. Eliza was much more powerful and useful to me than Jenny, but I couldn't admit that to her. "Emma, you have to believe me. I took Jenny's warning very seriously."

"Then why aren't you getting rid of Eliza?"

"Because she's one of my researchers, and just like any of my researchers I will do everything in my power to do what needs to be done to keep her here and productive."

She sneered at me and crossed her arms in anger, clearly unconvinced. I couldn't blame her. One of her friends had just died, and I was protecting the person who caused it.

"Please believe me, Emma. You've seen what Eliza can do. You know she's powerful. But I have control over her still. I won't be exposing anyone else to her who I don't think will be able to handle it."

"Will you tell her about Jenny?"

"No. And neither will you. In fact no one outside of Doctor Crebbs and the two of us is to know about this. Do you understand?"

She glared at me, but after a time she took a deep breath and nodded. The frown on her face abated.

"You asked me to handle it, and I will. Doctor Crebbs and I will remove the body tonight. Can I count on you to keep me informed on getting out without anyone noticing?"

"Where will you take her body?"

"She'll be cremated, and I'll give the ashes to her next of kin."

Emma nodded again. She knew I had done things like this before. She knew about the researcher who came back with the plague. She knew that this place was more important than one person's life.

"Why don't you take it easy for the rest of the day. Go home and relax." I flinched slightly as I remember the last words I had said to Jenny. Emma was a different case, I told myself. She was not nearly as stressed out and not exposed to Eliza. Since she had her eyes on everything that went on in this place, she knew there were some risks and less than ethical deeds that had to be done for the good of the lab.

"Thanks. Call me when you're ready to move her tonight." She stood and walked to the door. "And don't forget your *picture*." The word came out sourly.

I picked the frame up from her desk and looked at it. Whoever she got to frame it had done a good job. Thomas was waiting for me in my office. I took the frame with me and went to meet him. He greeted me just inside the door. He was holding the linked helmets. I glanced at him, questioning the helmets.

"Trust me," he said, "the fewer questions you ask, the better off you'll be. I've found a way for you to hide from Eliza, and not even realize you're doing it."

"What are you talking about?"

He handed me a helmet. "Like I said, the less you know the better off you'll be. But when there are things you want to hide, and you don't even want someone to know you're hiding them, you'll be able to. There will be no indication whatsoever that there's anything missing." He put a helmet on his head and waited for me. "It's like the brain remapping you exposed me to all those years ago. Except I'll be doing the remapping."

I grudgingly put the helmet on my head and tried to relax. Thomas had his eyes closed and had a focused look on his face. After a few minutes I felt a sharp pain in my brain, and then forgot about it.

"Think about something you'd prefer to not discuss with me," Thomas commanded, his eyes still closed.

That was easy. Jenny's death was an unpleasant situation that I had to deal with.

Thomas cringed, then refocused. "Okay." He took off his helmet and I followed suit. "Well?"

"Well what?"

"How do you feel?"

"Confused." I stared at him, uncertain what I should be expecting.

"I read your mind about Jenny. I'm sorry."

I shook my head. "The problem with sharing all my thoughts with you."

"Well you can no longer share the thought with me. At least, not the thoughts you just had."

"Of course I can. I can tell you about it right now."

"But I can't read it from your mind for myself. I've created—a hiding place, let's say. Anything you want to hide from anyone trying to link to your mind can be hidden there just by you desiring it to be hidden."

"Then how do you know about Jenny?"

"I saw it as it came to the forefront of your mind. Then it disappeared from view."

118 – The Children of Doctor Lancing

"Fascinating."

"So now think about the fact that you want to hide the fact that you can keeps things from her. Then the ability and even the desire will be hidden from Eliza."

I gave him another questioning look. "Isn't there some sort of damaging recursive loss there?"

He laughed. "Nope, no problem."

"What if I decide I want to hide something that comes up, like it did with you just now? Won't she notice that the thoughts disappear?"

"Yes, so I wouldn't recommend doing it in front of her if you can avoid it. It will take a lot of control to keep your thoughts in order. But you can handle it, I'm sure." He put a hand on my shoulder, mocking me.

"I appreciate the vote of confidence," I said and shrugged his hand off of me.

"Good luck," Thomas said as he turned away from me. "Because if she figures it out, you're in trouble." He left the room.

I picked up the picture again and headed to the dormitory where Eliza slept. There was no point in delaying a test run.

Eliza was watching a ball spin around her head. When she saw me her concentration broke and the ball fell to the floor.

"I think you can do better than that," I said, chiding her.

She smiled and the ball resumed its previous path as she spoke to me. "Jenny never showed up for work today."

"She's been very ill," I lied. "Doctor Crebbs told me she'd be out for at least a few days."

There it was, the mental intrusion. Eliza was following the thought to see if it led to any other information. Since it was a lie, there was nothing connected to it in my mind.

Interesting that she didn't quite believe me right away. It was another thought I didn't want her to see. I hid that as well. Thomas was right, I would need to be careful about keeping myself focused while I was with her.

"I think she's jealous of me." Eliza sat cross-legged on the floor. She kept her palms facing up as though in a meditative pose. She brought another ball into the mix. They orbited her head as though caught in her gravitational pull, like she was the center of the universe.

An apt analogy, I thought. "Undoubtedly. Who wouldn't want to be able to move matter with thought." I gestured at the balls circling her head with my empty hand.

Eliza noticed my other hand and again, the balls dropped.

"Well I know what we'll be working on tomorrow, Eliza."

She huffed. "What's that?" she asked and gestured at my hand.

"Emma got it for me." I handed her the photograph.

She looked steadily at it. For a moment her eyes looked like she was fighting back tears. She took a deep breath and laid the frame on the table next to her bed. "Thank you. It was a proud moment for me."

"It was a major breakthrough. Definitely a moment that needs to be remembered. I am very proud of you." I glanced at the balls on the floor as I turned to leave. "And I expect to continue to be proud of you. You're going to do great things, Eliza."

I caught her smile as I turned away.

"Nothing will be able to distract me tomorrow," she called after me.

"I'm counting on it," I said as I continued walking out. The door closed behind me and I set off for Jenny's apartment. It was going to be a long night.

Chapter 18

After Jenny's suicide I asked Emma to expand surveillance into the apartments. Not completely, I did afford my people some amount of privacy to take care of their human needs. They didn't know they were being watched, so it wouldn't have mattered anyway. I had more reasons than just Jenny's suicide to want to watch my employees.

My attention had been caught by one of the time travel researchers. Emma and Jim had taken to calling them "librarians" for some reason. Emma and Jim had been hitting it off pretty well. I had to remind Emma that Jim was almost certainly not a candidate for immortality. She backed off after that, but they were still more cordial with each other than most.

Jim had turned out to be an excellent intermediary between the librarians and the executive board. He understood the need for certain rules, but unlike Rachel, he could use his friendly nature to ensure cooperation with those below him. He was admired and respected, and intelligent. He provided another layer of distance between my researchers and myself. When he requested an audience with the board, I of course listened in from my office.

He was concerned about one of his librarians, a man named Noah Kent. Noah had a bit of a wild streak to him. Though Jim didn't think Noah would ever do something to harm the lab, he wasn't as strict about following the protocols as he should be. Whenever he returned from a mission he had cocky answers to the questions that were asked of him. He relentlessly hit on Doctor Crebbs and any other female of the support staff he encountered.

Jim's concern was that we weren't challenging Noah enough. He thought if we were able to send him on more complicated missions, he would be more focused on the work. He felt that Noah was likely to get sloppy when bored, but that he should be pushed, not fired, since he was an excellent librarian otherwise.

Rachel disagreed, and thought Noah needed to be taught a lesson. She instructed Jim to let Noah know that he would not be doing any missions for the next month. He had been doing at least two a month up to that point. She felt that how Noah reacted and what he did in his free time would be better indicators of how he would react to following the rules better. I let her judgment stand, though I didn't agree with it. I was surprised to note that Thomas backed her up.

Noah was not pleased, to say the least. After yelling at Jim for a while, he calmed down enough to apologize and ask for more information about why. He found the restrictions ridiculous, and told Jim as much. Jim tried to reassure him that they were necessary for the safety of everyone at the lab. Noah ignored him and stormed off into the habitat area. He kicked at the grass as he strode across the central courtyard, wandering aimlessly and having an argument with no one. He mumbled, but I caught words like "incompetent" and "useless." He gave me the distinct impression of an adolescent.

I watched as he approached the agricultural laboratory area and look at it with confusion. He had never been in any part of the complex other than his own apartment and my research section. Though normally I would keep people out who weren't involved in agricultural research, I let the doors slide open as he approached, curious to see what he would do. I figured there wasn't any harm in letting him into an oversized garden.

He ran into Montgomery Welsher, the head of the research farm. Montgomery expressed surprise at having a visitor, and mentioned that he didn't think other people were allowed in there.

Noah gave him a scandalous grin and asked what he was working on. Montgomery gave him the tour of the area. They stopped a few times to discuss research being done. Noah seemed fascinated by the cross breeding gardens. He chatted with Montgomery at length about what he had planted there and how things had turned out. He mentioned his mother used to play around with cross-pollination, but never to this sort of scale. He then asked Montgomery if he could have a bit of space, to try some things out. Montgomery furrowed his brow and looked over his shoulder, directly into one of Emma's hidden devices, but agreed.

I wondered why Montgomery had looked nervous. Agricultural experimentation was not likely to destroy the world. Regulations involving the farm were much more relaxed than the other research wings. All the same, I made a note to Emma that her devices were not as surreptitious as she thought and perhaps she should work on that. She had populated the agricultural wing with small robotic insects and birds. I had thought they looked convincingly life-like, but I didn't spend much time around animals. Perhaps they didn't behave as normal life would.

Noah went back to his apartment and started researching fruits and vegetables. It appeared Jim was correct in his assessment of Noah's focus. He hadn't hit on a single woman on the walk back to his place.

Banning Noah from traveling for a month had another unexpected positive effect. I decided to take a few more trips into the past, since Larry's load had eased. I went back in time again to observe myself as a child, and also to see if an adult perspective on my parents would give me better understanding of them.

I tinted my skin darker and had a prosthetic nose applied so I wouldn't look like I could be related to my family. I followed them to one of the services they had constantly dragged me to. The messages didn't seem any different. The place was conservative almost to punishment, and isolationist. My arrival at the church drew wary glances and whispers. Since I knew all the teachings, I was accepted as a visitor traveling through town to visit family.

I watched my younger self sit there in church, fists clenched into balls, back ramrod straight in the pew. Every now and then my mother would lean over and whisper fiercely into my ear. My father ignored me completely. I found that interesting, since it was my father who I remembered being more terrified of. Perhaps I was frightened of not knowing what he was thinking or what he might do.

The service ended after 4 grueling hours, and I made a hasty exit. The members I passed on my way out did not seem disappointed to see me leave so quickly. No one tried to make conversation or welcome me to the church. I lingered just outside the building, behind a tree, and waited for my parents and me to depart. I followed at a slight distance as they walked back to our house. For the first time I noticed a mark on the back of my neck, at the apex of my spine. Amelia had asked me about it a few months after we first met. Being on the back of my neck, I had no idea it was there.

It must have been a birthmark, but it was an unnaturally uniform circle. Most birthmarks I knew of were irregular shapes. I walked a little faster, trying to get a closer look. A smaller, darker circle was at the center. It looked like a scar. I must have been hurt badly when I was very young. I thought it an odd place to be injured.

It felt strange to be back in time. Cars were still being driven by the people inside them. People, aside from my family, were dressed in strange clothes. I watched as my parents steered me clear of other people on the street. After a while my younger self gave up on trying to take in his surroundings and simply walked with his head hung.

I had the feeling today might be one of the days I tried to run away. I was right. I never made it very far. Being so young, isolated and completely inexperienced in life made me terrified of the world beyond the end of my block. It was almost as though an invisible line kept me from crossing the end of the sidewalk into the next street.

I sat on a bench across from my old house and waited. The street was filled with children playing and people walking to and fro. Soon enough I heard the yelling start, and a short while later I watched myself bolt from the front door and run to the end of the block, stopping, paralyzed by fear to go any further. I watched as I passed by several children, neither of us acknowledging the others existence. Even as I hated my parents, I still obeyed their teachings and kept myself from interacting with others. It made no sense to me as an adult.

I desperately wanted to go talk to my younger self, to offer him encouragement or just a friendly word. To find out what it was that kept him from crossing to the other side of the street. I couldn't remember now. I wanted to talk to my parents and warn them that they were driving me away from them. To tell them that the level of isolation and punishment bordered on abuse, and if they didn't start treating their son better, the authorities would be notified.

Of course, I couldn't. I could only watch from afar as my life played out the way it was meant to. I sighed in frustration, walked to the side of another tree and braced myself for my return trip before pushing the button on the sphere.

As I tried to focus, I noticed a man who had been sitting on a bench a little ways down the street get up and head towards my parents' house. I put the sphere back in my pocket and followed. I got as close as I dared, trying to listen to the conversation as my father answered the door. He recognized the man, I was sure of that. There was yelling and the man gestured at my younger self, standing at the end of the block, paralyzed. My father sent the man away, angry.

I followed the man at a distance, but a few houses down the street he got in a car and drove away. I made note of the car type and which way it turned at the end of the street. I pulled the sphere out again, and again took a deep breath and focused.

I found that with enough mental concentration I could curb the effects of the return trip. I closed my eyes against the bright white room. There was no one here to take the sphere away or strip off my clothes. They knew better than that. My teeth clenched as I forced myself not to focus on the bile in my mouth and breath deeply.

I walked myself through the door to Doctor Crebb's examination room. She was waiting for me in case I needed her. "Welcome back," she said.

I handed her the sphere and continued through the examination room to the next door. The room beyond was where people were scrubbed clean and returned to their normal status. Vanessa met me to remove my nose and restore my original skin coloring. She did quick work and was silent throughout it. Normally she would be somewhat chatty, but in my case, she knew I didn't need to be investigated for any treasonous thoughts. I found though, as she was finishing up my skin, that I wanted to talk to her.

"Vanessa."

Her hands froze for a moment and an expression of panic filled her face.

I really needed to leave people with better impressions of myself. Here was a chance. "How would severe isolation and restrictions affect a small child?"

She let out her breath, pleased that I only wanted to consult with a psychiatrist. "It depends on the child. Some will rebel. Some will find mechanisms for dealing with any adverse impressions. Some won't even realize anything is wrong. In fact, if the isolation is severe enough, it's likely the child won't react in a negative way at all. It will just be a fact of life."

She stopped talking as she removed the last of the tint with a small laser tool. Her hand hesitated before moving away and turning her back to me.

"Hm," I said.

She turned back and hesitated again. "Would you mind telling me why you're asking?"

"Yes," was all I said. I didn't need to be psychoanalyzed.

The only people who knew why I was going back in time were Rachel and Thomas. I had managed to hide it from Eliza. As far as I was concerned, this was a private matter, and I had no obligation to discuss it with anyone else.

"One more question." I turned my back to her and gestured to the base of my skull. "Do you know what might cause a permanent mark around here?"

She walked over and removed my hand. "Looks like a scar of some sort," she said. "Maybe you should ask Doctor Crebbs."

"Thank you, Vanessa," I said, and left.

I stopped in to see Eliza, who was working with a new recruit, Peter. "Hello Eliza."

She didn't bother to speak aloud anymore, only in my head. *Peter is progressing nicely.*

I looked at Peter. He was sitting cross-legged on a cushion on the floor. He was staring intently at a card his hand. After a few moments he turned the card around and looked at it. I heard him quietly say "Yes!" and pick up another card to stare at it. I left the room without another word while Eliza continued to stare at Peter.

Thomas was waiting for me again in my office. "Have a good trip?"

"We're all still here, so I couldn't have screwed too much up," I told him. "I don't understand why I put up with my parents for as long as I did."

Thomas shrugged. He knew little of my background except for my relationship with Amelia.

"Amelia really did save me that day," I said.

"Maybe she gave you the opportunity to see a world that didn't revolve around your parents."

"Yes, but why her? Why not any of the other children on the street that I saw, day after day? What made her special?"

"Maybe she was just a hot six year old," Thomas said with a smirk.

I felt an overpowering urge to strike him just then. I controlled myself until it subsided.

Thomas realized he had crossed a line. He looked away from my glare. "Or maybe it was just fate," he said.

I laughed without humor. "Why would fate push us together only to drive her away so soon?"

"To push you even further. If you had never met her, you'd probably still be living in your parents' basement. If she wasn't going to die, you'd probably still be working for Kischukov."

The poke at my obedience reminded me of my previous curiosity. "You seem to agree with Rachel without thought."

He paused and looked introspective for a few moments. I knew whatever came out of his mouth next would be calculated.

"I've come to appreciate that people with a less scientific background can sometimes have interesting viewpoints," he said.

I said nothing, but stared at him inquisitively.

"And if it proves to be useless, no harm done to Noah."

I felt like he was holding something back, but I was still reeling from my adventure with my former self and didn't really want an in-depth discussion. I was tired of the subject, so I changed the topic of conversation. "Did you have a reason for coming in here, other than to ask me about my trip?"

"No."

"Then goodbye."

Thomas hesitated as though he was going to push me further, but got up and left. I went into my apartment, walked over to Amelia's pod and wiped the condensation off the glass to see her again. For the first time ever, I felt like I was looking at a stranger. "Who are you?" I asked her inanimate body.

Chapter 19

A few weeks later I decided to go see Larry. I hadn't visited him in a few months, and Noah's last return trip didn't go so well for him. He said he felt the passage of time between when he pushed the button and when he arrived here. That shouldn't be. I didn't want Larry to feel abandoned like Thomas had started to feel, so I went to make sure he was okay.

Larry did not look well. He had a helmet on. Eliza had rigged it to be wireless, so he was mobile. That meant though, that there was no reason for him to remove it, and it was showing. His hair under the helmet had been rubbed bare, and a red mark adorned the crook of his neck where the strap held the helmet on. He was exceedingly frail. He could barely move to acknowledge me when I came in the room, though when he smiled he seemed happy enough. I wondered if Eliza would reach a point where she wouldn't need the helmet at all. She seemed just a few steps away from being able to control his mind with no physical link.

Even as my concern for Larry built, I made a mental note to look for another candidate for controlling the sphere. I sat down next to him. "Hello, Larry."

He smiled again. Even though he had aged more than a normal person would have, I recognized the boyish grin from when we first met. "Hello."

"How are you enjoying your work?" I asked him.

"It's fascinating. I'm very happy."

"I'm glad to hear that." I didn't believe him. The smile seemed plastered on his face. It didn't touch his other features. "Do you move around much? Eat? Exercise."

"I'm well fed." He pointed to a container of nutritional packets. "I'm very happy."

I glanced at the container. I knew well the tasteless packets he was eating. I couldn't imagine sustaining myself on them for very long. "What about exercise? Do you walk around much?"

"There's no need for that. I'm very happy."

Something was wrong. "When was the last time you took off the helmet?"

His face showed a sign of panicked desperation, and his hand shot up to his head. "Helmet?" Just as soon as it happened, it went away. His face once again became one of placid contentment. "There's no need for that. The helmet keeps me very happy."

Something was definitely wrong. What had Eliza done to him? "Why don't we take it off for a minute?"

"No!" Despite his frail frame the movement away from me was strong and desperate. "No!"

"Okay, okay." I backed away so he would calm down again. "Why don't you want to take the helmet off?"

"I'm very happy."

Though he was smiling again, it was purely mechanical. It was almost as though Eliza had programmed in an unconscious response. If he always thought he was happy, he would never need for anything. Jenny had been right in her assessment. He was a shell. This was hardly what I could call a life anymore. "I'm glad to hear that, Larry. I'm going to leave now."

"Yes, it was nice to see you."

I left Larry to his room and walked back to my office. My legs trembled as I sat at my desk and took a deep breath. I tried to push the fear from my mind by focusing on the issue at hand. If Eliza had programmed him to do his job with no questions asked and no original thought of his own, why had it broken down on Noah's last return trip? I realized I would have to talk to Eliza about it.

I no longer bothered to speak aloud when I was in the room with Eliza. I would merely think what I wanted to say or ask and she would usually respond in kind.

"Good morning, Doctor Lancing," she said aloud.

It always made me a little nervous when she was formal with me. I was doubly nervous that she said it instead of thinking it. It usually happened when she was feeling especially smug, as though my doctorate was only a title and not something I had earned. I kept that thought suppressed. Whenever I talked to Eliza these days it was to the point and without any emotion. I tried not to let my mind wander. I relived my conversation with Larry in my head.

She responded in my mind this time. *Hm. I'm not sure. I should sit in with him the next time he sends someone on a mission, so I can monitor what's going on in his head that the helmet is not accounting for. He should be perfectly happy though.*

I thanked Eliza in my mind and left again, before she could engage me further. It was clear the helmet was making him think he was happy, but I doubted anyone could enjoy that lifestyle. I'd have to find another programmer and be sure Eliza treated them better. Until then, though I didn't condone what Eliza had done, I had no choice but to continue on. Time travel missions were the most lucrative part of the lab aside from our work with the Defense Department, and our operating expenses had skyrocketed since the lab had grown into a full-fledged complex.

I called to Thomas and waited for him in my office. "Eliza has been overstepping her bounds," I told him when he entered.

"What has she done this time?"

"When was the last time you went to see Larry?"

Thomas thought about it. "I'm not sure I've been to see him in a few years, actually. I never really worked with him much."

"He's not in good shape. Eliza basically has him in a mental state of euphoria. He's not taking care of himself because he doesn't think he has too. He's perfectly happy to simply exist to control the sphere for us."

"So what, he doesn't shower or eat until Eliza tells him to?"

"He doesn't even *move* unless Eliza tells him to."

Thomas nodded in understanding. "So what do you want to do?"

"We need to start over with someone new, I think. Larry is probably beyond help at this point, but if we could find a couple of children who show similar aptitude to him, we could spread out the responsibilities and maybe not have to have them in a constant state of mind control. There has to be a way to reason with them, so they'll do their work, and we can leave them be the rest of the time."

"The mind control was your idea in the first place, remember?"

"Yes. And I do think some control is needed. But like Eliza, everyone has their weakness. Perhaps we can exploit that to ensure cooperation rather than outright control."

"Why are you so mistrustful of people? What makes you think a programmer will intentionally screw up a mission?"

"I trust some people. I trust you."

"No you don't."

The observation stung. He was right though. I trusted Thomas more than anyone else, but I still had an irrational fear of betrayal. Perhaps it stemmed from my childhood of abuse. The people who were supposed to take absolute care of me kept trying to destroy me. "No. I don't. Not completely anyway, but close."

"Well, now that we've got that settled, it would appear you trust me more than Eliza."

"Absolutely." I rubbed my hand through my hair and pressed it against my skull. "I need a way to harness Eliza's power, so I can control the programmers on my own."

"I can do it."

I looked up at Thomas. "You've given thought to this?"

He nodded. "She is very powerful, but I'm sure I can find a way to control her, just as she controls him."

He was probably right. He had given Eliza a challenge when their minds were linked together. Eliza had been practicing delving into people's minds for years, though. If she somehow managed to destroy Thomas's mind, I couldn't take that. I wouldn't put it past her to try.

"You're worried about me," Thomas said, interrupting my thoughts.

"Yes. She's gotten frighteningly powerful. I imagine it's just a matter of time before she doesn't even need the helmet interface to control a person's thoughts."

"I can handle her."

"What makes you so sure?"

The side of his mouth twitched up. "I know her weak spot."

"And what makes you think she doesn't know yours?"

"We weren't linked together long enough for her to find it. And now I can use the same trick I taught you to hide it from her."

"Is it something she could exploit?" I asked. Curiosity flared in me against my will.

"It is someone she could hurt. Which would, in turn, be very upsetting to me."

"Aw, Thomas, I had no idea you cared so much."

"Don't flatter yourself, Lancing. But don't worry, she won't find it." Thomas sounded sure of himself.

"Okay. Let's see if we can find someone else with Larry's potential first. I don't want to expose you to Eliza any more than I have to."

"I'm telling you, I can handle it, but okay. Where do you plan on finding another kid like Larry?"

"Same way I found you."

"You're going to ask around cafes?"

"I'll research it. I'll check the medical journals that I haven't been keeping up with. Maybe tap some pediatric psychiatrists."

"Oh yes, that will go over well." He put on a face he did when he was doing an impression of me. "I'll take that crazy kid for you and fix him up real good. He'll send people back in time for me, and I'll keep him locked in a room to protect myself from him."

I glared at him. "I can be more discreet than that. I got you here after all, didn't I?"

"I just wanted to prove how much smarter I was than you."

"And you did. You no longer seem to have that drive though."

"I outgrew it. Eliza does not seem to be outgrowing it."

"Eliza doesn't want to grow up at all. She's got to be in her thirties now, and still looks like a teenager." I sighed. "The fatherly figure thing seemed to work for a while, but she's back to being her arrogant self. I'm getting tired of it."

"She's still useful. Leave her to me."

Part of me liked the idea of Eliza getting a dose of her own medicine from Thomas. The two of them had not been in the same room together since their first encounter several years ago. "First we find another child. Then we'll deal with Eliza."

"We? Are you going to let me come along?"

"Why not? You know what you were like at that age. And you can tell your tale of how I rescued you from a life of alienation and despair to bring you into my flock where you would thrive."

"Flock? That's an interesting way to put it. You haven't found any new children in a while, have you?"

"Peter was the last. Leaving him with Eliza was a mistake I won't make with anyone else."

"What did you do with that picture of the two of you?"

"I left it in the dormitory so Eliza would have to face it every day and remember what she did."

"I doubt she cares she killed Peter. She probably thought he was too weak to exist anyway. Did you ever tell her about Jenny?"

"No. There's a difference between killing someone accidentally and frightening someone so much they commit suicide."

"Maybe a good dose of reality is just what Eliza needs."

I sighed and slumped in my chair. I remembered the night Doctor Crebbs and I encased Jenny in the body bag, and dragged her out of the complex. I remember the day Eliza called to me frantically, and I found Peter lying on the floor, blood flowing freely from his nose, ears and mouth. Eliza seemed more scared than anything else, though she expressed no regret when it was all over and Peter had been removed.

"Given the harsh detachment she used to approach her work with Larry, I somehow doubt finding out about Jenny would phase her," I said.

Thomas was silent, an unusual state for him.

"You can't let it slip, Thomas. I mean it." I sat up in my chair, straightening my back. I hoped it conveyed the idea that I meant business.

"Fine." He frowned at me. "I still think it would do her good to know what she's done to people."

"I disagree. And I am the one in charge here." It felt disingenuous to pull rank on Thomas.

"Fine, fine. I'll hide it from her when I go in." He held his hands up in mock surrender. "Perhaps you're right. Perhaps she is too detached from humanity for it to make any difference. Maybe she should go volunteer at a soup kitchen."

For once, I laughed at Thomas's joke. The laughter quickly subsided as I thought about the idea. That many people with that many problems, and Eliza drilling into each of their minds with abandon. Maybe it would be good for her to experience the harsh realities of life after all. I shook it off.

"Enough about Eliza for now. If you're going to help me, we need to get moving." I ran my hand through my hair again, mentally sorting through the list of tasks I had ahead of me. "I'll let you research names instead. I think you'll have a better idea of what to look for. I expect you to have a list of at least ten potential candidates for recruitment into the time travel control by tomorrow morning."

Thomas stood and smirked down at me. "I'll have twenty." He started to leave. "Sorted by potential."

Thomas, I felt, had not completely outgrown his own desire to impress me.

Chapter 20

Thomas, true to his word, had found twenty candidates. I glanced through the profiles, eliminated some of them for logistical reasons and handed the remaining ones back to him. "Get the list down to the best five from here and we'll go see them tomorrow."

"You don't want to decide?"

"I have other things to do today. I need to take a trip back to my childhood. There's something that needs investigating."

"Your childhood? Don't you think you should let your past go? I mean it's not like it was good. You've already been back there twice, what more could you possibly want to see?"

"Thomas, this is none of your business."

"It is though. You're bypassing the board and not bothering to get anyone else's opinion on your trips. That's a bit hypocritical of you isn't it?"

I crossed my arms and sat back, irritated with him. "The board doesn't need to know all the details of my past life. There's nothing of interest to them. I'm not interfering. I'm just watching certain events unfold. I know the risks as well as anyone, Thomas."

"Fine. Have it your way, as usual." He left my office, peeved.

I went to see Vanessa to get my prosthetic nose attached and my skin tinted. I had Larry drop me off at a used car dealership not far from where my parents had lived, and I paid cash for an old car. It took me a few minutes to remember how to drive. I hadn't used that skill for several decades. I pulled up to the street at the end of my block and waited for the mystery man's car to appear. When it did, I followed it to the outskirts of the town and pulled into a space a few cars away. We were in the parking lot for a large building.

I followed him into the building and stopped short. It was familiar. I glanced around the lobby area. I had been in here before, I was sure of it, but I hadn't recognized the name on the building when we pulled up. I was trying to remember what this place was when I saw the man approach the elevators at the end of the lobby. "Excuse me, sir!" I ran after him.

He stopped a few feet from the elevators and glanced around. I waved to get his attention. He watched me with a curious expression as I approached. "Yes? Can I help you?"

"I believe you know Mark and Megan Lancing?"

"Of course. Brilliant scientists. We were very sad to lose them."

I tried to keep my face a mask. My parents were brilliant scientists? There's a laugh. "I think you must be mistaken. Mark and Megan Lancing are members of The Order of Vena. They would never have anything to do with science."

"Now they are, but not a few years ago. They used to work here. They were the most promising scientists in the field of brain usage expansion I had ever met. They destroyed all their work when they left, and no one has been able to come close to achieving the results they produced."

I struggled to come up with words. "I had no idea. Why would they change their minds suddenly and leave?"

He eyed me suspiciously. "Who did you say you were?"

I didn't have a well thought-out cover story. This was a mistake. I should have sent a librarian. My mind raced to come up with something reasonable. I tried to stick as close to the truth as possible. "I am also a research scientist. Doctor Lawrence Pope." It was Amelia's father's name.

"What field?"

"I also delve in brain manipulation." It was a strange coincidence to find out I had the same interests my parents originally had. I was still reeling from the revelation of their past.

"How do you know the Lancings?"

It was a difficult question to answer. I couldn't know them from their church, or I would never have contacted this man to begin with. "I live on their street. They were friendly enough, before they joined the church. I've seen their son many times, running out into the street. He's never talked to me though. I wanted to call child services on them a few times, but since I never really knew what was going on, it seemed useless. I saw you talking with them about him. I was just curious what you knew, if there was some form of abuse going on there."

He laughed without humor. "You could call it abuse, but they shield it behind their religion."

"But how could two scientists turn to such an extreme opposite? Abandon their field like that?"

"Unfortunately, their work drove them to it, in the end."

"What do you mean?" I asked.

"I hate to admit it, but their research methods were a little questionable. It's not easy to find volunteers for research involving the brain. I mean, only people who are already messed up would be willing to have someone experiment on their brain. But those people don't have the legal capacity to agree to such experiments, and whoever has power of attorney over them is not usually willing to gamble that things might get worse. So they had to find someone who wouldn't be able to say no. But to use your own daughter—" He stopped and shook his head.

"Daughter?" I have a sister? The information was coming too quickly. I was barely able to process the idea of my parents being scientists, and all of a sudden I have a sister? Where was she?

He let out a slow breath. "I told them to wait for the final results, but they thought the earlier they started work on their son too, the better the results would be." He took a deep breath before continuing, measuring his words. "When Jane died, that's when they finally realized they had gone too far."

Tears came to my eyes. I struggled to keep my voice level. "How did—Jane—how did she die?"

He shook his head again. "No one is really sure except the Lancings. Whatever happened, it convinced them that science was dangerous. They felt that their work could destroy the world. They were terrified that they had already done too much damage to their son, so now they keep him isolated."

"The mark on my—on the back of the little boy's head. The mark at the nape of his neck?"

"It's where they tapped into the brain stem."

A million questions swam in my head. I had a sister I never knew, and parents who were more like me than I could have dreamed; parents who did something to my brain. I swayed where I stood.

"Are you okay?" he asked.

"Yes," I said, lying. I felt unsteady on my feet. "I'm sorry, I have to be going." I staggered away from him.

"Wait—" he called after me, but I kept moving. I had to get out of there. I ran away from the building as quickly as I could without collapsing and darted into an alleyway. My mind was too much of a jumble to focus on anything as I pulled out the sphere and pressed the button.

I collapsed onto the mats and vomited. I didn't even care if anyone saw. I rolled over, away from the mess and lay on the mat, blinded by the glaring lights. I welcomed the pain and the tears the light brought to my eyes that I had been fighting against since I heard about my sister. I lay on the mat and let them stream down the sides of my face, until I felt the pool of salty water start to dampen my hair.

I got up and wiped the traces away from my cheeks before stalking into Doctor Crebb's area. My face became a mask. I didn't slow down as she greeted me and asked if I was okay. I continued through to Vanessa's area and told her "Later," as she tried to approach me with her cosmetic tools, keeping my head down and avoiding eye contact.

I almost ran back to my office and through to my apartment, stopping only when I stood over Amelia's pod. "Amelia," I whispered. "My parents—" I didn't know what to say. I slumped down into the chair next to her. She couldn't hear me anyway, but I felt the need to talk to someone. "My parents were brilliant. Just like me. And I had a sister. A sister! They killed her. They killed her for research." Tears came again and I wiped them away. "I'm just like them. Willing to do anything to test my research, prove my theories. I was wrong about them, so wrong. All this time I thought I was defying them." I placed a hand on the glass, wishing she were awake. "I wonder if they would have been proud of who I've become, had things gone differently."

I leaned over and placed my forehead against the cool glass, trying to sooth myself. I cried again. For the family I never knew. For the sister who I didn't even remember, and the parents I could have had.

Thomas was at the door to my office. I ignored him. He called my name, and I told him to go away. He yelled that it was important. I left Amelia's side, wiping my eyes, and went to meet him in my office.

"Nice nose," he said. "We need to talk."

"About what?"

"You."

I remained silent. I wasn't in much position to argue with him just then.

"Doctor Crebbs came to see me. I convinced her not to say anything to Rachel, though neither of us are thrilled about that decision."

"Thank you for your discretion."

"It's conditional. You need to tell me what's going on, Lancing. We can't have the head of our lab running off to the past whenever he wants and coming back in a state of—" he paused, trying to find the right word. "You have to trust me."

"I don't want to risk Eliza finding out."

"She won't!" he yelled at me. "To hell with Eliza, and to hell with the board, Lancing. Talk to me."

I groaned and slumped even further in my chair. "I don't even know where to start."

"What happened on your last trip that made you go back again?"

"There was this guy on the street where my parents lived. After I watched my younger self fail to run away for the millionth time, I was about to leave when I saw him approach the house. I watched as he argued with my father, but I couldn't really hear what was going on. He gestured to me, down the street, and my father yelled at him some more then slammed the door in his face. I tried to follow him, but he got in a car and took off. So I went back to follow him and find out what he had talked to my parents about." I paused, uncertain how much detail was necessary. "You remember when I told you about the dreams I had about my parents taking me to that big building with lots of people?"

"Yes," was all he said.

"Turns out it wasn't a dream. I followed the man there and stopped him. My parents had worked there, and taken me with them, before they became so isolated."

"So your parents had a life and jobs at some point. That's not so surprising."

I tried to keep my breathing steady. His nonchalance was not helping. "They were scientists, just like us. They did research on expanding brain usage."

"Fascinating," Thomas said, and meant it. He leaned forward, eager to hear more.

"They experimented on me, Thomas," I said, torn by anger at their betrayal and sadness at my loss. "They did something to improve my mind."

"Well that explains a lot about you." Again, it was a flat comment. He had known something about me wasn't natural.

"And—my sister." He was quiet again and I continued. "I had a sister," I said and shrugged. "And their experiments killed her."

Neither of us spoke for a long while. Thomas stared at the floor, processing the information. "I can't believe it."

We continued to sit in silence. I watched him and waited for him to say something else. When he spoke again it was slow and measured. "I'm sure they didn't know that was going to happen."

I didn't want him to defend them. I didn't want to defend myself. I was angry with him for trying to put them in a better light. "That doesn't excuse it! Don't you see? I'm just like them. How many people have we sacrificed in the name of science?"

"Progress demands sacrifice."

"I've been so callous over the years."

"But not with the people you loved, people you cared about. That separates you from them."

"You? Amelia?"

Thomas was taken aback. "I volunteered for that experiment. I know you think you tricked me into it, but I wanted it even without your psychological mind games."

I could barely look at him. "That doesn't mean my intention was not to use you."

"Sure. But you didn't know me. You couldn't possibly have cared about me at that point. Given the chance, I'm sure you wouldn't try something like that again."

"That's true." I welcomed the admission of even a small amount of empathy on my part. "I've been worried about you delving into Eliza's mind again."

"I appreciate the concern, but trust me that I can handle her."

"And Amelia?"

"What about Amelia?" he asked.

"She's as good as dead." I felt hollow as I said the words.

Thomas stood abruptly, pushed the chair away and paced, angry. "Amelia is not dead. We have had this argument a hundred times, Lancing! Someone someday will find the cure. And given what I've learned about the mind, I will be able to help her recover. We have forever. Therefore it is inevitable that we will fix things. I will not let her just die for nothing! That is exactly what your parents did, and you're better than that!"

I stood as well and leaned over my desk, ready to tear him down, but I realized he was right. I backed away. My parents squandered their lives. The man had told me they were brilliant. That may be true, but they were stupid enough to let one failure take all that away.

"You can't let this get to you, Lancing. We have done incredible things, and yes, some people have suffered. It happened, and you need to let it go. Where's your infamous scientific detachment now?"

My sadness at losing my family had turned back to rage at my parents' betrayal. They were inept morons for letting my sister die, and I wasn't about to make the same mistakes. "You're right." A smile crept across half of my face as I willed myself to prove it. I wondered if they were still alive. "I'm much better than them."

"Good," Thomas said. "Now get that stuff off your face, and let's go find some more programmers."

Chapter 21

Thomas had whittled his list down from twenty to the top five candidates, and we went to visit them. Two of them proved to be promising candidates for programmers. One was a ten-year-old girl, Quinn, whose parents, though hesitant, were willing to let us take her to the lab. The other one was a seven-year-old boy named Victor. His parents would barely let us talk to him, and flat out refused to give him up to us. The boy wanted to leave. Both Thomas and I could see the desperation in his face. His parents reminded me of my own, and I thought it criminal to restrict a mind with so much potential.

Against my better judgment, Thomas and I had returned later that night and rescued, or kidnapped depending on who you asked, Victor. We brought him and Quinn back to the laboratory complex with us. They hit it off even on the ride over. Victor didn't want to leave Quinn's side. With Jenny gone, Thomas was doing the initial brain scans. Quinn held Victor's hand throughout his scan and the two of them hugged when they found out they would both be staying.

We took them to Rich, who had covered the walls of his lab area with equations from his conversations with Larry. Both Quinn and Victor recognized them at once, and started talking to Rich with great enthusiasm about the tunnels they saw in their dreams. Rich's mental state seemed to improve when he met with people who understood his drawings and theories.

They spent a few days speaking with Rich before we brought them the sphere. When Rich saw the sphere he backed off into a corner. His one experience traveling with Larry had scarred him, and the day I left him in stasis while I went through my panic didn't help. I let him go back to his own room, to hide from the rest of us.

I gave the sphere to Quinn first, knowing that Victor would do everything in his power to get her back. As Quinn held the sphere, we had Victor cast his mind back to the previous night, when the room would have been empty. With his eyes closed, he gave a quick nod. Quinn pressed the button on the sphere and disappeared. Victor opened his eyes and saw the empty space where Quinn had been standing a moment before. His eyes widened in disbelief. "It really works!"

I patted him on the shoulder and smiled. "Of course it works. You didn't think we'd joke about something like this, did you? Now focus again. You should be able to see the end of her path in the past. Find the sphere button marking the end."

Victor closed his eyes again. For a moment he looked like he was about to panic, before let out a breath and opened his eyes again, just as Quinn reappeared.

"Someone was here," she said.

"What? What do you mean?" Thomas asked.

"Someone was here in the lab last night. I thought you said it would be empty."

"It should have been," I cut in. I scanned back in the surveillance of the room for last night and saw Eliza in the room, looking at Rich's papers. "What time was it?"

Victor looked for a moment as though he had done something wrong. "3 a.m. That was what you told me, wasn't it?"

"Yes, you did well, Victor." I scanned back again to 3 a.m. I did not see Quinn appear at all. Only Eliza was there, as she continued to study the equations. I wondered what she was doing in there. Why would she be trying to learn the secrets of time travel? I gave Thomas a glance that he knew meant something was up. "Are you sure about the time?"

"I think so. I mean, it was my first try, but I'm pretty sure I got it right. Or at least pretty close. I don't know!"

Quinn put an arm around him.

"Victor," I said, "it's fine. It's not an exact science. I understand that. You did exceedingly well for your first try."

"Who was that girl, Doctor Lancing?" Quinn asked me.

"Another researcher here. You'll meet her soon, maybe even today."

"I don't want to meet her," Quinn said. "She didn't seem friendly. She looked angrily at me. It hurt my head."

"She won't hurt you," I said. "She helps you focus on the task when you're sending and retrieving people in time."

"But Victor got me back here just fine."

"It was a short trip, and not very far. It gets more complicated as you go further back. It's just a precaution." Quinn looked unconvinced. Victor huddled against her, not sure what was going on. "I'll be right back, Thomas can explain it better and reassure you, it's fine." I glanced at Thomas, who gave me an exasperated look, and went to talk to Eliza.

She was sitting on the floor of the dormitory, pushing a ball back and forth with her finger. She made no sign of acknowledgment that I had arrived. I said hello to her in my mind, and she still did nothing.

"Eliza, care to tell me what you were doing in Rich's lab space last night?"

"It was that girl wasn't it?" She turned and glared at me. "She snitched on me! Who was she? She came out of nowhere!"

Eliza could have found the information easily in my head. I didn't understand why she wasn't just using her abilities to answer her own questions. Though it was against my nature to want her to read my mind, I focused on the answer and didn't speak.

I felt Eliza probe my mind. She looked downtrodden. "You're replacing me?"

I was confused. Had she not read my mind? "What are you talking about? She's a new programming recruit. She's not here for mind control."

For a moment I thought Eliza was going to cry. "She looks so young."

"She's ten. She'll grow older. We need someone to replace Larry."

"But I fixed Larry! You should see him now! He thinks of nothing but his mission and his happiness. He's very happy!"

My mind wandered back to my last meeting with Larry and my regret at what I had let happen. I realized I was not having a controlled conversation with Eliza, a normally dangerous proposition. "Larry is too limited. We need someone who can be controlled during their part, but left to themselves the rest of the time."

Eliza balked at the idea. "They don't need to have a life, they need to do their job."

"We've been lucky so far with Larry, but what if something goes wrong? The programmers would need to be able to think for themselves, on the fly."

"If I figure out the equations you wouldn't need a programmer at all, just me."

I gave her a patronizing smile. "You have enough going on at the moment. Your other work is too important to be wasting your time with programming." I thought again about the fact that Quinn didn't show up on the surveillance. I quickly hid the fact from Eliza. She didn't know that I kept tabs on everyone in the complex. She probably wouldn't like it. "I'll go get them, okay?"

"Okay."

I left her alone and went back to fetch Quinn and Victor. I trusted that Thomas had explained the situation well enough that they would not protest at meeting Eliza. It turned out that I was wrong.

"I'm not going to see her," Quinn said before I had even closed the door.

I looked at Thomas. He threw his arms up in surrender. "I tried. But it's hard to convince them of something I don't believe myself."

"Thanks, Thomas." I said sarcastically and turned back to Quinn. "Look, Eliza is not going to hurt you, she's just going to look into your mind and help you focus."

"No," said Quinn again, and hugged Victor tighter.

"Come on, Victor." I held out my hand to lead him to the other room.

"No!" he screamed, and cringed away from me.

All of a sudden, the room swam before my eyes. My body felt like it was being hit by invisible waves. My vision blurred and the hairs on my arms stood on end. I swayed backwards slightly and had to adjust my feet to catch myself.

The feeling passed and the room was silent. No one spoke. Everyone seemed as confused as I was, except Victor, who was shaking slightly. Quinn had stepped away from him.

"What was that?" Thomas finally broke the silence.

I watched Victor. He had stopped shaking and tears were welling up in his eyes. Quinn held a hand out to him. "Victor?"

He started crying with earnest. "I didn't mean to do it, I was so scared!"

"Victor," I said, "that was you?"

"I'm sorry, I'm sorry!" He ran to me and grabbed my shirt. "Please don't send me away, I won't do it again. I was just so scared!"

I took Victor's hands in mine. I could hear the chaos of the entire lab snapping out of their trances and wondering what had just happened. I wondered how far whatever it was had reached. "Victor, calm down. We won't send you anywhere. Just tell me what happened."

"I don't know. It just happens sometimes when I'm really upset."

"But do you know exactly what it was?"

He shook his head and sank it down to his chest. Quinn put her arm around him again. I scanned around the complex again, trying to figure out what it was. Eliza was curled into a fetal position on her bed, crying. "Thomas, watch them for a moment, I'll be right back."

I went to Rich's room. He looked up at me when I entered. "Who did that?" he asked me.

"It was Victor. Do you know what happened?"

Rich nodded. "He hurt time."

"What? What do you mean he hurt time?"

"He bent it. Couldn't you feel it? We're not right. We're still not right."

"I don't understand, Rich."

"It's wrong, we're all wrong." He huddled back in his corner and cried again.

Eliza was also still crying. I hesitated in my office, not sure which person to go back to. I decided Eliza could wait. I went back to Thomas and the children. Quinn was talking to Victor and trying to get him to stop crying. Thomas was pacing. He stopped when I came in and looked nervously at me. "Well?"

"I'm still not sure."

"Something's wrong," Thomas said. "Something's not right."

"Yeah, that's what Rich said. He said time has been bent. He says we're all wrong."

Thomas nodded his head. "Yes, it feels off."

"What does?"

He paused and tried to gather his thoughts. "I don't know."

"Victor." I turned away from Thomas. Victor looked up at me. Quinn had gotten him to stop crying. "How are you feeling?"

"Better. I'm sorry."

"You don't feel like something's wrong? Like something is off?"

"No." He looked confused at me. "Should I?"

"The rest of us do. Whatever you did, it's given us all a bad feeling. Quinn? Am I right that you're feeling it too?"

She nodded but didn't move away from Victor. I appreciated that she was trying to comfort him.

"So what did it feel like, Victor?"

"I don't know. Just a terrible fear, I only felt fear. And then it released and was gone. And I felt worried about what I had done, but the fear was gone."

I glanced at Thomas. "A defense mechanism?"

"In a boy who can see through time? Looks like it. That's rather amazing, Victor."

He continued to cling to Quinn. "You're not mad?"

I responded. "No, we're not mad. We're confused, and trying to understand it. We're scientists. This is what we do. We try to understand. But Thomas is right, it's an amazing gift." One that could potentially be used, I added silently.

Thomas continued to talk about what had just happened, but I had stopped listening. I could hear Eliza, calling out for help. She was terrified about what she had just been through and was still curled up on her bed, sobbing. Another voice filtered out from the general malaise and confusion of the laboratory residents. It was a familiar voice, and weak with fear.

I caught Thomas trying to get my attention as I turned to leave, but I only stopped long enough to reply, "Amelia's awake."

I heard Thomas's footsteps in the hall, chasing after me. Amelia was awake. I couldn't believe it. She was awake and she was making sense and calling for me. I flew through my office to the pod. It was still sealed and covered with condensation. I wiped the glass clean and stared down into the pod, intent on telling Amelia everything was okay, as Thomas would get the pod shut down and opened. Her eyes were closed.

"Amelia," I called through the glass. Nothing. "Thomas." I gestured to her.

Thomas looked in through the glass then checked the status panel on the side of the pod. "She's still in stasis. You said she was awake."

My heart sank before anger took over. "She was awake. I heard her."

Thomas gave me condescending look. It infuriated me.

"It couldn't have been her," he said. "Look at her."

"I am looking at her," I said. "I look at her all the time. And I swear to you, I heard her. She was afraid."

"It must have been someone else you heard."

"No. It couldn't have been. It was Amelia's voice. I know Amelia's voice."

Thomas moved around to stand next to me. His eyebrows were furrowed with concern. "Are you still hearing it?"

I stood still and listened. I hadn't heard it since I was back in the other room talking with Victor. It had been very clear though, and certainly Amelia's voice. "Thomas I think we should wake her."

"But her mind, and her disease. She won't have long to live."

"We'll give her the partial cure, she'll have a few years before we'd have to freeze her again—"

"No."

I turned to look at him, surprised by his forcefulness. "I am your boss, and this is my decision."

"I'll sooner quit than wake her up now."

I had never seen him so serious. "Thomas, please—"

"No. I won't be part of this. If you want to wake her up you'll have to do it yourself. But I'm warning you that you shouldn't. Just think for a minute. Let yourself calm down and think."

I recognized it as a line I had used on him once. "Get out."

Thomas left without hesitation. I looked back at Amelia. I had been so excited running to this place, to see her awake again. The pain of the reality was hitting me hard. Thomas was right, there was no point in waking her now. Perhaps the bend in time or whatever happened had led me to hear a version of Amelia from the past. I tried to think of a time she had called to me for help, but couldn't. I went back into my living room and retrieved a bottle of Scotch I kept around to have an occasional drink. I brought it back with me to sit by Amelia's pod and didn't bother with a glass.

Chapter 22

After some convincing, Victor and Quinn agreed to meet Eliza and let her work with them while they sent people back and forth in time. Eliza was behaving herself well. I explained what had happened with Victor and she realized that he might be the most dangerous person in the laboratory, aside from her. In fact, Eliza was being extra nice to everyone lately. It made me nervous.

I was still confused by what happened with Amelia. I also hadn't forgotten that although I didn't see Quinn go back in time in the surveillance footage, Eliza definitely saw her. I wondered what that meant for changing things in the past, and decided when I had some more spare time I would conduct some basic experiments with altering the recent past.

Thomas finally convinced me to let him work with Eliza. He came into my office one day carrying the helmets. I gave in after a brief argument, but told him if things were getting hairy he needed to find some way to let me know so I could remove the helmets and break the connection. He reassured me, once again, that he would be fine.

"What's your game plan?" I asked as I walked him to the door of Eliza's lab.

"I'm going to let her explore my mind for a while, see if I can follow what she's doing. See what she tries to get me to think. I've hidden everything damaging that I can think of. My mind should be basic enough it should make her question me. She'll know that there must be parts she isn't able to access, and I assume she'll try."

I nodded, knowing she would.

"Emma helped me rig my helmet into the security grid, so at the very least, you should be able to hear my thoughts. Emma says she'll be watching too, just in case. If things get dicey, she'll sedate Eliza instantly."

"Won't that knock us out too?"

"No, she's managed to narrow the sedation field. I'm stuck with the length of the tether, but as long as you're at least five feet away from her you should be fine."

"Let's go then." Thomas followed me in. Eliza was lying on her bed with her eyes closed. I had no idea what she was doing, but as soon as she heard the door open I felt her wandering around in my mind. "Hello, Eliza. I've brought Thomas." Her eyes popped open and she watched Thomas intently, probably already trying to penetrate his mind. "I'd like the two of you to link together. He's going to see if he can figure out why you had such an extreme reaction to Victor's little outburst last week, to see if we can find a way to protect you in case it happens again."

As I suspected she wasn't paying enough attention to me to realize I wasn't entirely being honest. Thomas held a helmet out to her and she took it without hesitation and put it on her head. He pulled a chair up to the bed and donned the second helmet, facing Eliza.

At first I could hear nothing. For a few moments they simply stared at each other. Eliza's eyes were focused on Thomas's. Thomas relaxed in his chair and seemed to gaze off into space. I also focused on Thomas. Finally, I heard him explaining certain things.

That's my mother. She was very supportive of me, but never really knew what to do with me. My father died when I was very young. There was a pause in his mental narration. *I didn't know him well enough to care.*

I could only imagine what was going on in Eliza's head. Given the exchange, I had to assume she was hoping that Thomas's father's death would be a raw spot for him, and she tried to dig further in.

That's an interesting path to go down, but try this instead.

Eliza visibly flinched and gasped. I couldn't tell what Thomas was showing her. She grimaced and set her eyes again.

They continued like this for at least half an hour. Every now and then Eliza would have some reaction to Thomas, but I couldn't tell what was actually going on. From what I could tell, Thomas didn't seem to be having any trouble directing where he wanted her to go.

"Ah, there you go," Thomas said aloud. Eliza was panting with effort. Her hands gripped the side of her bed and she leaned forward towards Thomas. At last she gasped again. Rage filled her face and she tore the helmet off then glared at me instead. I felt her probing my mind but there was nothing but honest confusion for her to find. Then suddenly, she was gone. The rage on her face turned to fear and I thought she was about to cry again. My confusion only deepened.

Thomas had removed his helmet as well. He was smiling and he gestured for me to join him outside the room. I squeezed Eliza's shoulder and said, "I'll be right back," then followed him out of the room. "What was all that about?"

Thomas set the helmets down on my desk and smiled. "She fell right into my trap, and in the process revealed all her tricks. Notice how she left you alone right before we left the room?"

"Yes. She looked like she was about to cry."

"She figured out that I was blocking part of my mind from her, and now she suspects that you are as well. She tried to probe into the buried part of your mind, but I stopped her."

I was still confused as to how all this was happening. "You stopped her from trying to get into my mind?"

"Yep. She didn't like it, apparently."

"What else?"

"Pretty standard stuff. She works just like the helmets do, but she's way more focused, so she doesn't need them like I do. There's nothing special about it though. She's like her own mental brain scanning machine." He paused and looked thoughtful for a moment. "It's actually kind of a nightmare in there."

"What do you mean?" An unexpected wave of concern washed over me. Eliza might be frightening, but she was still one of my children.

"To say she had a rough childhood is a drastic understatement. I think she'd give you a run for your money. There's a history of abuse. She spent a lot of time alone, which probably accounts for her ability to focus her thoughts so well. She's used to being trapped in her own mind a lot."

"What about the telekinesis? Can you tell how she moves things with her mind?"

Thomas shook his head. "That's still unclear. It seems to be an extension of the exploration process, and I think once I get more practice at delving into people's minds without the helmet, I may be able to extend to that power as well. The only problem is, where will I find willing subjects?"

I shook my head, "People are freaked out by Eliza. I don't think they'd take kindly to you messing with their private thoughts either."

"Quinn and Victor. And Rich. I doubt they would mind much. I'm not going to be trying to dig up repressed memories, or use their thoughts against them, like Eliza did with Peter. I just need to explore a bit. They trust me. They might let me. I'm sure they'd prefer to have me be the one watching them do their programming rather than Eliza."

"That's true. It can't hurt to ask. Leave Rich be though. He has enough mental issues already."

"Sure," he agreed.

"And Thomas, other than Eliza, I want you to have permission to go into people's heads. Okay?"

"Completely understand. I will never try to get into someone's mind without their consent."

I thought about some of the people I had used Eliza on. "Or an order from me," I added.

He nodded. "I'm going to go explore my new toy. You should speak with Eliza. You're the only person on this planet she has at least some respect for."

I nodded back and watched him leave before going back to Eliza's room. When the door opened she was sitting on the bed. She stared at me as I entered.

"Are you okay, Eliza?"

"Do you care?" Her words had bile in them.

"Of course." I went and sat next to her on the bed. "You're not reading my mind."

"You're hiding things from me."

"Of course."

"I thought you trusted me."

"I do, Eliza. But there are things that I don't want anyone to know. Things I prefer to keep private. Even from Thomas."

"What sort of things?"

"Memories. Things I'm not proud of."

"Are you going to get rid of me?"

"What?" I almost laughed at her. "Why would I?"

"You have your precious Thomas now. He's almost as good at this as I am. With practice, he'll probably be better. You won't need me at all."

Her childish attitude got to me every now and then. "That isn't true. Thomas can't move things with his mind."

"He'll figure it out."

"He has other things to focus on. Look, I'm worried about you. You seem like you've been stressed out a lot lately. I don't know if I'm just driving you too hard or what. But your reaction to that time—bend or whatever it was frightened me. You and Rich both seemed to take it pretty hard. We're just trying to find out why so we can protect you. You're very important to this lab, Eliza. And I appreciate how cooperative you've been."

Her eyes glistened and she once again looked like she was about to cry. "I'm trying."

"It hasn't gone unnoticed." I watched as tears finally did start to come to her. I sat with my arm around her and let her cry. "You know how you're in isolation all the time?"

She sniffed and looked up. "You haven't brought anyone else in here since Peter died, except Thomas and those new programmers."

"You make people nervous. You're always jumping right into their minds without even asking permission. There are times when that might be useful, but on the whole it's not very polite. It's unnatural, and it frightens people. Some people have very dark secrets or unpleasant past experiences they'd prefer to not have dredged up to the surface of their mind."

"They just don't like me reminding them of who they really are."

"No, they don't like it. That's part of why we keep you in here, alone. Thomas, as you know, has some of the same abilities as you. But he doesn't dive right into someone's mind and try to find his or her weaknesses. He respects their privacy."

"So you're saying I bring this on myself?"

"Yes."

"I'm not reading your mind."

"You could. I'm used to it." At the moment, I was feeling nothing but genuine concern for Eliza's state of mind. She was important to me, even if it was as a tool.

She shook her head. "I'd just like to be alone again for a while."

"Okay." I stood up to leave. As I passed by one of the beds I caught sight of one of the small red balls she had first levitated. I picked one up and turned back to her. "Hey, Eliza, think fast." I tossed the ball towards her but it stopped and hung in mid air between us. I smiled at her. "Not bad," I said. Her face remained flat. I turned and left.

Thomas was in the lab with Victor and Quinn. They had both agreed that they would rather have Thomas watching them while they did their work than Eliza. All in all it had been a pretty good day for me. When I got back to my desk Emma had an interesting report waiting for me. I settled in to read about a librarian's encounter with someone who seemed out of time.

Her name was Adelaide MacDuff. A few days ago she had returned from a mission involving Shakespeare. It was a fluff mission, requested by one of our more eccentric donors. Jim encouraged it. He thought Adelaide was an excellent librarian, and he knew she would enjoy the mission.

One of Emma's workers was monitoring Adelaide's actions since her return, and overheard her confess to Noah that she met someone who seemed to know more than he should and said things that seemed "out of place."

Adelaide had a wild imagination. It was part of what made her a good librarian. I wanted to dismiss it but figured I should investigate a little further first. I also knew she tended to take very thorough notes about her experiences on her missions.

I called to Jim and requested an unedited copy of Adelaide's journal from her most recent mission. Within a few seconds it showed up on my display. I read through the entries that mentioned the man she had suspected, and at first thought, I did think her imagination was running away with her. He just seemed like a creepy, unusual guy. As I read through the entries again though, one line in particular stood out to me:

> "Byron said something about me having nice teeth for such a lowly maid."

On first reading I passed over it as a compliment, but the fact that he emphasized her being a lowly maid was troubling. He was making the point that she didn't fit her part. Adelaide was right to suspect him, but what to do about it?

I thought it highly possible that Byron was another traveller from the future. William Shakespeare was a very important historical figure. I had no trouble imagining that other missions would surface involving questions about him. The question was, where did Byron come from? Certainly not our lab, since he would never have been allowed to cross paths in the past with another librarian. Someone else must have discovered the technology and started using it as well.

I didn't want to take my suspicions to the board until I had more evidence. Although I knew it was a flimsy excuse to get myself back in time again, I set off for the costuming department to find some Elizabethan era clothing.

Chapter 23

I was already wearing my Elizabethan garb and a wig when I went to see Victor. He giggled when he saw me.

"Victor, I need to go back in time on a rather important, but secret mission, so Thomas will not be involved."

Victor's body stiffened with apprehensive. "What sort of mission?"

I tried to reassure him with a warm smile. "Nothing bad Victor, just something I need to double check on one of our librarians past missions. A loose end that needs to be tied up."

"I thought you trusted Thomas. Why don't you want him involved?"

I sighed. I had hoped Victor would just cooperate and not ask too many questions. "What I'm going to do is a little tricky. I know Thomas would not approve, but I really need to get this sorted out."

"Why is it tricky? Shouldn't I have help if it's going to be tricky?"

"Tricky for me, not for you. I have absolute confidence in you, Victor. You remember the most recent mission you sent Adelaide on? To Shakespearean time?"

Victor nodded.

"She mentioned something in her journal that I need to see for myself. So I'm going to have to go to a specific time when she was still there, a specific date in her journal. That means there will be two spheres in the same period of time, like we do with scouts sometimes."

"Why isn't a scout going then?" he asked.

"Victor, I'm pressed for time, and want to keep this as quiet as possible. The fewer people I involve, the easier it will be."

"Rachel doesn't know either?"

I shook my head. "No, Victor. No she doesn't."

He smiled at that. "So it's a covert mission then."

"Yes. I'm trusting you here, Victor. You've been doing great work, and I have no doubt that you'll be able to get me there and back without Thomas backing you up. Give yourself just enough time to get your bearings straight, and then bring me back. Okay?"

"Okay. When are you going?"

I looked up Adelaide's last entry mentioning Byron in my mind for the date. "Friday, September 18th, 1598, in the morning. Just outside Shakespeare's house. I believe Adelaide spends all day in the house, so you shouldn't have any trouble dropping me somewhere that I won't accidentally run into her on my arrival."

Victor screwed his face up in concentration. "Okay, got her. Ready when you are."

"Thanks for doing this, Victor." I gave his shoulder a squeeze. "Remember, you can't even tell Quinn about this."

He frowned. I knew he wouldn't like that.

"Do you still have the place, Victor?"

"Oh yes!" He shook the thought from his head. "Ready."

"Good." I flipped the lid of the sphere open and pressed the button. The instant I arrived on a hill beside his house, I regretted not taking longer to think through what I was going to do. I should've made a plan. I had nothing on me but some coins in case I needed money.

I walked to the hedgerow at the edge of the road that passed by the house and sat in the grass. I had no idea what time Byron came to the house and left again, so I'd just have to wait for him. I also had no idea what Byron looked like. Adelaide had no reason to suspect him outside of their conversation, so he must blend in well. I had to hope that he would be the only visitor to the house today.

Adelaide had not mentioned another person, as far as I could remember. I suddenly wanted to double-check the journal entry to be sure, but my link to the lab did not work when the lab did not exist.

I cursed myself. My impatience could be my undoing. I felt naked without my connection to the lab, without being able to watch people and bring up documents with a single thought. I wasn't prepared for this. I hadn't thought I would need to be.

There was nothing to be done. I didn't want to take multiple trips. The risks of being caught at this were bad enough.

I sat and tried to formulate a plan. The less interaction I had with him the better. I'd wait for him to leave Shakespeare's house, then follow him on foot—and hope he's not riding a horse. Again, I cursed myself. I could try to go find a horse, or buy one, but then I might miss Byron when he arrived. It wasn't far from the house to the town, Adelaide mentioned walking it quite often, but I wasn't even sure which direction that was. Again, if he was on a horse, I wouldn't be able to keep up with him. I'd just have to assume that was the direction he was headed in. I cursed myself again.

I thought again about going back and reformulating my plan. The longer I waited, the more risky it was that I'd run into myself again. Though I'd be prepared—I scanned the road to see if another version of myself had decided to come back later—I had no idea if two of me, in the same time with the same sphere would be difficult for Victor. I decided to stay. If nothing else, I would wait to see who Byron was.

I settled into the grass to wait. I could travel through time. So long as I didn't do anything really stupid on this trip, I could always come back again some other day, once I knew who I was looking for.

The countryside was dead. I could hear voices carrying from the house from time to time, but after an hour I was bored. I should've brought a book or something. No one came along the road. I lay back in the grass to stare at the sky. It was gray, but didn't look like it would rain.

It was the first time in decades I didn't have something occupying my attention. My mind wandered to Amelia. So many things had gotten in the way of my plans for the two of us. I had learned to be patient, though the fear nagged at me that I would never find a cure or be able to fix whatever mental destruction she was suffering, despite Thomas's recent assurances. I tried to push the fear away.

I imagined Amelia there by my side. She'd say something reassuring. She always knew what to say. There was a patch of clear sky that was a dazzling blue against the gray clouds. I focused on it, and imagined the rustling of the grass was the sound of wind blowing through palm trees on a beach.

Amelia reaches out to squeeze my hand and says, "You'll figure it out. You're brilliant."

I sit up in my beach chair to watch the waves roll in repeatedly. "I'm out of my element."

"You've never had an element. You'll fit right in."

I smile and stretch back out, contented. "You're right. What's the worst that can happen?"

"You accidentally kill Shakespeare and as a result are never born?"

"If that's the case, Victor is no longer waiting for my return. I'll be stuck here."

"With me? I think I can live with that." A breeze blows across the beach again, sending goose bumps across my skin that had been warmed by the blazing sun. "How did I hear your voice? When Victor had that episode?"

"I don't know anything that you don't know."

I decide it can wait. I close my eyes and squeeze her hand again.

"Sir." Amelia's voice had deepened. In actuality, it sounded like a man's. Confusion overtook me and I opened my eyes to look at her again, but she was gone. Instead of Amelia lying next to me, the disembodied head of William Shakespeare's was peering at me curiously. "Sir," he said again.

I sat up, still at the bottom of the grassy hill. "Oh!" The rest of his body, hidden by a large neck ruff, came into view. I silently cursed myself. How long had I been asleep? Had Byron already come and gone? I cleared my throat to speak. "Pardon sir, I've been—deep in my cups." I paused. "Mine cups." Was that right?

He raised his eyebrows and looked at me with an expression that was both amused and confused. "Though hast not stumbled upon a brothel, my good man. Thou art ensconced in my shrubs."

"Aye, I was in the village one afore I befell mineself here. I beg your pardon, Sir."

He slapped my shoulder and gave me a hearty laugh. "Indeed, I know it most intimately! Many a night have I stumbled whence," he said and gestured at the road, "much as thy tongue stumbles in search of recovery."

I grinned sheepishly and shrugged.

"I must depart," he said and gave my shoulder a pat before turning to the road.

I glanced over at his horse, loosely tethered to a fence lining the road. Shakespeare was not home when Byron stopped by, I was sure of that. I must not have missed him, unless Shakespeare was coming home and not heading out. "I myself wilst be moving onward. Where go ye?"

He gave me a crooked smile and raised his eyebrows. I swayed where I stood to play up the idea that I was drunk.

"On to that self-same village," he said as he mounted his horse. "I have business to attend, then I shall join my friends at the tavern meself."

"What friends?" The question felt too nosy. I was sure he would scurry off without another word.

"Sir Henry Wriothesley and Sir Byron Goodfellow. Beest thou acquainted with the gentlemen?"

I shook my head no.

"Prithee, relieve thyself not upon my foliage. Fare thee well, my good man." He gave me a nod before clomping off.

I sat back in the grass, reeling. Though I was not quite the fan Adelaide was, I had to admit it was humbling to meet him. And by dumb luck, I now knew where Byron would go when he left the house.

I looked down the road. Shakespeare was gone from view and the area was deserted. I wanted to head straight to the pub, but I still wasn't sure what Byron looked like. If Shakespeare didn't address either of his friends by name, I wouldn't know which was which. I decided to stay until Byron arrived for his visit, then walk to the town center.

I didn't have to wait long before I heard horse hooves clopping along the road. I took a good look at Byron from my cover in the shrubs. He certainly looked like he fit in here. I waited for him to enter the house before clambering through the hedge onto the road and beginning my walk.

I met no other travelers on my way. The town square itself was larger than I expected, but it was not hard to pinpoint the tavern from amongst the shabby looking buildings. I entered and nodded hello to the surly looking woman behind the bar, then took a seat in a far, dark corner. Apparently my nod was taken as a sign that I also wanted a beer. She brought it over in a grubby looking mug and slammed it down on the table with an air of impatience. When she continued to stand there I realized she must want payment. I pulled out one of my larger denomination coins and hoped it would be enough. She took it and huffed away for a moment, returning with my change that she also threw down with little concern, before resuming her surly post behind the bar.

The place was empty. I wondered if it was too early in the day for me to be drinking. I took a sip of my drink. It was awful. I was never much of a beer person to begin with, and hoped the alcohol was killing off the germs that certainly lined the inside of my mug. I took a larger sip, deciding that a bit of a buzz might make the beer more tolerable, so long as I could keep my wits about me.

Beer in this time period must have been stronger, since two mugs in and no concept of the passage of time later, I became dizzy and nearly fell over in my seat when my head snapped up at the sound of the door opening.

Byron walked in. The most ridiculously dressed man I had ever seen followed him. His neck ruff had to be a three-foot diameter and was starched perfectly straight. Every separate piece of puffy clothing on him was a different garish pattern. The feathers on his hat almost brushed the ceiling and were dyed bright colors. It had to be Henry, I decided.

I couldn't help but snicker at him. It was a mistake, since it caught their attention. I swayed dramatically and lifted a mug to them. The man I assumed had to be Henry sniffed his disapproval and the two of them took a table in the middle of the room. Henry almost took up a table all by himself. Byron received a mug similar to mine, but the tavern woman gave Henry something in a more slender, fancy cup. I eyed it longingly, but didn't want to try to ask for anything else, lest I betray my unfamiliarity with the drinks of this time period.

I tried to listen to their conversation, but found my mind wandered quite often. A lot of names were dropped, with a lot of "Sir of this" and "Duke of that," but none were familiar to me. Henry giggled like a young girl a few times and I tried to hide my laughter with fits of coughing into my mug. It was not long before the door opened again, and William himself entered to join them.

He had removed his ruff and was looking less formal. His business must have been with someone important. I crouched at my table in the dark corner and hoped he wouldn't notice me. He greeted Byron and Henry and proceeded to yell at the innkeeper for two rounds of drinks. He sat down with his back to me, next to Henry. Byron sat on the other side of the table, but ignored me now that William was here.

I once again tried to focus and listen. Thus far, Byron had done nothing to make me suspect him of being from another time, but I hadn't had a chance to see him alone. I loathed the idea of trying to make conversation with him after he left the bar, but I wouldn't have any other choice if I were to judge his fitness in this time. The three of them talked about a play. The premise sounded familiar, but again Adelaide would have known better than I which play it was. I finished my drink and tried to leave as discretely as possible, intent on sobering up before confronting Byron.

"Soft, my good man!" William bellowed. I stopped and turned to face his table and nod. He swayed in his seat, the drinks already having an effect. "I merrily gaze upon thy sweet face again!" He smirked.

I felt like there was a joke in there that I was missing. I smiled and nodded again. "I must be departing."

"Marry, nay! Stay and take a drink with us. One drink!" He stood up, grabbed me bodily and thrust me down into the seat next to Byron. I nodded by way of greeting to both of his friends. "My friend is short in tongue but where drink is concerned." He laughed and slapped me on the back again before yelling for another round and sitting back down.

I was already too far-gone. There was no way I would be able to have a conversation in proper Elizabethan tongue with these men. I cursed myself for what felt like the millionth time that day and tried to stop the room from swaying. William and Henry seemed like chatty men. I hoped I could get away with a mostly head gesture conversation.

"Thou couldst not stay away? We've news to celebrate, worthy of our drink. I have commissioned another play!"

I lifted my newly arrived mug by way of congratulations. "Huzzah!"

The other three fell silent. Was that wrong?

Henry sniffed again, "Bit out of fashion, sir." He sneered on the last word.

I lifted my mug to my lips again and shrugged at him.

"Whence came thee, lad?" Byron asked.

Something was hidden in his expression. His eyes were narrow and his mouth was not quite a frown, but was not friendly. I felt like he knew I didn't belong here. "Cambridge." It was the first place that came to mind, one of the universities I had considered attending.

"Thou art far from home. I trust with good intents? What bringst thou to Stratford?"

Even in my drunken stupor I could tell he was being too nosy. I lifted my mug again. "The drink!" I smiled broadly at William, hoping he would take over the conversation and kill the line of questioning.

It worked. He bellowed with laughter and knocked me on the shoulder again. "Verily, here sits a wanton tosspot! Byron, have you heard of the Duke this morn—"

I smirked behind the mug lifted to my mouth and tried to disappear under the table. William had saved me from the inquisition. I finished my drink as quickly as possible and William did not protest when I got up to leave this time. He made me promise to meet him there again in three days and I agreed, hoping he would forget in the mean time. I staggered out of the pub in search of a well and a place to bunker down and wait.

*   *   *   *

The square was deserted by the time Byron emerged from the pub and bid his friends farewell. I had finally sobered up enough to walk without listing. I tried to creep softly behind him so my boots wouldn't make scuffing noises in the dirt. He was heading across the square towards where his horse was tethered. I silently cursed again, and wondered how I'd be able to follow him once he mounted his horse.

He slowed ahead of me and spoke as he turned. "They should've sent one of the ninjas. I mean really, you stick out like a sore thumb. I had you pegged from the moment I walked into the pub."

I stopped a few feet away from him and put on my best accent. "I know not of what you speak. What is this, ninja?"

Byron blew a raspberry that morphed into a laugh. "Seriously? I would've thought you'd be better prepared for the language than that."

I said nothing, kept my face level, and waited for him to explain.

"Okay, I'll play along." He took a step closer. I held my ground. "A ninja. One of your spies—oh, I forget what you call them. Your pre-mission mission people." He plastered a look of bravado on his face. It was his turn to wait for me.

Panic locked me in place. How could he know about us? There seemed no need in lying, but I didn't intend to give away more information than necessary. "Scout."

"You're clearly not a scout. Who are you? Why did they send you? Is that little minx of a maid in on this?"

"Since you appear to know more than I do, why don't you tell me who you are and what you're doing here?"

"My name is Byron Goodfellow," he said with a flourish and bow.

"Your real name."

"My real name is not important. I was sent here by my employer, on a mission of great importance that has nothing to do with you or wherever you come from. Strictly need to know if you get my drift."

"When are you from?"

"Ah, that is a more difficult question to answer." He smirked at me.

"The future?" I asked.

"Yes, but not your future."

I tried to figure out his statement. Did that mean he was from my past, but future of here? "Why are you harassing one of my librarians?"

"Your librarian?" he asked, emphasizing the first word. "So you're the one in charge, are you? Well you don't look like Jim, so that must make you—"

"I'm Doctor Lancing." Announcing myself gave me yet another boost of confidence. I drew myself up to convey my importance.

"Ah, Lancing. Good." His face fell flat and all manner of amusement left his features. He was all business now. "I have a message for you."

"A message from whom?"

"Amelia."

My composure crumbled at once. "How do you know Amelia?"

"That's really not important. All you need to know is that I work for her."

"Where is she?" I leapt at him and grabbed the edges of his jacket, terrified that he was about to disappear on me. "Tell me!"

"You're really not in a position to demand anything from me," he said, and gave me a sour face that demonstrated that he wasn't pleased with me handling him.

I let him go with a slight shove. I had no advantage here, and it was irritating me. "Why isn't she here to tell me herself? Why send you?"

"She's very busy, and I was already here on some other business. Besides, her Elizabethan is worse than yours." He chuckled as I felt a bit of jealousy flare at his suggestion of familiarity.

"What other business?" I couldn't keep the anger out of my voice.

"Again, none of your concern."

I chewed the inside of my cheek to keep from unleashing another verbal assault at him. I spoke deliberately and tried to keep my feet planted. "What is the message from Amelia?"

"She says to not let her out. She cannot be released from the pod in your lifetime, or she will surely not survive, and you will never see her again."

In my lifetime? For an eternity? I was overcome with a mixture of rage and sadness. Amelia would never come out of that pod if that were the case. I tried to come up with more questions, to keep him talking, but I couldn't think of anything to say that would make any bit of difference given the news I just heard.

"Now I must be off, Willy will be waiting for me." He smirked and turned to leave.

"I never find a cure then?"

"What?" He paused and turned back to me.

"She dies if I take her out of the pod. That means I never find a cure, and I shouldn't even bother trying."

"Now now, you know rules are in place for good reason. I can't reveal too much or I risk destroying what's there," he turned again to leave.

"Wait!"

He stomped a foot and turned again, irritated. "I've told you everything you need to know, you won't get anything else from me."

My eyes pleaded with him, though I didn't know what I wanted. My mouth opened but no words found their way out.

His face softened in pity. "Remember, don't let her out, or you'll never see her again." He turned one last time to leave. I watched as he mounted his horse and rode slowly out of the misty square, half expecting him to disappear.

I couldn't help but let a tiny glimmer of hope plant itself in my stomach. He had said if I let her out, I would never see her again. That could imply that if I left her in there, I would see her again. Perhaps it was some sort of riddle. Deep down, I knew Amelia was alive somewhere, somehow. Her voice had called to me across some ethereal barrier. She was waiting for me. I squashed the hope down, but remembered where I could tap into it again if needed. It would sit there and not be nourished in the mean time.

I played through the conversation in my head again, and another thought struck me. He knew Jim. How was that possible?

I glanced around me at the deserted square, and walked into a dark, narrow passage between two buildings before opening the sphere and sending myself home.

Chapter 24

I could sense the tension and anxiety emanating from the return chamber before I even heard the frantic call from Thomas. The aides who usually remove everything from the room were panicked and didn't know what to do. I focused on the white room and saw an old man, writhing on the floor. I quickly did a mental scan of the records. Noah was supposed to be returning today. Instead, there was a screaming old man who had come back. How had he gotten a hold of the sphere?

Another aide was trying to gain control of the situation when Doctor Crebbs finally went inside the return chamber and sedated the old man. The aides carried him into her office for her. They got his clothes off and strapped him down to an examination table and left in a hurry. I watched as Doctor Crebbs tried to bring him out of sedation. He immediately started screaming and thrashed against his restraints. She sedated him again and did her examination.

I called Thomas to my office. Rachel protested that he needed to stay and help her and the rest of the board deal with the situation. At Thomas's mention of my name she went quiet. She knew I would be keeping an eye on the situation and keeping Thomas up to date.

"You know as much as I do," he said as he entered my office.

"I want you to go in there with Crebbs. See what you can get out of his mind."

"You know Eliza's better than me."

"I don't need him dissected, I just need to know what he's thinking."

"Okay," he said and left.

I watched him enter the room where Doctor Crebbs was doing her examination. She nodded as he entered and stood by a machine that was running some blood work for her. The monitor next to it suddenly displayed a bunch of text that I couldn't read from my vantage point. I heard her gasp though.

Her voice wavered as she spoke. "This is Doctor Crebbs. DNA analysis confirms patient is Noah Kent. Patient—"

Rachel broke in, "Pardon Doctor, repeat that please?"

"Patient is Noah Kent. Patient bone and tissue samples compared with initial indoctrination samples indicate an aging of about seventy-two years." She continued with her examination. She tried to revive him again but he only screamed some more.

"Noah?" Thomas said. "Doctor that's impossible. This man is at least sixty years older than Noah should be."

"Yes, he is. I told you, seventy-two years."

That quieted Thomas. He believed her, and so did I. For some reason Noah came back much later than he should have. "Can you wake him up again?" Thomas asked and held out a helmet.

"I'd rather not, he's very disoriented and somewhat violent. You saw yourself, he just screams."

"He's in restraints. I just want to know what's going on in his head for a minute. Doctor's orders."

Crebbs knew she was being overruled and made a face she knew I'd see. "Just for a minute. I'll try a mild sedative at the same time, see if that helps." She took one of the helmets from Thomas's hands and put it on Noah's head.

She gave Noah another injection. Thomas hovered a few feet away, out of Noah's field of view with the other helmet on his head, ready to go. Noah gradually came to and looked at his surroundings again. He started to cry. He either didn't notice or couldn't care about the helmet on his head. Doctor Crebbs looked at Thomas, who gave her a gesture to wait a minute. Noah continued to cry while Thomas focused on him. He nodded, took the helmet off and placed it next to the bed. He left her with Noah and headed for my office.

Doctor Crebbs left Noah awake and tried to pat his arm reassuringly before removing the helmet. She let him cry it out for a little while before giving him another, stronger sedative. It would relax him enough to be moved, but keep him awake. She called for guards, who released Noah from the restraints and moved him to a secure room. He sat at the table and continued to cry, though it had dissipated quite a bit.

Thomas had returned to my office and sat in the chair opposite me.

"Well?" I said.

"It's hard to say. He doesn't have any idea where he is or what's going on. He's terribly frightened and feeling helpless at the moment. He wants to go home. I don't know exactly where that is, but the visions in his head were definitely not from this time. Gas lamps, colonial looking furniture maybe."

"So it sounds like he came from around the right time period."

"Later, I'm pretty sure. He kept picturing a woman and some children. He's very fond of them. I might be able to get more later, when he's calmed down a bit. But his mind is just full of pain and confusion right now."

I sank in my chair, hating the idea of delaying further investigation. "Okay. We'll leave him some time to calm down. He has that other librarian friend, what's her name?"

"Adelaide MacDuff, I believe."

Of course, I thought. She was one who noticed Byron in Shakespeare's time a few weeks ago. "Send her in. See if she can get anything out of him. Maybe a more familiar face will trigger something in him."

"I think she's on vacation."

"Well then bring her back early," I said, snapping at him for no good reason. I was unhappy about the situation, but it wasn't Thomas's fault.

"I'll get Jim on it." He stood up and left, unfazed by my outburst. Thomas knew not to take it personally.

I checked the records again. Victor had brought Noah back. I wanted to know why he had waited so long. I headed to the programming room where he was still pacing. He furrowed his brow in doubt and spoke quietly to himself, apparently wondering what had gone wrong. He stopped pacing and looked frightened when I entered the room.

"Calm down Victor. You're not in trouble."

He nodded and took a deep breath to calm his nerves. He hadn't had an outburst since his first one, and triggering another wouldn't help now.

"Tell me what happened," I said as gently as possible.

Victor sat in the only chair in the room. "Everything seemed fine. I came here a few minutes early to clear my head and focus. I found the sphere just like always, and the end of the sphere's path. The person attached to it, though he seemed a little off, was definitely Noah. I didn't really think anything of it when I brought him back here. Why would I?"

It seemed as though Victor had acted according to plan. I was worried that I was going to have another Larry situation on my hands. Larry's behavior had become more and more erratic. People were returning at strange hours instead of when they were supposed to. They were getting more and more ill with each trip and complaining about it not being instantaneous like it always was. Once Victor and Quinn had proved to be perfectly able programmers, I took Larry out of commission.

Nobody leaves the lab. There's too much going on in this place that could be damaging if it were to get out. Eliza, under Thomas's supervision and with Doctor Crebbs' help, had dealt with Larry. He left the time travel research wing and was given the impression that he had always had a knack for gardening. Jim befriended him and helped him get over the disorientation of not being able to remember most of his life. I was told he had become an excellent gardener, who simply suffered a few rather disturbing nightmares about people trying to control him.

I snapped out of my reverie to respond to Victor. "Why indeed? How did he seem off to you? Can you explain it?"

"Physically it's Noah, just with some minor biological changes. Nothing that would've ruled him out as the right person. And I was surprised that he didn't have anything with him. When I sent him there a few days ago he had a small case with him. Noah's a man of habit, he always returns exactly as he left."

"So you could sense that he was older?"

"Well everyone's a little older when they come back. Adelaide was gone for months, that was definitely noticeable."

"People don't age that much in a few months."

"No, but her physique definitely changed. And the way she held herself. But she was definitely still Adelaide. It's hard to explain the difference. I've gotten used to the way the librarians are."

"Anything else?" I asked.

"The sphere's own timeline was much too long. And Noah's path was somehow wrong too. Almost as though he had veered off course. He was harder to pick up. It wasn't exactly how I expected it."

"What do you mean his path was wrong?" I kept my voice level, but it was my turn to panic. If Noah had stayed past his expected point, who knows how many times he could have pulled his timeline off course. Little things, we had discovered, didn't matter. When a person crosses the street a few second later because a librarian was in their way, they hurry a little bit later on their own. Small things had a way of fixing themselves. It was like time wanted to continue on its expected path. Victor noticed this after my trip back to Elizabethan times. Since it was not a routine mission he had spent much more time observing the path of the sphere while I was gone. As he described it, it had separated itself from Adelaide's sphere in the same time period. "Can you see alternate paths?"

"I can't really see them, but I can sense that they're there."

"So if Noah was actually on a different path, you wouldn't have been able to get him."

"I don't think so. I haven't had a chance to try it out, of course. But I don't think so. But then..." He trailed off in thought.

"Then what?"

"Well if there are two paths in time, wouldn't Noah exist in both of them?"

I had no idea. We hadn't experimented with things like this for fear of what might happen in the present. "That first time you sent Quinn back in time, do you remember?"

"Yes."

"She stumbled upon Eliza. Eliza remembers this perfectly. But our surveillance system did not pick up on Quinn's existence in that moment at all. I've searched through it myself. Why would Eliza know about it, even though there was no record?"

Victor was silent. He bit his lip and furrowed his brow. "I don't know." He sounded disappointed in himself.

"Okay, let's explore this a little. Cast your mind back in time, to when you sent Noah back. Can you picture it? The start of the sphere's run?"

Victor closed his eyes. "Yes."

"Good, now follow the sphere to about when you expected Noah to come back."

Victor's brow furrowed even more. His eyes were crushed closed and he gripped the arms of his chair, focusing. "It strengthens and weakens, my sense of it." He furrowed his brow again.

"Why didn't Noah push the button and come back when he was meant to?"

"I don't know. I can't tell. But the button wasn't pushed, I'm sure of it. Not for at least sixty years."

"We have to find out what happened."

"I told you, I can't tell."

"No, Victor, I'm sorry. I meant we as the lab."

"You're going to send someone else back?" he asked.

"I think we have to. You've done this before, two spheres in the same timeline. Although admittedly the two people didn't interact with each other."

"As long as they don't try to come back at the same instant, I think it'll be okay. I should be able to keep track of each one separately. It's the same sphere, but its path will be later."

"We'll send someone back and find out what happened, then bring them back and figure out what to do with the man who already came back."

Victor squirmed in his chair and twisted away from me. "I don't think I can change what's happened. The sphere is already back. I can't alter its course now."

"We'll deal with that when we have more information."

"Who are you going to send?" Victor asked.

"This is really a job for Jim, but I don't think I'd get him to agree to it." I paced as I tried to work it out. "I could go, but I doubt Noah would trust me. Noah and Adelaide seem to be good friends, but that could make her unpredictable. She might ignore her instructions, thinking she can remedy the situation for Noah by disobeying orders."

Victor was silent and staring at me. He did that when he felt like he had nothing left to contribute to a conversation. I had forgotten he was there altogether while thinking through my plan. I patted him on the shoulder. "Thanks Victor. Why don't you go home now and take it easy. I'll call you if I need you."

He nodded and left. I followed him out and went back to my office. Thomas was waiting for me. "Jim has gone to fetch Adelaide and bring her back."

I nodded. "I'm sorry I snapped at you earlier."

He ignored my apology and went straight to business as usual. The incident was already settled in his mind. "What are you going to do?"

"We'll see what this Adelaide can get out of Noah and formulate a plan from there."

"You want me to go see him again?"

"No. He seems to have suffered enough traumas for one day. Let's see how she does with him."

Thomas nodded and left again to return to the board room where a bunch of self-important people who thought they knew everything were arguing about what should be done. They thought it was intentional on Noah's part; that he had been trying to steal a sphere for himself. They didn't think anyone should be sent back to find out what happened, and that the man who came back should simply be disposed of.

Thomas sat quietly and listened, knowing I had already made my decisions.

Chapter 25

I was disturbed to find out that Noah had lived a full life. He no longer had memories of this place or who he really was. He completely adapted to his cover story, stayed in Massachusetts, got married and had children and grandchildren. This didn't seem like the life of the man I had been casually observing for the past eight years.

I decided that Adelaide would be sent back to find out why Noah didn't return when he was meant to. She would come back with information, and we would decide what to do then. My feeling was that the Noah who had returned would need to be disposed of. He was too old to be very useful to us. He was also too mentally damaged to be let go. I had no idea what sort of memories someone else might trigger, trying to help a poor homeless man who had been left on the street with no idea who he was. As irritated as I was at the situation, I couldn't bring myself to leave him to Eliza.

Adelaide had advocated for sending him back to live his life out with his family, but that could also have disastrous effects. Thomas found out in another mind reading session that Noah had befriended one of the major instigators of the American Revolution and was adamantly against that idea. We couldn't let him interfere with such a significant event in history, so there was no way I would allow him to go back. That left him to a life locked up in a room here, or no life at all. I declined to inform anyone about my decision, but I knew Rachel was on the same page.

We gave Adelaide some time to prepare herself. It was mostly for surveillance reasons. She had been very vocal about her displeasure with us for not sending the older Noah back, so I had wanted to keep an eye on her and see if she would try to warn him about anything. She kept visiting him but said very little about what she was about to do. She declined to voice what she thought might happen to him. It made me trust her a little more, but not much. She was a tool at this point, plain and simple. I needed her to get Noah's trust and find out what happened, and then return to us. At that point, she would be out of the equation and could go back to her work.

The day of her trip arrived. Jim went to collect her and Victor was all set to send her back. We were only going to give her a few hours to accomplish her mission. If her sphere path didn't end in that time...well I really didn't know what we would do at that point. We couldn't force her to come back. It was a bit of a gamble. Victor was only going to give himself five minutes on our end. Once she was sent, he would take time to relax and refocus on the sphere, then bring her back.

Her trip out went fine, Victor assured me. I stayed in the room with him and also with Thomas. Thomas had gotten to the point where in close proximity to a familiar mind, he no longer needed the helmets. It made things easier on Victor and Quinn, though since Victor had already proven himself trustworthy with abnormal mission parameters, I decided to use him. Just under five minutes after Victor sent Adelaide off, Victor started looking down her sphere path. When he clenched the arms of the chair again and I heard Thomas gasp, I knew something was wrong.

"Wait, no!" Victor said.

My breathing accelerated but I kept myself silent. I didn't want to disrupt Victor's focus any more than whatever had caused his outburst. Sweat broke out on his forehead and his breathing was labored.

"No, no, it's not the right one. It's his old one!"

I waited while Victor cringed again and shook his head and Thomas collapsed to kneel beside his chair, hands raised to his head.

"I can't—" Victor opened his eyes in panic. "She's not here," he said. "She's not here! Where did it go?"

I cast my mind to the return chamber where, instead of finding Adelaide, Noah was kneeling down on the mats and vomiting. I watched as Noah looked around and got his bearings. He spat the last bit of bile out, wiped his mouth off and began to laugh.

"Where is she?" The words seethed through my teeth, too late for me to realize Victor's state.

The wave hit me and I collapsed. It was much more intense than Victor's first outburst, but through it I could see him trying to focus again. Thomas had collapsed to the floor and was clutching his head. It was the last thing I saw before I passed out.

*　　　*　　　*　　　*

I came to when Thomas slapped me in the face. Victor still looked frightened and clung to his chair. "Victor," I said, and tried to keep calm. "I'm not mad. I just need to know where she is."

He shook his head and started to cry. "I'm not sure! She's somewhere in the future. I couldn't get her back in time. It was so messed up!"

I went to his side and crouched next to the chair, trying desperately to ignore the sound of Amelia's voice in my head. "Victor it's okay. I just need to know what happened. Calm yourself, and talk me through it." I could see Noah being taken to Doctor Crebbs for his examination. He was asking about Adelaide.

"Okay," he said between sobs, and took a few deep breaths. "Her sphere path ended, but she wasn't alone. Noah was attached to the sphere as well, and his own kept going on. It was taking too much time to sort it out so I just dumped them as soon as I could. Both of them."

"But Noah came back," I said in my most level voice, encouraging him to continue.

"Yes," Victor responded. "His sphere reactivated. Only it wasn't his sphere, he had Adelaide's. By the time I figured out that it wasn't Adelaide but was Noah, I had already brought the sphere back here. And then the other sphere, Adelaide had it. But I couldn't bring it back here at the same time and I just wasn't fast enough. I got confused because it was the old sphere, crossing it's own path. I lost track of it."

"Do you have any idea where she is, Victor?" It was hard to keep my voice from rising when my mind was filled with rage and feelings of betrayal. *This was not Victor's fault*, I tried to remind myself.

"Somewhere in the future. I can't be sure."

I fell back onto the floor. I had Noah and his sphere back, but who knew where Adelaide was with hers. Not only had I been betrayed, I had no idea how or why. My mind tried to focus and I kept my voice as calm as possible. "Don't worry, Victor," I said. "I'll find her."

I picked myself up off the floor and went straight to Eliza's room. She seemed surprised to see me as she uncurled from the fetal position she had been in. The trails left from her tears still tainted her cheeks. I said nothing and stared at her, thinking about what had happened and what information I needed. She stared back and me and I felt her probe my mind. An excited grin crept up into her face and she nodded at me.

"Come on," I said to Eliza. As we walked towards the return chambers, I contacted Emma and requested that she bring the older version of Noah from his temporary quarters back to a controlled room.

Noah was still getting his medical examination. Eliza and I waited just beyond her door while I watched the examination. Noah still had a stupid grin on his face. I was determined to find out what he knew and what he was hiding. The Noah in her office was the one I had expected to return a week ago. He was the right age and his mental state was the same as when he had left, cocky as ever.

After what seemed like an eternity, the door opened and Noah walked through it. He stopped in his tracks when he saw Eliza and me. He had clearly been expecting the grooming staff to get him back into shape for the present time period. I threw some clothes at him. "Come with us," I said.

He dressed quickly, and I led him and Eliza back to the room where Emma had brought the older version of Noah. The older version of Noah looked at us curiously when we entered. Noah glanced at him, looking confused. "Take a seat," I said to him, gesturing at the empty chair next to the table.

The two of them sat across the table from each other and glanced at each other. It would have been comical had I not been so enraged at the idea of being betrayed. The younger Noah leaned over the table and stared into his eyes, working it out. "It's him, isn't it? The other me," he said. His voice was angry.

I turned to Noah. "Where is she?"

He was still staring angrily at the old Noah before he turned to look at me. "What?"

"Where is she?" I asked again.

He tried to keep his face blank, but I caught the twitch of lip that indicated he wasn't going to be cooperative of his own will.

"I'll ask you one more time," I said. "Where is Adelaide?"

He shrugged, and stared back at his older self again. He was about to say something when I glanced at Eliza and nodded. I didn't know what she was doing to him, but for the moment I didn't care. He fell out of his chair with the pain of it. "Where is Adelaide?" I asked him again.

He was gasping with pain but in between managed to squeak out, "I don't know," again.

I nodded to Eliza once more, and once more he screamed and twitched on the floor. The older version of Noah was watching in terror. "What manner of monsters are you?" he asked us.

I placed my hand on Eliza's shoulder and Noah fell silent, curled in a ball on the floor. "Where is she," I asked the older version of Noah.

He looked at Eliza and then me with terror in his eyes. He couldn't say anything. He only managed to shake his head before he started to scream.

I watched him writhe on the floor as well. The anger built inside me. I finally called to the guards to have him and Noah removed. Eliza stopped whatever it was she was doing as soon as she heard the door open. There was a smug look of satisfaction on her face. It gave me pause. I once again looked at the two version of Noah, lying on the floor in the fetal position in various states of wailing and clutching themselves. Disgust momentarily replaced the anger. I pulled Eliza from the room with me and thought of nothing but sending her back to her lair. She complied without a word.

I went back to my office and took a few minutes to compose myself before calling on Thomas again. I began to feel ashamed at what I had allowed to happen, though the rage still simmered below. Neither of them knew anything, I was sure of that.

Thomas arrived and sat across from me. I was certain he could see the pain in my face. "Anything else from Victor?" I asked.

"No," Thomas said. "He's feeling pretty bad about himself, but I've calmed him down. I don't think he'll have another episode."

The word triggered the memory. "I heard Amelia again."

"Did you go look to see if she was awake."

I shook my head. "I know. Deep down I know she's not. Whatever it is that's causing me to hear her, it's not real." *At least not in this time*, I thought to myself. I had not shared the details of my Shakespearean adventure with Thomas.

He nodded. "What now?"

I thought about it. The older Noah didn't know anything. I wanted to get rid of him. The real Noah didn't know anything either. I wanted to get rid of him too. He at least could still contribute to society. I would have Eliza erase his mind as I had Larry's and force him to do some menial task around the complex. Then I could watch him and revel in his mediocrity. It would be enough. I contacted Emma and asked her to keep both of them under constant surveillance for the next few days. I was too tired to deal with it now.

"I need a break," I told Thomas. "Go back to work. Business as usual. I'll deal with both Noahs later."

Thomas nodded and left to rejoin Rachel and update the board on the situation. Everyone else had gone back to their normal lives. I had no normal life that I knew of. I went back to my quarters and stood by Amelia's pod. I fought the urge to wipe the mist away and look at her. Deep down I knew nothing had changed. She would understand that the things I did had needed to be done, to protect this place and keep it going. "I'm sorry, wife," I said to the still pod. My doubts overcame me and I wiped clear a section of glass. She remained as still as ever.

Chapter 26

I prepared memos to issue to people about each Noah. I thought it would distance me from the act if I ordered other people to do my unpleasant business. Then I realized this might be the perfect time to try out Thomas's new mind interaction device with Eliza. He claimed to have developed a new helmet. It would connect to Eliza's mind and offer the user her powers. The only problem was, she would have to be operated on. The other side was no longer a helmet, but electrodes that needed to be attached directly to certain parts of her brain. He did not think injectable electrodes could be positioned with the sort of accuracy he needed. That meant opening up her skull to expose areas of her brain. I was not looking forward to that sort of procedure, and had no idea how to get her to even agree to it.

I couldn't deny, though, the incredible power it would yield me. To no longer have to rely on Eliza and her mental instability to take care of mind control for me would be a relief. If it also allowed me to manipulate matter from a distance, that would be an even greater advantage. Perhaps, once we had it set up, I could get the information I needed out of Noah myself.

Noah had been back for a week and I still had no idea what had happened to Adelaide MacDuff. The older Noah was being kept in captivity again. The younger was back at his quarters with strict orders to remain indoors. Today he was supposed to have his memory erased. I sat in my office, staring at the memo and weighing my options.

I could have just let his memory get erased, but the urge to probe his mind on my own was overwhelming. I was sure the answers I wanted were in there. After all, Eliza might have found something and not told me about it. I felt like I couldn't trust anyone these days, except maybe Thomas. Amelia as well, but I couldn't talk to her.

I stood up and paced back and forth in front of my desk. I was frustrated with my situation. Thomas would not approve of what I was about to do, but he had long since outgrown any desire to chastise me for my less than ethical decisions. He often knew there was no other choice. Amelia would not approve either, I was sure. Even if she had been awake to talk to, it would not have gone well. The conversation would almost certainly have ended in one of us departing angrily. I would have given anything for her to even be able to stomp out of my office right then.

I felt so alone, and I knew exactly whom to blame.

I tossed my lab coat onto my desk chair and stalked out into the hallway, calling to Quinn to meet me in the programmer's room. I grabbed the sphere from its safe keeping space, the guard standing back and avoiding eye contact as I took it. My mind ranged through the various accusations I would make as I approached the programmers room. I realized I was having imaginary arguments as I reached the door and paused to collect myself before going in.

Quinn was not as worried about me bypassing protocol as Victor usually was. I explained the street where my parents lived and the tree I usually arrived behind to hide my sudden appearance. She confirmed that the tree still existed, and did not hesitate at all when I pushed the button.

It looked different. My other journeys here had taken place in the past, when I was much younger. Quinn had left me in the present day at my request. Everything looked more modern and sleek. It wouldn't have surprised me to find out my parents had moved away from this place to avoid having to adjust to the new technologies that had developed, and gone to live on a farm somewhere. I held my breath as I walked up to their door and knocked.

No one answered for a minute. I knocked again and rang the doorbell. I heard a shuffling noise approach the door. I stared into the camera that would show them who was at the door. My mother opened it just a crack, and peered out with narrowed eyes. She had gotten much older than I expected. Her face was heavily lined and her eyes sagged with tiredness. She even seemed shorter. I quickly calculated that I hadn't seen her in over forty years.

"What do you want?" she asked. Her voice was guarded and unfriendly.

"Megan," I said.

"Do I know you?" She glanced up and down at me. I was not dressed like a church member, so I knew she would not want to talk to me.

"Is Mark home?"

Her eyes narrowed further and her frown became a grimace. "Mark died five years ago." She tried to close the door on me, but I stuck my foot against the frame to keep it open. Her eyes widened in alarm. "Get out of here, or I'll call the police!"

I stared at her for a moment, unable to form any words. I thought some show of sympathy was probably due to her, but I couldn't summon any. I was surprised at my own lack of sadness upon hearing of my father's death. I was never close to him. He rarely even talked to me, it was always my mother who took care of me and taught me. Still, he was my father. I flashed back to the death of Amelia's father and how she hadn't seemed phased by it. I finally understood how that could be. "Don't you recognize me?" I asked her.

"No, go away!"

"Perhaps this will jog your memory," I said as I twisted my back towards her, awkwardly trying to keep my foot against the door. I pulled the back of my collar down to expose the scar she and my father had given to me so many years ago in their experiments.

"No," she whispered, and I felt the door give against my foot as she backed away. Her hand flew up to her mouth and tears filled her eyes. "No," she said again, and gasped for air.

Her voice cracked as though she was in pain. I wasn't prepared for tears. I expected her to be angry with me for showing up at her doorstep. "Hello, mother. Bet you never thought I'd show up again. So sorry I missed my father."

She backed behind a chair and grasped it for support, shaking her head. She closed her eyes and a few tears escaped. She began chanting a prayer underneath her breath. I recognized it as one from the Order of Vena, and it enraged me to the point where I could finally ignore her tears.

"Don't give me that bullshit!" I yelled and pointed at her. "I know the truth, and you can't hide behind your religion! I know you don't believe it!"

"Of course I do," she snapped at me, gaining a small amount of courage. "It's you who lied all those years, pretending to be the good son."

"I was a good son. A very good son."

"You abandoned us and everything we tried to teach you! That makes you a traitor!"

"No, I'm not a traitor. In fact, I did exactly what you wanted of me. I actually followed in your footsteps without even knowing it."

She clung to the chair still, confusion twisting the features of her face. She gasped for breath, but said nothing.

"I always wondered where my propensity for learning came from, and now I know," I said as I pointed to the scar at the base of my neck. "A fine job you did, too. I had no idea my superior intelligence wasn't natural until recently. And it's come in handy, despite your efforts to suppress me."

She shook her head. "We were trying to protect you. The technology was dangerous—"

"Oh yes, I know just how dangerous it is. See I know something about the inner workings of the brain, mother." I spat the word out, ashamed of her. "I spent a lot of time perfecting my own neural pathways so my brain will never degrade. I will remain this age forever."

Her hand flew to cover her mouth as it fell open in shock. She shook her head again. "You can't do this. You must not—"

I slowly approached her as I spoke, my face twisted in sarcasm and rage. "I never would have accomplished all this without you and my dear departed father. And to think, all that time I thought you were holding me back, when really I should be thanking you. Thanking you for messing about with my brain in the first place. Thanking you for isolating me from everyone, so I wouldn't trust anyone. It's much easier to use people to your advantage when you have no means of empathy for your fellow man. I suppose I learned that from you as well."

She took a deep breath and lowered her hand back to the chair. When she spoke it was barely above a whisper, and her voice broke repeatedly. "We tried to protect you. We were worried about what might happen if we finished— We were saving you."

"Saving me from what? From what you did to Jane? Perhaps I should bring you back to my lab and do the same for you!"

Her eyes flashed as she gritted her teeth. Pain and anger warred in her face. "No! How do you—Who told you about Jane?"

"One of your old friends at the lab you spent so many years convincing me didn't exist. He told me all about your callous disregard for human life in pursuit of science."

"We were helping people. We were going to make everyone so much smarter," she tried to argue.

I stopped on the other side of the chair, and leaned in to yell at her face. "I may have inherited your callous detachment when it comes to scientific pursuit, but at least I never killed anyone I cared about!"

She broke down and collapsed on the floor. "No!" she wailed. Her hands gripped the sides of her face and her body shook with the force of her sobs. "Please," she managed to gasp in between sobs.

My resolve fell at the sight of my mother contorted in pain. I tried to shake it off and regain my emotional distance. *She doesn't deserve my sympathy*, I tried to tell myself. It's her fault I am who am I. I felt my own tears welling up to the surface. "How could you," was all I managed to get out before breaking down and turning back to the door.

I was desperate to get away. She wasn't supposed to get my pity. She was supposed to feel my wrath. She had destroyed my life.

But my mother was alone, just as I was alone.

I heard her cry out my name as I closed the door. My hands shook as I pulled the sphere out of my pocket and pressed the button, frantic to get back to my safe haven of the laboratory. I didn't even try to hide. I disappeared from the doorway of my childhood home. I left the sphere with Quinn and staggered back to my office as quickly as possible, passing my desk and heading into my apartment. I collapsed next to Amelia's pod and stopped trying to fight the tears.

Chapter 27

Emma called to me urgently. I cast my mind out to the dome as I rose from aside Amelia's pod and went to my office. There were people climbing up the outside glass of the central habitat. They had drawn a crowd of curious onlookers in the main courtyard. I dismissed it and tried to ease Emma's worry. I figured they were probably just thrill seekers trying to get some attention. It didn't matter though. The glass in the structure was unbreakable. They would never be able to get inside the dome. In a few minutes they would get bored and climb back down.

They had quite a bit of attention, most of the lab was out there watching, including Quinn and Victor. I found that odd since Quinn and Victor never left this section of the lab. Quinn looked as though she was trying to pull Victor back inside. He looked terrified, but refused to go. If it kept up, he would have an outburst. Well good, I thought. When the wave hit the people climbing they would lose their focus and grip and fall to their deaths; problem solved.

The climbers had stopped at a panel near the top of the dome. I wondered what they were waiting for. None of them seemed to be moving. I looked back to Victor, who was starting to tremble. Any second now, it would be over. Quinn backed away from him with a confused look on her face. Victor was looking up at the group of people outside the dome. He closed his eyes and I could see his body knocked backward from the force of the wave.

I thought that was strange. Previously Victor's wave flowed outward from all sides of his body. He remained in place. A noise came from the top of the dome and I looked back to where the climbers had congregated. The glass between them shattered and fell over five hundred feet to the grass below. The people who had been watching were starting to back away and some started to run. A small section of the metal frame was bending inward. It almost looked like it was melting. The climbers wasted no time in repelling down into the dome. I stood up in panic, uncertain what to do. They had guns strapped to their backs.

I called to Quinn, Victor, and Thomas. The executive board was in a meeting, but Thomas saw what was going on and left immediately. The board was used to him departing abruptly upon a call from me, and thought nothing of it. I told Emma to mobilize whatever guards we had. People were running in earnest away from the intruders now. Victor stood, frozen. I saw the trembling begin again. I couldn't find Quinn, she had just been right beside him. She barely ever left his side.

When I awoke I found I had collapsed back into my desk chair. The disorientation passed and I tracked the intruders down to the boardroom. They had the board surrounded at gunpoint and were waiting for the members to wake back up. Victor had knocked everyone out but them, it seemed. Why wouldn't they have been affected, I wondered. Perhaps they had been too high up still for the wave to hit them as they descended into the dome. The pack of guards that had taken position to defend the wing before they had been knocked out by Victor lay in various parts of the hall. Each of them had been shot in the head, point blank.

I sat frozen in my chair. What would happen if they came down the hall and found me? My door wouldn't open unless I allowed it, but they had managed to force their way into an unbreakable dome.

They broke into an unbreakable dome using Victor.

I seethed with rage. Victor must have been in on it. It couldn't be, I tried to reason. Eliza had been inside his mind countless times. She would have seen something, unless she was in on it too and kept it from me. I looked into her room. She was just starting to wake up too and seemed confused and upset as well. *A very good actress*, I thought.

Thomas was getting up off the floor. He had been on his way to my office when the wave hit. He looked around and started to head back to the boardroom before I called to him. He stopped at my call and at the same time, saw a guard dead on the floor. He turned and ran back to my office.

"We need to hook up Eliza, now."

"Now? What's going on? Why is there a dead guard on the floor?"

"Thomas I don't have time for this, just read my mind and be done with it!"

I waited a moment while he caught himself up. "What's going on in the board room?"

"Rachel and the others are waking up. Rachel is demanding to know what's going on. They're talking about going back in time— Come on, we have to get Eliza ready."

"That procedure will take hours. We've got to help the people in the board room now."

"And how do you suggest we do that, Thomas?" I was enraged at having been betrayed by my own people. I wanted Eliza under my control so I could use her to kill the intruders in the boardroom from a safe distance. "All the guards are dead. If we go in there those people will shoot us. We're out numbered. We need Eliza to do this."

He hesitated for a moment before agreeing. "Okay, fine. Let's go."

I stood up. "Wait for me in the operating room. Get whatever you need ready. I'll get her." Thomas exited through one door and I went to gather Eliza. I had to set my mind straight so she would come willingly. I couldn't let any of my suspicion of her involvement in what happened be known to her.

The people in the boardroom were introducing themselves as Gardians to the rest of the board. I had heard of them, a sect that split from Wiccan culture because they had violent tendencies. They were demanding that Rachel let one of them go back in time to prove that Jesus Christ was not a religious figure, but a fictional character or the embellishment of a normal human. Rachel was trying to explain the procedures and necessary precautions that went into sending someone back in time. It was a delay tactic. She was counting on me to do something to intervene.

I entered Eliza's room. She immediately scanned my mind. I let it drift over the last few minutes and ended with an urgent desire for her help. She stood up and asked silently, *What do you want me to do?*

I gave her a mental image of the people in the other room and what I wanted to do to them.

But I can't get to the people in that room, these walls are too thick.

"I know," I said. "That's why Thomas and I are going to help you." I tried to frame it that way in my mind. We wouldn't be controlling her so much as guiding her at what to do. With my mind already synced up to the rest of the lab we hypothesized that I would be able to use Eliza's power remotely.

My train of thought was cut off by the sound of a gunshot. I felt Eliza probing my mind again as I focused on the board room. One of the Gardians had grown tired of Rachel's arguing and shot another board member to show how serious they were. Rachel realized she would have to cooperate. "We have to hurry."

Eliza nodded and followed me out to meet Thomas. Rachel had asked one of the board members to find Victor. I had completely forgotten about Victor. He was back in this section of the lab with Quinn. He seemed confused about what had happened.

I opened the door to a small medical room that Thomas was preparing for surgery. Eliza didn't even flinch when she saw the bed. She climbed right in and lay down. Before she could think about it, Thomas had given her a sedative and she was out cold.

Victor and Quinn had been collected and taken back to the boardroom along with the sphere. Quinn was protesting the idea of sending someone back who wasn't a member of the lab. She was saying he wouldn't do it. One of the Gardians pointed at the dead board member, but Quinn held her ground. She held her ground right up till the moment a Gardian pointed a gun at Victor's head. Victor began to tremble, and for a moment I couldn't see Quinn. Another Gardian grabbed the gun and slapped the woman across the face. She then worked on calming Victor down. She obviously knew what he was capable of. But they hadn't been affected by his last outburst, so why would she be worried now? If Victor wasn't in on it then someone else had to be helping them. Given how they were treating him, I didn't believe he was cooperating. I felt a little better letting myself believe that he hadn't betrayed me. Victor stepped forward and agreed to do what they wanted after Quinn continued to protest.

Rachel had a protocol in place for this sort of situation. I groaned when I remembered what it was. "Thomas you have to hurry."

He was cutting away part of Eliza's skull. "This isn't an eye exam, it's complicated brain surgery. I can't rush this."

"Maybe I can delay them somehow."

"What?" he asked over the sound of bone being split with a laser.

"Keep working. I'll be right back."

I left the room and paced my office. I needed to find a way to stall them. I sent a quick message to Rachel. A Gardian heard the notification and asked her what it was. She told them it was a message from her boss. They seemed very interested to find out she wasn't actually the person in charge. They told her to read it out loud. When she did, all it said was "Vaccinations." I hoped it would be enough.

She explained to the Gardians that librarians needed to be inoculated against certain diseases before we send them on missions. They asked why her boss would be concerned about the health of someone who took over his lab. Rachel knew it was a delay tactic on my part, but explained to them that we didn't want diseases being brought back and infecting the entire lab. It wasn't about that particular person, but the possibility of spreading a contagion to the rest of us. They relented. It bought me some time, though I doubted it would be enough.

I could tell Thomas had cut away most of her skull and was now working on getting the electrodes hooked directly into Eliza's brain. He was close. I went back in, sat in the chair next to the bed and put the helmet on my head. I tried to avoid watching Thomas attach the electrodes to her brain. I kept imagining a girl, even younger than Eliza, who looked like me lying there with her brain cut open. I wondered, against my better judgment, if this was how my sister looked when she died. I shook the thought from my head and tried to focus on the task at hand.

Once I had access to Eliza's power I needed to eliminate the Gardian who was to go back in time. Then I would deal with the ones in the boardroom.

"Just a few more minutes," Thomas said as he checked something on a monitor and attached another electrode.

Rachel was walking with Victor to the room he normally worked from. Quinn had been left in the boardroom as collateral. A Gardian had just been inoculated in Doctor Crebb's office and was heading back to the boardroom to collect the sphere. Rachel convinced the guard who escorted them to the room that Victor would need to remain calm, and an armed guard wouldn't help with that. The guard agreed and left them in the room alone. Rachel explained to Victor what he had to do, the protocol for this situation. Victor refused at first. He didn't want to kill someone. Rachel told him she couldn't save Quinn unless Victor sent the Gardian away. I knew it was a lie. Rachel had no means of protecting Quinn. She had to get Victor to cooperate though. He nodded finally, agreeing to do it.

"Thomas," I said urgently.

"Almost got it—"

The Gardian who had been inoculated took the sphere and was heading to the departure chamber. She pushed the button just as Thomas flicked a power switch on and said, "Done."

It was too late. Victor had sent the Gardian and the sphere back to a prehistoric time when the earth was nothing but rivers of lava. She would have been killed instantly, and the sphere destroyed. That was Rachel's protocol, so that no one else could take over the sphere. It was gone. I couldn't tell what happened next, as I was assailed by the power of Eliza's mind.

Chapter 28

I looked up into the face of a woman. It was hard and lined from too many years of stress and anger. I felt paralyzed by my fear. "That's enough lies out of you, Eliza," she said.

"I'm sorry, mother."

I barely saw the hand before it contacted the side of my face. My head was knocked to the right with so much force I staggered to catch my balance. My cheek felt hot and when I raised my hand to it, there was moisture. I pulled my hand away and saw blood. I pushed my anger down inside myself. It would not be good to upset her. The room swam. A man walked away from me through the woman and she disappeared.

I ran down the street and yelled after him, but he wouldn't stop. A tall man in a lab coat appeared in my path. He held his arms out to embrace me, but they turned into snakes and wrapped me in a crushing hold. I cried, and promised to do better. The snakes released me and slithered away, leaving him with no arms. He turned and followed the other man down the street. I tried to chase after him as well, but he moved as though on a conveyor belt and I couldn't catch up.

I heard a giggle to my left. There were young children watching me. They were dressed in khaki pants with white shirts and black ties. They wore lab coats that were too big for them. The sleeves were rolled up and the hem hung to their ankles. Red rubber balls encircled them, floating through the air like a carousel. They pointed at me and laughed.

The anger welled up in me again, and this time I let it encompass me. The children stopped laughing as the balls dropped to the ground. They trembled where they stood as their eyes rolled into the back of their heads and blood started to pour from their noses. It dripped down their torsos, staining their sparkling white lab coats.

I heard another familiar voice, calling for me. No, it was calling for Doctor Lancing. I recognized the voice. It was the man who was always trying to drive a wedge between Doctor Lancing and me. He called again. The noise was deafening. It came from every direction.

Dirt walls rose up from the ground and encased me. It became quiet. There was no light and no sound. I relaxed in the peacefulness.

I heard a different voice calling for Doctor Lancing. It was a woman. It was soft and familiar. A small light appeared at my feet. I stepped back, away from it. The voice rose up from the bright chasm. The light grew and enveloped my feet. I closed my eyes and tried to scream as it swelled to encompass me and the voice grew louder.

I found myself in a box. It was cold and smelled. The lid was clear glass. I saw the doctor on the other side. I pounded on the glass and called to him. My voice had become the woman's. He didn't hear me. My voice changed back into the man's as I called again—

Thomas was standing over me, the helmet in his hands. "Are you okay?"

I didn't realize I was panting from the effort. "Yes. It's just going to take some practice to get some control over her mind."

"I was starting to worry. I was trying to monitor your mind, but I could only get flashes of what was going on. I think Eliza may have known and tried to keep me out."

I nodded. "There were a few moments, I think, where I was in control. How long was I hooked up to her?"

"About ten minutes. What's going on with everyone else?" Thomas asked.

I searched back in the surveillance files over the last ten minutes. Rachel had helped Victor escape through an air duct before confronting the Gardian who escorted them to the programming room. She asked to be taken back to the boardroom. The Gardian beat Rachel across the face with the butt of her gun before agreeing to escort her. Rachel had staggered back down the hall with blood dripping from her mouth. She still managed to have a smug look on her face as she walked.

I thought if I could get to Victor, I could scare him into knocking everyone out again. Then he could take the Gardians' guns and bring them back to me where they couldn't get to them. It would at least even the playing field. "We have to find Victor, quickly. We need his help."

"I thought you said Victor was in on it."

"I'm not sure about anyone anymore, but we need Victor." I paused. Rachel had returned to the boardroom and was explaining where Victor had sent the other Gardian. "Rachel has returned to the boardroom. She's explaining that Victor sent the Gardian back to prehistoric times. She's telling them that she is dead and the sphere has been destroyed."

Thomas's face fell in disappointment. "That was your emergency protocol?"

"Rachel came up with the idea. She didn't want the sphere to fall into anyone else's hands."

"The sphere's gone then. I've got to get back to Rachel," Thomas said.

"You can't go in there, Thomas, those people are dangerous."

"I can't just think of myself. The entire board is in there, I've got to help them!"

"Thomas please, it's too dangerous for you to go. You—" I was distracted by an overwhelming wave of fear coming from the boardroom. Before I could even explain the situation to Thomas, I watched as one of the Gardians ripped out Rachel's throat. I gasped at the brutality of it. Another seemed to plunge her hand into a board member's chest and pull his heart out as it continued to beat and sputter blood all over the boardroom table. She chanted something as she held the heart aloft. Yet another sliced open a board member's gut with a knife she had shoved in her belt, and then yelled something in a language I didn't understand.

"No," I whispered, frozen in shock and fear.

"What is it?" Thomas asked frantically. "What's happened?"

"They've killed the entire board."

Thomas had to steady himself against a wall. "Rachel?"

"Dead."

"I have to help them," Thomas said as he went for the door.

"Don't be a fool!" I tried to grab him and hold him back but he shook me loose and ran out of my office. "Thomas!" I let the door close behind him and panicked. I couldn't go out there. If they found out who I was I would be killed for sure. But Thomas was in trouble too now. I needed Victor or Eliza. I searched about for Victor but couldn't find him anywhere.

I tried not to pay attention as the Gardians departed the boardroom and headed this way. I went back into the room with Eliza. As I lifted the helmet to put it back on I saw Thomas try to wrestle a gun from one of them. I paused with the helmet in my hands, held just above my head. I watched as Thomas collapsed to the floor, the second time today that I failed to stop a tragedy. *At least his death was quick and painless*, I said to myself before I lowered the helmet and lost my mind in Eliza's.

I tried to cling to the elements of myself that presented themselves in Eliza's visions. I focused on each part until it overwhelmed Eliza's thought and became my own. She fought me to retain control for a few more minutes until her world shrank further and further into a small point. Everything suddenly became peaceful. All images were gone except for a pencil floating in the space in front of me.

I opened my eyes and saw the pencil floating in the air. I focused on it, and made it spin in a complete circle. I set it on the floor, marveling at the newfound ability control objects.

I picked up a scalpel with my mind. It was still bloody from Thomas's surgery on Eliza. I made it spin in the air as well, building speed before I flung it towards the wall, where the blade embedded itself. An enormous grin erupted across my face. It was an amazing experience. I could've spent all day just playing with things in this room. A banging noise brought me back to the present.

Without moving, I focused on the door to the room and caused it to open. I could see my desk through the doorway in the other room and could hear pounding on the door. The Gardians, I knew, were trying to find me. I closed my eyes and let my mind wander into the hallway beyond my office. I saw them trying to smash a chair into my door. I saw Thomas lying on the floor in a pool of his own blood just a few feet away. They had just left him there. I knew I should be angry, but I was inexplicably tranquil.

I left my mind drift over Thomas, and through him. I found the bullet that had pierced his heart and pulled it out. It landed with a soft clatter on the floor of the hall. The Gardians couldn't hear it over the noise they were making. It was an awful lot of noise.

I focused on the Gardian closest to the doorway and squeezed her heart. She gasped and clutched her chest, her face contorted in pain. The other ones stopped banging on the door to see what was wrong before she collapsed to the floor. Too easy, I thought, remembering the brutality they had shown in the boardroom. The next one was looking at the other remaining Gardian, alarmed. I began to pull her intestines back in on themselves, up through her stomach and esophagus till a fountain of bile and filth and pink flesh poured from her mouth in a stream that took longer than I would have thought possible.

The remaining one shot herself in the head before it was even over. A few Gardians remained scattered about the complex. I gave them quick deaths, feeling avenged and now wanting to move on with things. They wouldn't know what was coming for them anyway.

The hallway outside my door was in a rather macabre state. I focused on the closest dead body, the woman whose heart I had stopped. I focused on the heart then moved outward into her chest and lungs. The human body is a bunch of molecules, I told myself. I focused on the parts, breaking them down into their constituent atoms. The gases dissipated and all that remained was a pile of dust. I did the same for the other bodies in the hall. I swept the dust from the three guardians into a gentle tornado, watching as the piles joined and twirled in the hallway before settling into a larger orderly pile near the door.

I focused on Thomas again. It seemed a simple matter to close the channel the bullet had made through his skin and his heart. The bleeding stopped. Thomas was not breathing. His heart was not beating. I made it pump. It pushed the blood through his veins and into his brain, but there was nothing there. No activity.

I began to explore the pathways of his brain. There were too many. I was getting lost. I backed out and stopped forcing his heart to beat. It did not continue on its own. I reduced his body to dust as well, and then took the helmet off, disappointed in my inability to save Thomas.

I wiped the tears from my eyes as I tried to focus on the events of the past few hours.

I realized the older version of Noah was still being kept imprisoned and isolated. I remembered that I was supposed to deal with the original Noah before all this happened. It hadn't been much more than an hour ago when

Victor punched the hole in the roof of the dome. I hadn't even thought of trying to focus his outbursts to use them as a weapon. Someone had thought of it. Maybe it was Victor, maybe someone else. I made a mental list of all employees who knew of Victor's outbursts. It was a very short list, and I couldn't believe any of them would have wanted this to happen. I would have to investigate the matter further. I just had to find Victor.

I surveyed the state of the lab. People were milling about again in the habitat dome, uncertain of what to do. I tried to find Jim. Jim was a well-respected member of the lab. People would listen to him. I couldn't find him. I called to Emma. It took her a moment to respond, she was still reeling from the events of the afternoon.

"Where's Jim?" I asked.

"He escaped," she said. "He took Noah and they left through the passage in the farm house."

As she spoke I followed them in my mind, out along the path to the hatch in the field next to the lab.

"They ran into—"

"Adelaide MacDuff," I answered. I watched as they were joined by a young girl and held hands. Adelaide opened a box, pushed a button and they all disappeared.

"How did—"

"Never mind, Emma. Never mind." I was so angry I could barely feel it. I left Eliza in the hospital room, left my office and went to my quarters. I pulled a chair up beside Amelia's pod and wiped away the condensation. She was so still, and so beautiful. "I'm sorry." I folded my arms onto the top of the pod and collapsed my head into them, and then cried myself to sleep.

Chapter 29

The next morning I pulled off my lab jacket and did something I hadn't done in more years than I could say; I left my wing of the laboratory. I scattered the larger pile of dust as I walked away from my door. I stopped only to scoop as much of Thomas's remains as I could into a plastic bag. I would find a more appropriate vessel some other time.

I felt good as I walked down the hall, past the dead guards and the bloodstained door of the boardroom. I was oddly optimistic. I walked to the habitat dome, glancing up at the hole in the glass above me. A few people were still milling about. None of them recognized me. Few of them even knew I existed.

I walked to Emma's quarters and knocked on the door. She was not surprised to see me standing there as the door slid open. "Come in," she said and gestured to the inside.

She looked only slightly older than she did thirty years ago when I hired her. "Nice to see you face to face again, Emma." I sat down on a couch in her living room and looked around. I hadn't been inside anyone's living quarters in a long time, though I could see them in my mind. Emma had posters of very old Kung-Fu movies covering her walls. "Nice place."

"What's going to happen to us?" she asked.

Right to business, as usual. I noticed her eyes were puffy. She had been crying. Of course, I had forgotten, Thomas was her brother. "I'm not sure. The sphere is gone. We can no longer send people back in time."

"What about Rich? Can he make another sphere?"

"Rich is in no shape to do much of anything these days. I might just set him loose. There's little harm left that he could do. The time travel was our most lucrative research project. Without it, I'm not sure we can keep this place running."

"What about the military contracts?"

"Maybe. But Rachel handled all that. I have no desire to take it up again."

She looked down at her lap and nodded. "What will you do?"

"There's always more research to be done. Now that I don't have a big lab to run, maybe I can get back to basics. See if anyone will fund me to find a cure for Sunithe's disease." I smiled at her. Unless Thomas had confided in her, she wouldn't understand the implication.

"And me? What do I do? After everything I've done and seen, what am I supposed to do now?"

"Whatever you want to do. You're free to go anywhere, do anything. You're a smart girl, Emma."

She sniffed and nodded again.

"You could go home. I'm sure your mother would like to see you. And someone should tell her about Thomas."

She shook her head. "I can't go home. It's been too long. Our mother stopped trying to get in touch with us years ago."

"I'm sorry."

She gave me a sympathetic look. "It was my choice to come here with Thomas. I never regretted it for one second, and I doubt Thomas did either." She paused and wiped her nose. "He was in love with Rachel. Perhaps you should find somewhere to bury them together."

"Rachel?" Things suddenly made sense. Why he was inclined to agree with her so often, and why he ran out after she had been killed to try to do something. I felt like such a fool.

"You didn't know?"

I shook my head.

"For such a smart man, you don't know much, do you?"

"He kept it from me. He was probably right to do so." It saddened me to realize I had not had Thomas's complete trust. "I tried to warn him. I tried to save him."

She said nothing, just nodded slightly.

"Do you know what happened to Victor?" I asked.

She shook her head. "I lost Victor as soon as he climbed into the vent. For all I know, he's still up there. Or he might have found a way out and ran off. Quinn was in the boardroom when they started killing people. For whatever reason they decided to spare her. She seems to be in a state of extreme shock. Doctor Crebbs found her in there when she was looking for survivors and is watching her for now. Victor would never leave without her. He'll turn up at some point and possibly take her off to wherever it is he's escaped to."

The idea of the two of them escaping together warmed my heart and made me think of Amelia and me all those years ago. Then I realized I would be my parents in this scenario and the memory was soured. I moved on. "I need to tell people about the lab closing. Do we still have that emergency alert system?"

"Yes. I'll have to check and see if it works, we've never had a reason to try it out."

"Please do."

I walked out into the courtyard again, saying hello to the few people I passed by. I went to Adelaide MacDuff's quarters and overrode the lock. Her place felt unimpressive. She had a few decorative touches strewn about, but it felt unlived in. I rummaged through her kitchen cabinets to see what sort of things she ate. I went into her bathroom and looked at what she kept in her medicine cabinet, spilling the contents out as I went and not caring to put them back. It wasn't like she would ever be in here again.

I thought maybe I could find something that would explain what had happened. I started rifling through her drawers, trying to find a secret diary or papers of conspiracy. I tore the place apart, but found nothing. The disappointment passed quickly. It didn't matter.

I left her quarters and squinted up into the sunlight. I was certain that I was pasty white. Perhaps the first thing I would do upon leaving here would be to take a few days vacation on the island and work on my tan. Or maybe I'd just move there. Set up a small lab, do some research, bring Amelia's pod along.

That was appealing. I could go back to what I was doing at Kischukov Laboratory. Do a few popular research projects to bring in funding, and then work on Sunithe's disease in my free time.

Even if I found the cure, I couldn't wake her. I had been warned. Her mind was almost certainly too far-gone at this point for it to make a difference. I attempted to ignore the sense of foreboding that tried to invade my thoughts, and hold on to my indifferent acceptance of the state of things. Every moment of hope that tried to peek its way into my bleak future was pushed aside.

I strolled back to my office, picking up the plastic bag of Thomas's remains along the way. I would have to talk to Emma to determine what should be done with them. She might want to have them for herself, and I'd have to respect that wish.

As I walked through the hall I thought about what this place would be like when deserted. The halls dark, the labs collecting dust. Rats running around the ventilation shafts.

Big rats, I thought. I paused just outside my office to put the bag of remains down on the floor again, and went back to the room where programmers usually stayed when they were sending people back and forth through time. There was only one vent in the room. The cover came off easily. I stood on a chair to peer down into it. It was empty. I noted how far down it went before turning to the right. It would head into the dormitory area where Eliza used to stay.

I scanned back to the moment when Rachel had sent him into the vent, then ran through the surveillance on the dormitory for the next few hours. He never emerged from the vent, unless he hid in there all night. He was a clever kid, but Emma was right. He'd come back for Quinn at some point. I thought about alerting Doctor Crebbs to keep Victor here if he returned, but then what? Could we start over? That didn't appeal to me.

Thomas was dead. Eliza was incapacitated. Quinn was suffering from shock. Peter had died, and Larry's mind had been wiped. Now Victor was gone. My children were all gone. It was time to move on to the next phase of my unending life.

Emma contacted me to let me know the alert system was online. I sat at my desk and she patched me in.

"Laboratory workers," I started out. "This is Doctor Lancing, your leader. I realize most of you have never met me or even knew of my existence. I started this lab over thirty years ago. I have been very proud of the work that has been accomplished here. We have made significant advances in many fields of study, but it is time for it to end. The events of the past few days have been tragic. We cannot recover from our losses.

"I urge all of you to take the next few days to gather your things together and prepare to leave. You all have brilliant minds, I am sure you will have no trouble finding work in another lab. The main gate will be left open. You are free to leave. The support systems will be shut down in one week. Good luck to you all in your future lives. I am very proud of all of you."

I wished the speech could have been more profound, but I was never very good at public speaking. I thanked Emma and told her about Thomas's remains. She told me to keep them and do whatever I wanted with them. She said she would be gone within the hour. I wished her well. I tried to imagine her on a beach on an island like mine, drinking a cocktail in the sun, but couldn't believe she'd ever be out of reach of a computer.

I wasn't sure what to do about Thomas's remains. He had never shown much interest in the agricultural wing. I had never asked him what happened on the island when he went to convince Rachel to join the lab. Perhaps it was there that he fell in love with her. I decided to take both of them with me and bury them on the island.

Doctor Crebbs contacted me to let me know that Quinn was awake and seemed to be doing much better. I decided to visit her personally. Doctor Crebb's office was in the return chamber area. I went back out into the hallway and backwards through the time travel mission recovery rooms. Just before I reached the door I mentally glanced in to see the state of things. Doctor Crebbs was hovering over an empty bed.

My temper flared as I burst through the door. "Where is she?" I said as I entered.

"What are you talking about?" Doctor Crebbs asked. She was standing next to the bed, her hand on Quinn's shoulder.

"Quinn. You're here."

She nodded.

"Of course she's here," said Doctor Crebbs. "Where else would she be?"

I closed my eyes to focus on the room again. I could see Doctor Crebbs and myself, but the bed was definitely empty. "Quinn." I opened my eyes again. "Where is Victor?"

"I don't know."

She seemed sincere. There was disappointment and desperation in her voice. "And where are you?"

She looked confused. "I'm in Doctor Crebb's office."

"Are you sure about that?"

She looked to Doctor Crebbs for help, then back to me.

"Lancing," said Doctor Crebbs, "what's going on?"

"I can't see you, Quinn." Curiosity reared in my mind.

"But you're looking right at me," Quinn said.

"What are you doing? You must be doing something to stop me from seeing you."

"I really have no idea what you're talking about!" Quinn was starting to get upset.

Perhaps it was an unconscious thing. I looked back again, for places and times where I knew Quinn would be. I remember her first trip back in time. Eliza had seen her, but she had not shown up on the surveillance. I went back to the room where we all were before she disappeared. She wasn't there either. Somehow Quinn was keeping herself invisible from our surveillance system at certain times.

When the room started to shimmer I knew I was too late. I woke up on the floor next to Doctor Crebbs. The bed was empty. Victor had come and gone and taken Quinn with him. I shook Doctor Crebbs awake and told her before heading back to my own office again.

I opened the door to Rich's room. It was empty. He must have gone with Quinn and Victor, I decided. I didn't bother to look back and see.

I had my own arrangements to make. I decided that the island would be a good start. I would take Amelia's pod with me. I still had the portable power source that Thomas had made. I had to arrange transport and alert the island staff that I would be coming.

I made sure all my research files were in order and gathered the reports on everything that had been done on Sunithe's disease into one place. I was glancing through the most recent progress report when Emma called to me to say goodbye. I put the paper down and watched as she walked across the courtyard for one last time and left the complex. She didn't turn to look back even once.

I was alone. No one was left who had been here from the start except for Amelia's cold, unmoving shell of a person. I scanned back through the courtyard. People were still milling about, talking about their plans, where they were thinking they would go. One group was chatting about me, wondering if I was a real person when one of them gasped and staggered backward.

I looked to see what he had seen and was shocked to see Noah, Adelaide, and that strange little girl suddenly standing in the middle of the courtyard. My shock quickly turned to rage.

Chapter 30

My rage grew as I watched Adelaide try to reassure the people around her. It was clear she had no leadership abilities. Her public speaking skills were atrocious. Her voice cracked with her nervousness. She was going to try to get the lab back under control. Where was Jim? She left with Jim. He was a much better candidate for leading this place.

Jim must have known what would happen to Noah had he stayed here. I supposed it was only fair that he would want to spare one of his librarians from that fate. He had befriended Larry after his reintroduction to society. He must have known the mind erasure wasn't a pleasant ending to a career and plotted to get Noah out. Why he would then abandon them, I wasn't sure. He must not have known how inept she would be at this.

The Adelaide woman seemed to be so sure of herself, and Noah swaggered around like he owned the place. This could not stand. Because of them, my life had fallen apart. I wasn't about to let them take over the place I had built from the ground up.

I watched as they headed for the time travel research wing and word began to spread amongst the remaining researchers. I began to scan through everything I had on Adelaide. She was the one who had taken Jim and Noah away and brought Noah back here. She was the one with the box; it looked liked she was using it as a sphere. She was clearly the one deciding things.

Adelaide had been a model researcher. She had the natural thoughts of mistrust that came with a secretive upper management but had never betrayed any thought of rebellion. She was an eager worker. She studied hard for her missions and took her job very seriously. Perhaps Noah's impetuous side had gotten to her. Addy, as he called her, was not one for throwing a wrench into the works.

Yet somehow when she was sent back to find out what had happened to Noah, she managed to send him back and go somewhere else herself. She would've had a sphere with her to return, so where was that sphere now?

They entered the return chambers and moved through to find Doctor Crebbs in her office. She was rummaging through files and was pleasantly surprised to see them. I watched their happy little reunion, bile building in my mouth. Noah had a moment of indignation when he realized she would have been the one to erase his mind, with Eliza's help. She calmed him with her cool doctor's logic. She refused to stay on, claiming that she had enough of the distasteful tasks I had assigned to her. Funny, she never complained to me directly about it. I guessed that the loss of a salary made those things less palatable.

They continued through to the white room itself. I wasn't sure what they expected to find in there. It became clear when they explained the room to the young girl that they were giving her a sort of tour. I realized at that point, that she was the one who had been controlling their passages through time. She was gifted like Larry, Quinn and Victor! If I could get control of her and their sphere, I could go back in time and prevent this mess from happening. Thomas would still be alive. No one else would be gone.

I thought about using Eliza to crush them from afar and take the sphere for myself. No, I wanted to see Adelaide's face. I wanted to look her in the eye when I destroyed her. I wanted her to know who her destroyer was.

They left the return chambers and arrived at the boardroom. Blood still stained the handle. I hadn't bothered to clean the room up, though I had reduced the bodies to dust. Adelaide refused to go in, a coward. Noah went in and saw the gore still splattered about the walls and floor. It couldn't be a pleasant sight, none of them died cleanly.

Adelaide told Noah he could wait there and continued on down the hall. Of course in his arrogance he followed them anyway, just a few seconds behind. I realized why she didn't want Noah to accompany them for the next part; they were going to see the older version of him that was still being kept locked away. I had completely forgotten about him during the chaos of the past few days. I watched as they entered the room.

He was not in great shape, but it didn't matter. I knew Adelaide's mind at this point, I knew she would send him back to his family, as she had argued for that a few weeks ago. I watched as the young girl handed Adelaide the box that had taken the place of the sphere. I leaned forward in my seat with anticipation. All I had to do was get that box.

Noah came in shortly after them, enraged when he realized who he was looking at. Adelaide took the old man and disappeared. When she returned she yelled at

Noah. It looked like she had some fight in her after all. It would make destroying her even better.

I grabbed a syringe from the medical room and filled it with sedative. Emma had shown me how to work the directional gas sedative, but I couldn't be sure I'd catch them standing close enough together to get all three of them. I left my office and stepped into the hallway, waiting for her arrival, hiding the syringe in the palm of my hand by my side. I pondered what to do with them, once I had them in my control.

Noah I would kill. He was of little use to me, and had always been an annoying showoff. Perhaps I would put Adelaide in a stasis pod for a few years and see how she fared. The young girl, I'd have to try to convince to join me. If not, I could always use Eliza's mind control to get her to obey me. Surely I could reason with her that her life would be better if she listened to me, rather than me having to force her to behave.

I watched as Adelaide floundered. She was frightened of me. That was good. Noah puffed his chest out and led the way. A moment later he turned the corner and stopped dead. Adelaide hurried around the corner and pushed past Noah, stopping as well as soon as she saw me. Her friend crept up from behind, and she and Noah flanked Adelaide. I could feel her fear as I stared down the hall at her. I couldn't help but let a small grin escape my lips as the adrenaline built in my system. "Adelaide MacDuff," I said to her. We had never met, but I knew her well.

She couldn't seem to move. I let her fear feed my confidence. Noah mumbled words of encouragement to her. He told her I was just a man. How little he knew. Would "just a man" live forever? Could he crush people into dust with the mere power of his mind? These two had no idea how much more than a mere man I was. I almost laughed at their ignorance.

I marveled for a moment at how unremarkable Adelaide was. Yet she had managed to contribute to the destruction of everything I held dear. Everything except my Amelia. Undoubtedly her part in the past few days must have been accidental. There's no way she could have known about everything going on behind closed doors. Perhaps Jim had passed her information. He had more access than her, and he had befriended Larry. Larry's mind had been erased, but maybe some of it could have been recovered. I didn't understand what Eliza had done to him. My own experience with mind erasure made memory recovery impossible, but perhaps Eliza used a different tactic. I forced myself to refocus. I needed to deal with Adelaide.

The little girl stood at Adelaide's side. They exchanged a glance and started walking slowly towards me. This was my competition? A young girl and the great Adelaide were going to stop me? I had felled many greater than the two of them in my day. She spoke my name. I could hear the uncertainty in her voice.

I matched her forward pace. "I knew you'd show up at some point," I said. She remained silent, unimpressed with my visionary mind. "It's like a drug, isn't it? The power of the sphere." I knew I had caught her attention. After all, she couldn't resist coming back here. Couldn't resist using the sphere for her own purposes. "It's how I got you all to obey. Best not ask too many questions, don't make too many waves? Heaven forbid you be denied access to your venerable sphere." She rolled her eyes at me. My temper flared slightly. She must have learned that bit of arrogance from Noah. I was done toying with her.

My face became a mask again when we stopped a few feet from each other. I cast my mind out to Eliza, to see if I could get to her. Maybe I'd give Adelaide a bit of a scare first. I heard her breath accelerate. She was very frightened. She didn't even know me, but she could tell I was a dangerous man. It gave me a thrill of power. The small girl peered out from behind Adelaide. "Who's your little friend?" I asked, knowing full well she was the one controlling the box. The box was there, in her hand, daring me to snatch it away from her. I couldn't get Eliza to respond. I would have to do this on my own. Adelaide had not responded to my question. "What's in the box, Addy?" I asked with an air of knowing condescension.

I saw her cringe slightly at my attempt of familiarity. She raised her hand and slowly lifted the lid to the box, opening it towards herself and keeping the button hidden from me. "Nothing," she said with a slight smirk.

Did she think I was an idiot? I already knew the box was a sphere. My impatience got the better of me, and I swooped forward to wrench her wrist around with my free hand. The box was empty. Where was the glowing, red button? I was confused, I had seen her use the box myself, and I knew it was their method of travel. I still didn't know what had happened to the sphere she brought back with her from her trip to find Noah. Where was that sphere, and why was this box empty? I became angry and squeezed her wrist even tighter. "What-" I began to say when the hallway disappeared and we were standing in a dark forest. I let go of her wrist, but I knew it was too late.

Panic filled me again. I still had the syringe, but a circle of people with hooded cloaks and torches now surrounded us. I was powerless outside of my lab. I surveyed the scene quickly. The young girl had another box. That must be the one she used, the other had been a decoy. Adelaide called for someone named

Sarah and a cloaked figure moved into the circle towards her. This woman called Sarah asked her something and gestured to me. Adelaide dropped her empty box on the ground and began to address the crowd. "As promised, I have delivered the man who will deceive you and kill many of your people. Do with him as you like."

They were Gardians, I realized. She was leaving me here with the Gardians, to do whatever they pleased with me. I glanced around the circle again, enraged. How dare she do this to me? She was nothing before she met me and started working at the lab. She was backing up to the young girl again, no doubt to return to our time. The cloaked figures started closing in on us and I leapt forward to grab Adelaide's arm. I was a second too late. My hand closed on empty air.

I only had a few seconds to assess my situation. Ketelzene and my mind kept my body young and strong, but these people were likely to do hard manual labor on a daily basis. They would be fit. I could never take on so many at once. The syringe would do me no good now. I dropped it on the ground to free my hands. My only chance would be to break through their ranks and run, but then what? I would be stuck in this time period. I'd have to live through the next several hundred years before I could get back to a time when I could go back to warn myself about any of the events leading up to this point. I didn't even have a cure to give to Amelia to prevent any of this from happening all over again.

It was still better than letting these people get to me.

I was about to run to try and break through the least dense section of the circle when one of the cloaked figures drew a dagger from her belt and ran it across the torso of the figure standing next to her. The woman screamed and collapsed as the one with the dagger turned to her other side and quickly stabbed that person through the stomach. I caught just a glimpse of the dagger, bathed in red and glinting in the torchlight as she pulled it back out of the woman's abdomen.

The circle was breaking. There was confusion amongst them about what was going on. As the dagger swung around to hit another figure, I took advantage of the confusion to snap the neck of the nearest cloaked figure. The one next to her came at me with a dagger that I rerouted into the heart of someone approaching me from the opposite side. A quick elbow jab to the face and the dagger was dropped. I retrieved it and finished off the remaining person on my side of the circle. I turned to watch the last person standing get slashed in the leg and drop to the ground. The dagger sliced through her neck and the remaining cloaked figure wiped it clean before sheathing it.

I was breathing calmly though the adrenaline hadn't worn off. The figure approached me and I bared the dagger towards her in warning.

"You won't be needing that now. You're safe," she said, as she picked up a torch and approached me. With her free hand she pulled her hood back and moved the torch to illuminate her face.

My breath stopped and I dropped the dagger in shock. Suddenly nothing mattered anymore. My life up to that point became meaningless. Only the future stood before me. A future with my love, alive and well. I sucked in a breath and said, "Amelia."

Immense thanks are due to my sister, Nicole, my editor. She is the greatest finder of plot holes, and helps keep my canon honest. To my husband, Sean, for his continued support and encouragement of my storyline. To my sister Heather, for pointing out my repetitiveness and annoying habits. To St. Elmo's Coffee Pub, for yet again providing me with my favorite writing space. And once again to Nanowrimo for pushing me to write and write and write.

31877693R00141

Made in the USA
Middletown, DE
15 May 2016